D0297934

Suspects All!

Suspects All!

The Mulgray Twins

ROBERT HALE · LONDON

© Helen and Morna Mulgray 2011
First published in Great Britain 2011

ISBN 978-0-7090-9281-0

Robert Hale Limited
Clerkenwell House
Clerkenwell Green
London EC1R 0HT

www.halebooks.com

The right of The Mulgray Twins
to be identified as the authors of this work has
been asserted by them in accordance with the
Copyright, Designs and Patents Act 1988

2 4 6 8 10 9 7 5 3 1

Typeset in 10.25/13.25pt Sabon
Printed in Great Britan by the MPG Books Group,
Bodmin and King's Lynn

In Memory of
Frances Hanna
who never lost faith in us

Acknowledgements

Special thanks to our agent, Frances Hanna, Acacia House Publishing Services Ltd, 82 Chestnut Avenue, Brantford, Ontario for her advice and hard work over the years on our behalf.

Grateful thanks also to all who have aided us in the research of this novel, and in particular to:

Mariano Medda and David Menzies of Glasgow Botanic Gardens who let us into the secrets of orchid propagation.

The Royal Dick Vet Hospital for Sick Animals, East Bush, Roslin and Dr Alexander Campbell, Manager of the Veterinary Poisons Information Service, London, who very kindly gave of their time to answer our questions on the correct emergency treatment for Gorgonzola.

Harry Cummings, retired Chief Superintendent Lothian & Borders Police for helping us to determine a site for the English Criminal Courts where the guilty were weighed in the scales of justice and found wanting.

Our editor, Gill Jackson of Robert Hale, for her patience when dealing with the problems we cast in her way.

For those readers interested in the phenomenon of cats that paint (or find the idea totally incredible), we refer you to the amazing works of art in '*Why Cats Paint – a theory of feline aesthetics*' by Burton Silver and Heather Busch, published by Ten Speed Press, Toronto.

CHAPTER ONE

They call Madeira 'The Floating Garden', but it wasn't a flower that was floating in Funchal harbour. Face down, the body rocked gently in the swell, the black jacket and trousers traditional Portuguese funeral attire. Dead men tell no tales, they say. Not true. Not true at all. That last meal, how death came and when – through the medium of forensic science, these things the dead tell us as clearly as if their cold lips had whispered the words. But for the moment, Luís Gomes wasn't saying anything, unless he was communing with the fish.

I don't suppose that Luís Gomes, barman at the Massaroco Hotel, had expected to be a corpse by three o'clock in the afternoon. Nor was I expecting him to die. When earlier this morning Gomes had leant over the bar and whispered that he had something to tell me, I felt like kissing him on both cheeks and toasting his health in *poncha*, the local rum-based drink. Of course I did neither, merely nodded and stirred the large glass of milky coffee he'd just handed to me.

'Meet me in the Beerhouse on the harbour at *três á tarde*. I tell you something then,' he'd muttered, casting a nervous glance round and moving quickly away.

Premature rejoicing is not something I'm prone to, but I must say I had high hopes of that meeting at three o'clock in the afternoon. What Gomes had to say could be the pulled thread that would unravel the web of evasion and subterfuge inextricably linked with any drug network. I saw myself knocking triumphantly on Comandante Figueira's door with something at last to report....

I was in Madeira as the result of a tip-off to HM Revenue & Customs. An English-run drug ring, it seemed, was making use of the Massaroco Hotel in Funchal, so HMRC had requested the cooperation of the Portuguese equivalent of the UK's Serious Organized Crime Agency. For the past month they'd arranged for me to pose as the English employee of the Agência, a Madeira travel agency based in the hotel – ideal for snooping into any murky goings-on. But to date my gleanings had been negligible, or to be painfully honest, zilch, zero, *nada*.

As a result, my twice-weekly meetings with steely police comandante, Justinia Figueira were becoming strained. She was making it increasingly clear that my unproductive presence and all the paperwork it generated were causing an intolerable disruption to her department. Portuguese is a squishy, squelchy language lending itself well to the expression of scorn. And it surfaced once again when she'd addressed me this morning in her almost perfect English.

After I'd admitted that yet again I'd nothing to report, she'd hissed, 'What evidence do you have that this English-run drug network exists? Why is London thinking you will be finding anything in the Massaroco Hotel, Deborah J. Sshmit?'

These soft Portuguese sibilants were indicative of her attitude to DJ Smith, lowly officer from HM Revenue & Customs. Not once in the past month had she bothered to pronounce my name correctly.

A blood-red fingernail stabbed the desk calendar. 'I give you twenty-one days. Are you listening? Twenty-one days. If you do not have by then, how do you say, a breakthrough, it will be a case of goodbye to you, Sshmit.'

Twenty-one days, when I'd been unable to dig up anything in the last *twenty-eight*. I'd used the Portuguese police files to enquire into the backgrounds of the hotel staff, I'd forwarded to London the passport details of new arrivals at the hotel, I'd made copious notes on each English guest checking in – and what had I come up with? *Nada*, nothing, zilch. Until Gomes set up our meeting.

As is standard practice in my line of work, I arrived half an hour early for my appointment at the Beerhouse, a restaurant-bar on a pier jutting out into the harbour at the western end of the palm-lined Avenida do Mar. The glass walls were topped by a shiny white roof rising into a strange collection of conical peaks, calling to mind a double row of baked meringues. The overall colour scheme was white – white tables, spindly-legged metal chairs and sun umbrellas, today furled against the stiff breeze.

I ordered a drink at a table with a view over both the inner marina and the main harbour. A thin scarf of grey smoke drifted up, swirled and dispersed from the squat, black-rimmed funnel of the latest cruise liner to dock. Canvas sails puffed out by the wind, the tiny *Santa Maria*, an exact replica of Columbus's ship, was gliding past the liner's towering sides. In the distance, traffic thrummed softly along the busy *avenida*. I sipped my beer. Soothed and lulled by the melodic *plink plank* from the tangle of slender masts of cabin cruisers, catamarans and other small sailing boats in the inner harbour, I let the minutes drift by....

At 3.15 I wasn't worried. On the whole, the Portuguese don't make punctuality a high priority. For Luís to be quarter of an hour, even half an hour late for our appointment was neither here nor there. But by four o'clock I had to accept that he wasn't going to turn up, that he'd chickened out through fear of reprisals. I signalled to the waiter and paid the bill. 'Back to square one,' I sighed. I pushed back my chair.

It was then that I saw the small crowd peering over the railings. A crowd gathers a crowd. I wandered across to see what was going on. I don't know what I expected to see, but it certainly wasn't a body floating face-down in the water.

A fast-flowing river tumbles down from the hills above Funchal and drains between high concrete walls into the outer harbour. About fifty metres out, where the brown silt of the river merged with the faded blue-green of the harbour water, a black rounded hump was wallowing sluggishly.

We watched sombrely as the orange and black *socorro do mar* lifeboat nosed up to the corpse and arms reached down to heave the body aboard. As the head and torso rose from the water, the pale face stared back at its audience. Beside me an old woman muttered a prayer. With a roar of opened throttles, the boat arced back towards the entrance beacons of the inner harbour, churning the brown waters and sending angry waves slapping against the seaweed-covered rocks beneath the Beerhouse pier. As it shot past, I could see directly down into the boat.

My breath caught in my throat, my heart thumped and pounded in my chest as the dark eyes of Luís Gomes stared sightlessly up into mine. I gripped the railing with such force that the rough metal cut into the palms of my hands. Luís had served his last drink. And I had just lost the only lead I had.

Comandante Justinia Figueira didn't wave me to a chair. Things were serious. Out of her hearing, those who worked at Police HQ referred to her as The Ogre and at this moment her glare was directed at me.

11

'Useless! Utterly *useless*, Sshmit!' The sibilants scythed through the air with the swish of scimitar blades.

I stared at the vase of orange and blue Bird of Paradise flowers on the corner of her desk. Spikily beautiful, these *Strelitzia reginae* signalled 'Admire but do not touch'. The same could be said for Justinia Figueira with her shoulder-length midnight-black hair, lustrous dark eyes, perfect olive complexion and fiery Latin temper.

'Luís Gomes was your best lead. Your *only* lead. And you have, as you English say, blowed it.' With sinking heart I noted the lapse in her English, further evidence that she was in a towering rage.

I transferred my gaze from the spiky blooms to the equally spiky *comandante*. 'Perhaps if I go over my report....' I indicated the single sheet of paper lying disregarded on her desk.

'The report is clear, Sshmit. It is the essential detail, yes, the essential detail, that is lacking.' She plucked up the sheet and waved it aggressively, dangerously close to shredding it on the sharp beaks of the Bird of Paradise flowers. 'You state here that you ordered a coffee and Gomes poured it for you. As he put the cup down, he said to you....' She rasped an elegant finger down the page till she found the place. 'Yes ... his words were, "Meet me *três á tarde* at the Beerhouse on the harbour. I tell you something then". After that you leave the hotel and the next time you see Gomes he is dead.' She looked up and I nodded. 'Obviously someone must have heard this conversation. Where is the list of those who were there?'

That was a difficult one. In my undercover role as a client liaison for a travel company with a chain of hotels on the island, my daily office hour in the Massaroco Hotel could be pretty hectic. Today had been fairly typical. Just who had been in earshot when Luís had muttered these words? I played for time.

'As you know, *Comandante*,' I said, 'after the office hour I have established the routine of having a leisurely coffee in the Massaroco's Mimosa Bar with the barman, Luís. It's an ideal opportunity to steer the conversation round to the current crop of guests and their bad habits. There's nothing people like more than a discreet gossipy moan.'

The Ogre drummed impatient fingers on the desk. 'What I want to know is *whose* eyes were watching and *whose* ears were listening. And what we must then establish' – she reached out, snapped the head off one of the strelitzias and jabbed its point ferociously in my direction – 'is whether some careless action of yours, Officer Sshmit, has led to the death of this man and jeopardized the success of the operation. I will expect your completed report at 1800 hours.' A curt nod of dismissal signalled the end of the interview.

That gave me barely an hour. Back in the office assigned to me for the duration of my deployment with the Madeiran Drug Squad, I stared at the blank sheet of paper in front of me and tried to recapture the scene in the café-bar of the Massaroco Hotel six hours previously. I had been writing up my client notes and mentally filing away snippets that might tie in with the tip-off on HMRC's confidential hotline for reporting smuggling or other suspicious activity, information that had brought me all the way from London to Madeira. So I had only a hazy recollection of who was still there and who might have overheard Luís making his rendezvous with me.

With a marker pen I drew a crescent shape to represent the bar and circles for the nearby tables. A red blob denoted Luís behind the bar, and another, myself on a bar stool. At eleven o'clock this morning, how had it been?

... Most of the tables were empty. Sunny weather and a popular excursion to the wine lodges had combined to make it a slack time for the Mimosa bar. Charles Mason, nicknamed by me The Playboy, bleached and spiky gelled hair a foil to that golden tan and carefully cultivated dark designer stubble, had been standing at the far end of the crescent-shaped bar, elbow propped on the black marble top.

In an assured manner verging on the arrogant, he was chatting up pretty but empty-headed Zara Porter-Browne. The powerful Madeira rum they were tossing back seemed to be cementing their relationship in a rosy glow. His punchline had evidently scored a hit, for her high-pitched giggle soared up to the timber roof, bounced off and came tumbling back. They'd soon reached the intimate stage of sipping their drinks through intricately intertwined arms. She was hanging on every word as he launched into another tale of prowess (his). The words 'hooked a shark' drifted along the bar....

Who else was there? I frowned in concentration.... Yes, artist Celia Haxby.

'If I could just interrupt your thoughts for a teeny moment ...' she'd said, as she unfolded a map of the island and smoothed it out on the bar top.

Although slatted blinds blocked out the bright rays of the sun from the café bar, she was wearing a floppy chrome-yellow sun hat, a seemingly essential accessory to that brightly coloured artist's smock and blue-and-white striped calf-length trousers. If Charles Mason was working hard on his playboy image, she was working equally hard on hers as the flamboyant Arty-Crafty Artist.

She'd stabbed a finger down on the map. '… and if you could just point out the picturesque village that the old bulldog Winston Churchill favoured for his paintings, I'll just bag a taxi, pop along there and complete a few canvases myself.' Her tone intimated a supreme confidence that *her* work would one day be equally sought after.

'That's it here, Câmara de Lobos.' I'd underlined it on her map. 'It's only a few miles from the Massaroco. You can easily get there by taxi or bus.'

My ignorance of artistic ways drew a snort of derision. 'Bus? *That's* no use! I'll need' – she ticked off each essential item on fingers that still bore traces of paint – 'my easel, stool, paint box, tube of brushes and, of course, canvases.'

There'd certainly be some difficulty dragging all that gear onto a bus. I'd smiled and said something like, 'Well, get the taxi to drop you beside the Churchill Restaurant. The view over the harbour to the village on the hill is much the same as when The Great Man sat and painted there, very picturesque.'

Then…? She'd picked up the map and stowed it in a bag slung round her waist, and muttering, 'Now I think I'll go and cheer up poor Dorothy Winterton. What we both need is a good cup of tea,' she'd sailed off, her brightly coloured smock billowing out like a taut spinnaker. In the curved bar mirror I'd watched her heave-to at a nearby table where Mrs Winterton, middle-aged, recently widowed, sat greyly toying with a slice of the heavy black Madeira honey cake.

For the next five minutes or so I'd been busy writing up the day's client business, in my mind the forthcoming tall glass of coffee and the possibly fruitful exchange of gossip with the cleaning staff who would soon come clattering in on their lunch break. What had happened after that?

If I looked at the desk diary that I'd been writing up, the notes should help me remember…. Two brown stains disfigured the current page. Celia Haxby had been responsible for one of them when she'd banged down the teapot on the bar in front of the startled Luís. *Clunk splat*! A watery brown splodge spread over the paper as tea spurted from the spout.

'The water is *not* boiling!' she'd boomed. 'It is absolutely *essential* that the water is *bubbling* before you pour it into the teapot.'

Mesmerized, Luís had stared at her like a snake cornered by a mongoose.

She'd flicked open the teapot lid and eyed the faintly steaming contents, lips pursed in a moue of distaste. '*Bubb-ling*. You understand? If the water is not boiling, the tea is not tea. It is *dishwater!*' She'd pushed the offending pot across the counter.

As if suddenly awakening from a trance, Luís grabbed the teapot and scuttled off to the sink.

Celia leant toward me lowering her voice to a conspiratorial whisper. 'Dorothy's a *leetle* down.' She'd rolled her eyes to indicate the mouse-like Mrs Winterton. 'I thought it might cheer her up a bit so I asked her to come with me to that Churchill place. You know, she was *pathetically* grateful....'

In the curved glass of the bar mirror Mrs Winterton had seemed quite perky. She was nibbling animatedly at the wedge of thick dark cake and washing it down with the previously neglected glass of sweet Madeira wine.

Daa daa da-da da da-da. The chirping ringtone notes of *Land of Hope and Glory* warbled on and on. *Daa-daa da-da da daa.* Oblivious to the malevolent glances being cast in his direction, or merely ignoring them, David Grant, Exotic Flower Importer & Exporter, hadn't been in a hurry to answer his phone. The crumple-suited figure lolling on a barstool had taken a leisurely sip or two of his drink before answering the call.

Celia Haxby hadn't bothered to lower her voice. 'If there's one thing *worse* than having to listen to those frightfully *inane* mobile phone conversations, it's being disturbed by them when one's relaxing over one's cup of tea.'

'Grant here,' he'd shouted into his phone. 'Yes, I left a message about that orchid delivery you made yesterday. I wanted *phrags*, not paphs. No, they're not the same ... I'm not paying for stuff I didn't order. I'll go over that list again....'

'This is absolutely *frightful*. He's showing *no* consideration for others!' Scooping up the newly refilled teapot, Celia flounced off to rejoin her protégée.

After that, it had been impossible to concentrate on writing up the desk diary. In fact, I'd found Grant's loud one-sided conversation so irritating that a large chunk of it had burned itself into my memory.

'Fifty boxes of strelitzia … one hundred of cymbidiums, that's the green ones, and another hundred of the yellow…. No? Well, make it fifty yellow, fifty pink….'

I'd caught Luís's eye and pointed at my empty glass.

'I'll have another *galão*, Luís. Got anything interesting for me today?'

It had been a spur of the moment question. But, as he'd handed me the glass of milky coffee, his hand shook and for the second time a brown splodge disfigured the page of my diary. He'd leant forward and flicked his eyes sideways in the direction of Crumpled Suit.

'There is something….' Another sideways flick of his eyes. '*Três á tarde*, I tell you more.'

'OK, three o'clock. Will I meet you here?' I'd said, casually lifting the glass to my lips but never letting my eyes leave his.

Again I glimpsed that flicker of fear. 'No. At the harbour. Meet me *três á tarde* at the Beerhouse on the harbour. I tell you something then.' A quick rub of the bar top with his cloth and he'd moved away.

Shortly afterwards I'd left for my next office hour, this time at police HQ. That unmistakable glint of fear at the back of his eyes had set my pulses racing. It was the breakthrough I'd been waiting for. Even in retrospect I felt the surge of excitement. But perhaps I *had* betrayed a hint of it to watching eyes…. Could I have been responsible for Luís's death, as Comandante Figueira had suggested?

I stared at the five names I'd jotted down on the sheet of paper. Five names. Porter-Browne, Mason, Haxby, Winterton and Grant. It could have been any of them. Or none. Luís could himself have aroused suspicion when he stumbled across whatever it was he had seen or heard….

Comandante Figueira had demanded a list of those present. But she'd want more than that. She'd expect a list of suspects ranked in order of probability. Wearily I pushed back my chair and moved over to gaze thoughtfully out of the little window overlooking the old town wedged between the sea and the soaring cliffs, a district of cobbled streets and narrow alleys, a tumble of pantiled roofs, not so much red as burnt orange or toasted honey.

Back at my desk I tore a sheet of notepaper into six squares and wrote a name on five. On the sixth square I drew an enigmatic black question mark to represent person or persons unknown. I spread the squares out on the desktop.

David Grant, Exotic Flower Importer & Exporter, had to be front-runner in the field of possible suspects. His expensive gold watch, his well-manicured hands, his leather shoes spoke money, but this was at odds with his somewhat unkempt appearance. Greying hair, untidily cut, brushed the collar of a reefer jacket over open-necked denim shirt. And if I was looking for something that *might* tie in with drugs – these boxes of orchid flowers would be ideal for their transport and concealment.

I swept aside desk clutter and moved the square bearing his name to the top of the cleared space. At the bottom of the space I placed Dorothy Winterton. Except in the realms of an Agatha Christie whodunit, nobody in their senses would suspect her of anything more serious than getting a free lunch by sneaking out an extra roll from the breakfast table. On the other hand....

Deciding on the top and bottom names had been easy. The order of the names between, that was the problem. Ten minutes later, it was still the problem. None of them could be ruled out. Flamboyant Celia Haxby, for instance, would have plenty of scope for skulduggery under the guise of eccentric artist. And could anybody *really* be as silly as the empty-headed Zara Porter-Browne? Resignedly, I concluded that they could. On the other hand, a razor-sharp brain might be concealed behind that gilded butterfly exterior. Charles Mason, Playboy of the Western World, was fake, false and phoney. But was he a criminal?

What was the right order – Mason, Haxby, Porter-Browne? Haxby, Mason, Porter-Browne? Porter-Browne, Mason, Haxby?

With an exasperated sigh I gathered up all the cards, shuffled them and placed them in a neat pile face down on the desk. One order was as good as another. So suspect Number One would be.... I turned up the top square. The black question mark stared up at me. Murder by person or persons unknown. That would have to satisfy the information-hungry *comandante*.

'Excellent.' The *comandante*'s voice was unexpectedly mellow. 'You have done well, Officer Smith.'

I could tell right away she was genuinely pleased. For the first time Smith had received its correct pronunciation.

She smiled. Two neat rows of perfectly matched teeth reminded me of a crocodile about to dine on a tasty morsel. 'But I do not think you are right in saying that we are dealing with an unknown perpetrator.

No, Officer Smith, we will find the person we are looking for among the five people you have named. Of that I am sure. What you must do, my dear Officer Smith' – the crocodile smile grew more expansive – 'is cultivate each one individually. All are suspects. But you must discover whether in the background of one there lurks most suspicious circumstances. Everyone has his secrets. Peel away each layer like an onion. This I leave to you.'

The perfect teeth closed with a decisive snap.

In a bit of a gloom I went back to my rented apartment, the Casa São Jorge, on the Estrada Monumental near the Lido, a picturesque old two-storeyed house long descended into gentle decay. I'd fallen in love with this building, straight out of *Hansel and Gretel* and *Sleeping Beauty*. The passage of time and the rains of many winters had stippled a soft patina on the pale stucco walls of the old *quinta*. The faded dark-green shutters were peeling and flaking back to the paler green of more prosperous days, and sections of the ornamental wooden fretwork edging the steepled roof hung crazily askew, threatening to slither down to the garden below.

I made myself a cup of tea and sat out on the veranda considering the *comandante*'s order. *Cultivate each one individually. Everyone has his secrets.* All very well in theory. In my client liaison persona it would be easy enough to engineer a chat or two, but winkling out secrets, even peccadilloes, would necessitate a lot more. I couldn't look to her for much help. She'd made it clear she wasn't going to allocate personnel or resources to me unless I could produce conclusive evidence that Luís's death was tied in to drugs and the Massaroco Hotel. I would need to shadow my suspects 24/7 to have hope of spotting any suspicious behaviour. Impossible, even if I could narrow them down to the one person....

I gazed out over the garden that was slowly reverting to a tangle of palms, magnolias, camellias and other greenery under-carpeted with ferns and clumps of luminous white Madonna lilies, the funereal kind. A shiny black seed from a neighbouring kapok tree drifted lazily by on its fluffy white parachute. I made a grab for it, but when I opened my hand there was nothing there. A metaphor for my present impasse.

I leant back in my chair and looked up at the precipitous slopes that enclose Funchal. Sunset was flushing the tops, but far below, the darkening hillsides sparked with pinpricks of light from the white, red-tiled houses crowding up the slopes on every patch of available land. A gust of cool night air stirred the purple racemes of the wisteria that twined tightly round the veranda supports. I picked up the tea-tray and carried it indoors.

It was time for my weekly phone call to London to check up on Gorgonzola, my red Persian cat, whose present abode during my posting to Madeira was the HMRC kennels in England. Since I'd rescued her from drowning when she was a new-born kitten, there'd been a particularly close bond between us. Once she'd proved to HM Revenue & Customs that she was the equal of any dog as a sniffer-out of drugs, she'd become a colleague as well as a pet. In my undercover work she was invaluable – for who takes notice of a moth-eaten moggy padding by? This was the first occasion we'd been parted for more than a few days, and at first I'd been a bit worried about how she'd get on, but she seemed to be coping pretty well.

Phone to ear, I stood in the open doorway looking out over the garden.

'Hi, Mike. DJ here. Just checking up on how Gorgonzola's doing. Been behaving herself, has she?'

When I didn't get the usual, 'Everything's fine, DJ,' I knew something was wrong.

'Erm ... she's a bit off her food. I was hoping you'd call. If you wait a minute, I'll read you the vet's report.' The receiver was clunked down. A long pause, then, 'Still there, DJ? Right, four days ago she suddenly stopped eating, lay in her bed, eyes closed. The vet says ...' – paper rustled – 'that he can find nothing physically wrong, but that she shows all the symptoms of pining for her owner ... already lost weight ...' – more rustling of paper – '... and there will be cause for concern if the situation continues ... not refusing water yet, but if she does ...' He cleared his throat. 'The situation today is just the same, I'm afraid. She just lies there, eyes closed. It's as if she's given up. What do you want us to do?'

I hadn't been expecting bad news, so this was all something of a shock. I found myself on the veranda sitting on the cane chair with no remembrance of how I'd got there.

'Give me time to think, Mike,' I said. 'I'll call you back.'

In the few minutes that had passed since I'd carried in the tea-tray, all colour had left the sky. Fingers of grey cloud had infiltrated through the mountain passes and were creeping stealthily down, smudging out the clusters of lights crowding the hillsides above Funchal Bay. The garden beyond the veranda was a shadowy jungle of ill-defined shapes. Down at the harbour, ships' riding lights reflected in the still black waters, and a cruise liner, all decks brightly lit, nosed its way cautiously to its berth. I took all this in, and yet it didn't really register.

Gorgonzola's willpower had been evident from the moment I'd spied her, a half-drowned kitten, clinging desperately to the half-submerged log in the river. That willpower had pulled her through the days that followed. Despite all the odds, she'd survived. She was quite capable of starving herself to death, under the impression that I'd abandoned her. As I've said, we'd hadn't been parted, before this, for more than a few days even when I was on a case, so to her, four weeks would be an eternity. I had no way of telling how much longer I was going to be in Madeira. It could be only a few days more, if the *comandante's* patience ran out, but if I managed to uncover something interesting....

I made my decision. I flipped open my phone and called Mike.

CHAPTER TWO

'*Cultivate each one individually. Everyone has his secrets,*' the *comandante* had said. The next morning I began with Celia Haxby.

I spotted her multi-hued smock in the gardens of the Massaroco Hotel and peered over the shoulder as she sat, brush in hand, in front of her easel.

'That's—'

'Ah, Deborah, you've tracked me to my *leetle* retreat.' Another wodge of khaki-green paint splashed onto what could only be described as a nightmarish chiaroscuro. She gazed at it for a moment, then laid down her brush and stood back. 'Now do give me your *honest* opinion.'

Her interruption gave me the chance to continue diplomatically, '— captured the essence of Madeira.'

The yellow sun hat nodded in emphatic agreement.

I pursed my lips. 'You know, I can't quite put my finger on it, but your style has quite a hint of ... could be a....'

I paused, confident that Celia's conceit would supply the answer and save me from committing myself. The pause lengthened embarrassingly.

She was gazing up at me expectantly. 'Yes?'

'Gaugin. South Seas period,' I said, tone confident. No other names had come to mind. 'I'm such a novice in these matters,' I added, to get myself off the hook if I was completely on the wrong track, 'but I would definitely say Gaugin.' I rushed on. 'That – that exotic dash of colour is so ...' Words failed me to describe the clashing hues of the Haxby palette without causing offence.

'Well,' Celia simpered, lowering her eyes modestly, 'I *do* think I've managed to capture just a *leetle* of the ambiance.' She squirted half a tube of crimson onto her palette, briskly mixed in some chrome yellow and daubed randomly at the already overloaded canvas.

'Aaah!' I gasped.

'Years of practice,' she murmured.

I seized my chance. 'That's just what I wanted to talk to you about. Do you think that you could *possibly* find time in your busy schedule to give me an interview for the monthly *Visitors to Madeira* feature?'

Celia frowned. 'I don't.... No, I don't really....'

I waited. The *comandante* would not be satisfied if I failed at my first attempt to peel away the layers that concealed the secrets of Celia Haxby.

That artist was studying her creation with narrowed and far from critical eyes. 'Mmm. Gaugin, you said?'

'Oh yes, Celia, definitely Gaugin,' I gushed. 'But Gaugin with something *more* ... something....' I paused, lost again for words.

'Yes?'

Was Celia genuinely fishing for compliments, or was she slyly playing me like an expert angler with a wily fish?

I plunged on. 'Perhaps something of the Van Gogh, his kinetic energy, the sense of natural forces pitted against each other.' To be honest, there really was more than a hint of the madhouse about Celia's spectacularly awful oeuvre.

'I see what you mean.' Celia held her head to one side, considering. 'It hadn't occurred to me before. But yes, I agree.' She dipped her brush in the black and signed her name with a flourish, then shot me an appraising glance. 'It takes someone other than oneself to see the obvious, doesn't it?'

I nodded. But just who had been pulling the wool over whose eyes? The verdict was open on Celia Haxby, painter extraordinaire.

I was pondering my next move when my mobile rang.

'It's Mike, DJ. I've just checked in Gorgonzola at Gatwick. Everything's fine, just fine. You said the cat would get into a strop when she saw the travel box, but she let me put her in without a murmur, no bother at all.'

My heart sank. Something was very wrong. To Gorgonzola that carrier box was like a red rag to a bull. *Every* time I produced it there was a battle of wills.

'So there's nothing to worry about,' Mike was saying cheerfully. 'She'll be with you in about three hours.'

*

Below Funchal Airport an empty pewter sea stretched emptily out to the mist-shrouded horizon where the Desertas Islands floated, insubstantial shadows on the edge of the world. A black speck drifting across under the low ceiling of cloud resolved itself into the daily British Airways flight from Gatwick. The plane banked steeply to line up with the long concrete pier of the extended runway and commenced its final approach.

I'd just have time to make my way to the viewing terrace to see it land. There it was, nose and wing lights bright, a grey silhouette against the grey rain clouds. The twin runways, sliced out of a steep hillside dotted with red-roofed houses, seemed almost within touching distance. From where I leant on the rail of the terrace I was close enough to see the curtain of spray as the wheels touched down. With a roar of reverse-thrust the plane rolled to a stop. Gorgonzola had arrived.

I turned and made my way anxiously down to the Customs office in the Arrivals hall. What state would she be in after those days of self-imposed starvation? I handed over the necessary papers and watched the official saunter off through a swing door, willing him to hurry. But it took longer than I'd anticipated for us to be reunited. Ten minutes, fifteen, thirty minutes passed before he reappeared carrying the regulation cat box. There was more delay as he methodically checked my papers and the pet passport.

At last he looked up, '*Bem, senhora.*' He handed back the papers and lifted the carrier onto the counter.

I put my face close to the grid and said softly, 'It's OK, G. I'm here now.'

I'd hoped for the usual indignant mew of cat suffering the outrage of close confinement in hated box, but the only response was a faint thump as she shifted position. Self-abasement on my part and eating a lot of humble pie usually put things to rights after a separation, but this time, to make her feel secure and wanted would take a lot more than that well-practised routine. This time I'd have to pull out all the stops. And I'd just the thing that might do the trick, the CD of a doleful dirge-like Spanish *madrelena* I'd managed to track down in a music shop in Funchal. When we were in Tenerife on Operation Canary Creeper, it had become G's favourite form of relaxation. At the first soaring notes she would roll over, paws limp, purring loudly. I'd play that CD to her on the way back to the house.

In the twelve miles from the airport to Funchal, the *via rápida* dives through ten tunnels, a journey that takes the sedate airport bus forty minutes. Taxi drivers do it in twenty. Today, eager to get us back to my Hansel and Gretel cottage, I kept pace with the fastest of them, the mournful *madrelena* loud in my ears, setting my teeth on edge.

Funchal is a city of narrow roads clogged by moving and stationary cars. A big advantage of the rented apartment on the Estrada Monumental was the easy parking. Two imposing wrought-iron gates welded open by rust and the luxuriant plant growth of decades gave access to a driveway paved with black and white pebbles in an intricate design. I switched off the engine, cutting off the *madrelena* in mid howl.

In the blissful silence came the sound I'd been hoping for, the low rumbling *purrrrrr purrrrrr* of a contented cat. G and I were a team again. But I'd have to pick my moment to inform the *comandante* of G's presence. I wasn't looking forward to telling her that the HMRC agent I'd summoned to help me unpeel those onion layers of hers was a cat. But this was Saturday and the *comandante* wouldn't be at her desk till Monday.

Later that afternoon I homed in on Dorothy Winterton as she sat at a table on the terrace. She was wearing a green silk polka-dot dress, on her knee the Agência's distinctive blue information booklet. The lavender-blue flowers of a nearby massaroco, the plant from which the hotel took its name, toned with the soft blue rinse of her iron-grey permed hair. Yesterday's little outing with Celia didn't appear to have done her much good. She looked as colourless and depressed as ever. Perhaps, of course, a morning spent in the company of Celia in full-blown artistic creativity would leave anyone looking limp and faded.

'Good afternoon, Mrs Winterton,' I said brightly. 'Enjoying the sunshine?'

'Not really.' Dorothy Winterton's grey eyes peered at me over the top of the enormous lenses of her spectacles and her thin lips tightened to an almost invisible pale line.

Pointedly she raised a spindly arm and consulted her watch. 'Five o'clock. That's when it stated that your office hour would be held today.' She stabbed at the Agência's booklet to emphasize her point. 'It is now,' – she consulted the watch again – 'three minutes past.'

From her disgruntled expression it was clear that no excuse would soothe the savage breast. Even, *I'm so sorry. I was giving the kiss of life to Mr X who has just suffered a massive heart attack*, or *I'm sorry but I was telephoning the airport arranging for the ashes of Mr Y to be flown home*. Both explanations would be treated as completely inadequate. I settled for an unqualified and abject apology.

'I'm so sorry, Mrs Winterton. I shouldn't have kept a valued client waiting. It will not happen again.' I'd read her character correctly. A satisfied smile played briefly across her lips. 'Now do let me order you a drink while I give you my undivided attention.'

She awarded me a nod of gracious forgiveness. 'A glass of Henriques & Henriques, medium dry. Large.' She levelled a sharp glance at me over the top of those enormous lenses. 'I always go for the expensive. That way I can be sure of getting the very best.'

I waited till the glass of nutty brown Madeira and a thin slice of dark honey cake were set on the wicker table beside her, then asked, 'Just how can I assist you, Mrs Winterton?'

She didn't reply immediately. Now that she had me at her disposal, Mrs Winterton seemed to be in no hurry to broach the urgent matter that had demanded my presence at precisely 5 p.m. She slid the Agência's blue booklet back into her bag, took a leisurely sip from her glass and nibbled daintily at her cake before replying.

'As you can imagine, the recent death of my husband has had a catastrophic effect on my health.'

I gazed across at her. Why did I have the feeling that far from being a cry from the heart, this was merely a device trotted out to elicit sympathy from the listener?

She pulled out a lace-edged handkerchief. 'But when I chose Madeira to recuperate,' – she took off her spectacles and dabbed daintily at her eyes – 'I didn't realize that there would be all those hills.' She waved a thin arm. 'Everywhere, hills.' Again, her lips compressed into a tight line of discontent.

'I'm not very fond of driving, you know, so I have decided I need a chauffeur-driven service—' She broke off and delved into her capacious handbag.'

At home in England she'd probably potter along in her car, top speed 35 m.p.h., behind her a hooting backlog of frustrated drivers. As I reached into my briefcase for some leaflets, it slid from my knees. I leant forward to pick it up and caught a glimpse of some small packages beside the Agência's booklet in the interior of her handbag.

She located and drew out some pages of newsprint and handed them to me, 'I've seen some advertisements in that tourist paper *The Madeira Times*. Quality and reliability. That's what I'm looking for. Which would you say was the best of these firms?'

'There's a good firm not far from the hotel. You can phone them, or go in person.' I sketched a quick map on the back of the flyer and handed it over. 'You're most wise to choose a chauffeured car, Mrs Winterton. Most of the roads are impossibly narrow and steep, with dangerous hairpins and you'd have to cope with drivers who treat the road as a racetrack.'

'Yes, you're right, my dear. Peace of mind, that's what I want.' A look I couldn't quite decipher flitted across her face.

She slipped the flyer into her bag and zipped it up, then with a curt nod headed off through the gardens in the direction of the hotel, her thin shoulders squared against anticipated onslaught from a hostile world.

Cultivate each one individually. Everyone has his secrets. I reviewed my little *tête à tête* with Dorothy Winterton. Everything she'd said and done had been in keeping with the stereotype of the elderly upper-class English lady abroad: the colonel's widow, stuffily old-fashioned, self-centred and autocratic. And yet ... how to explain those little discordant notes. What were the small plastic-wrapped packages glimpsed in the depths of her bag? Was she one of those foolish women who used their handbags as a portable safety deposit box for euro notes, passport and jewellery? Was that why the handbag sported a high security combination lock? Should I upgrade her from the bottom of my suspect list? Possibly yes.

No other guests sought me out. In contrast to yesterday, office hour today had been quiet. I snapped shut my briefcase and followed the route Mrs Winterton had taken through the grounds of the hotel.

The Hotel Massaroco prided itself on its gardens planted with clumps of the blue Pride of Madeira, flamboyant purple jacaranda and tumbling bougainvillea of every hue imaginable. Gardeners in wide-brimmed straw hats weeded the flowerbeds, ensuring everything was neat and tidy.

That's why the crumpled piece of paper tossed carelessly into a flowerbed made me slow, then stop. I've always had a short fuse about sweet wrappers, empty cigarette packets and pieces of orange peel dropped for others to pick up. The offensive paper had lodged itself in a clump of thorny-leaved bushes. I reached over and extricated it from its resting place. As I tossed it into the wicker litterbin discreetly positioned only a few metres away, a gust of wind caught it, sending it fluttering back to the ground at my feet.

Staring up at me was the map I'd hastily sketched for Dorothy Winterton, the information she'd requested, the paper I'd last seen being carried away in her tightly zipped bag.

Cultivate each one individually. Everyone has his secrets. On Monday I turned my attention to David Grant, Exotic Cut Flower Exporter. It was still dark as I made my way to the Mercado dos Lavradores, the flower and fish market at the eastern end of the Avenida do Mar. Though I passed it every day on my way to the nearby police headquarters I'd never actually been inside. I'd had to spend all my time learning the ropes under the *comandante* and establishing my cover by visits to the Hotel Massaroco for the Agência, so any market activity was well and truly over when I finished work. All I'd seen of the market to date had been the blue and white picture-tiles at the entrance, and the women in their striped skirts and straw hats seated outside under the red tulip trees selling their exotic orchids, proteas and carnations from tall vases and wicker baskets.

Early as it was, the fruit and vegetable courtyard was crowded and noisy. From my position on the gallery above, I had a bird's eye view of the stalls piled high with pyramids of oranges, greyish-green custard apples, lemons and wrinkled purple passion fruits.

On the other side of the courtyard, half hidden from me by the spreading branches of a tree and a bougainvillea-covered pergola, I spotted David Grant in close conversation with one of the flower sellers. I hurried down and positioned myself on the steps overlooking the covered fish market where he'd be sure to see me on his way to the traders' car-park.

I half-turned away and stared down at the array of fish lying on the rows of tables running the length of the light airy hall. I didn't have to feign an interest. The fish market was just as interesting in its own way as the flower market.

I didn't see him approach. I was too busy exchanging stares with one of the huge-eyed espada fish, draped like a patent leather scarf over the marble slab. Midnight black like the ocean depths from which it came, it lay shrouded in diamond chips of ice, its gaping mouth edged with fearsome saw-like teeth.

'Debs from the Agência, isn't it?'

My thoughts elsewhere, I must have stared at him blankly.

A trifle disconcerted, he repeated, a shade less heartily, 'Debs from the Agência?'

Quite often I'd seen him lolling at the far end of the bar, but we hadn't even exchanged pleasantries. Why had he made a point of speaking to me now?

'Mr ... er – I've seen you at the Massaroco Hotel, haven't I?' My furrowed brow and distant smile indicated that I had no interest in him at all and couldn't quite place him.

Wrong tactics. I saw the flicker of irritation.

'It's Grant. Dave Grant.'

A silence fell like a stone between us.

That had obviously not been the best way to make his acquaintance and peel back those layers to find the most suspicious circumstances in his background. Grant was the type who needed someone to feed his ego, hang on his every word, bolster his self-esteem.

The silence was broken by the high-pitched notes of *Land of Hope and Glory* trumpeting forth from the inner pocket of his linen suit.

He whipped the phone out and held it to his ear, 'Grant. Yes, I'm in the market now,' he bellowed. 'The price of cymbidiums has risen to a high?' A grunt. 'It's always the same story. End of season scarcity and market forces. Do I want the usual? Yes, good quality, mind you. None of those common colours. OK, I'll take a hundred and twenty boxes.'

He slipped the phone back into his pocket and made a brief note on the small clipboard he carried.

I saw an opportunity to polish his ego. 'One hundred and twenty boxes! I see I'm in the presence of a business tycoon.'

'Well, Debs, I think you've hit the nail on the head there.' His lips stretched into a self-satisfied smile. 'Want to see me in action? I've an order to pick up.' He didn't actually say, 'I'll grant you the privilege', but his tone said it for him.

'Oh, that *would* be interesting,' I said, and meant it.

'Right then.' He turned briskly on his heel. 'Follow me.'

We headed across black and white mosaic tiles to the flower stalls. He stopped at one stacked with more orchids than I'd ever seen *en masse* – green orchids, white, pink, cream, yellow. I recognized the familiar rounded blooms of the phalaenopsis or moth orchid, and the tiered spikes of cymbidiums with their strap-like leaves, but the purple daffodil-like types and the waxen-pouched oddities were new ones on me.

'Just watch this.' That smile took another curtain call.

The next few minutes were a revelation. A quick assessment of the flowers, a rapid negotiation of prices with the vendor, an entry on the clipboard, and the deal was done. Thoughtfully I made a note on a mental clipboard of my own. I was up against an astute and agile brain. Ruthless about beating down any opposition, quick to seize advantage of any weakness, he was certainly capable of running an illegal operation.

His fingers caressed my shoulder. 'Well?' he asked.

'Absolutely amazing,' I said honestly.

He nodded, matter-of-factly accepting the praise as merely his due.

I waved a hand at the organized chaos going on around us. 'And I'd no idea that it would be as busy as this so early.'

'Early?' A snort of derision. 'It's eight o'clock. The market's beginning to wind down. The rest of the morning's a good show for the tourists, but the real business has already been done.' His fingers tightened on my shoulder. 'To play the market you've got to get out of bed early.'

On the word *bed* the pressure on my shoulder increased. His eyes wandered over me, assessing, undressing.

'You mean, you've been here for *hours* already?' I stepped back as if in amazement, forcing him to loosen his grip.

'Since six. The early bird catches the worm, y'know, Debs. Have to beaver away. Can't afford to let the other guy steal a march. Now that order there,' – he tapped the clipboard – 'I took a five minute break and that *filho-da-puta*' – a nod in the direction of a swarthy middle-aged man – 'got his foot in the door. But I snookered him on the next deal when—'

The chords of *Land of Hope and Glory* cut him short.

'Y'see, Debs, I'm available 24/7.' One eye closed in a meaningful wink. He held the phone to his ear. 'Grant. Yes. Right away.' He slipped the mobile back into his pocket. 'All work and no play makes Jack a dull boy. Gotta go. See you later, Debs.'

What a beer-bellied, oily, smug, far from charming Prince Charming! That chat-up routine, arrogantly certain of success, held no interest for me. But something else did. I gazed after him speculatively. I had been keeping watch from the shadows on the first floor balcony of the flower market since 5 a.m. He'd said he'd been here since 6 a.m. but he hadn't made an appearance till 7.30. I was absolutely certain of that, because if he *had* been (in oily Dave-speak) beavering around, that light suit would have stood out like a sore thumb among the dark jackets and shirt-sleeves of the locals.

David Grant, Cut Flower Exporter, didn't know it but he'd just elevated himself to one of the prime suspects on my list.

I didn't go back to my car immediately. A stroll along the seafront promenade would give me a chance to sift through the questions thrown up by my encounter with that ghastly lothario Grant. I'd just drawn level with the Beatles' Boat café-bar when a luminous day-glow figure caught my eye. It was Zara Porter-Browne, draped like some exotic wilted orchid over the rail on the upper deck. Today her shoulder-length hair was a vivid emerald green, exactly matching the silk mini-tunic that set off her bronzed skin to perfection. Three days ago when I had watched her giggling *tête-à-tête* with the Playboy of the Western World, she had been an unremarkable brunette.

The early morning sun twinkled off the brass rails on either side of the drooping figure, throwing golden rays skywards like the search-lights of 20th Century Fox. From what I'd seen of Ms Porter-Browne, I'd have staked a bet that 8.30 a.m. was still the middle of the night for her. I stopped and took a closer look. She *had* probably been there all night. The silk tunic was crumpled, the green hair disarranged, the eye make-up smudged, the green eyes red-rimmed.

It was obviously not a good time to cultivate her acquaintance, but too late, unfortunately, to make a tactical detour round one of the pavement kiosks. I turned my head away and pretended a sudden absorbing interest in the bus disgorging its passengers at a nearby stop.

'Yoohooo, Bo-a. No, no,' – a wild giggle – 'Debo-ah!'

I swung round, looked up in feigned surprise. 'Oh, hi, Zara. Er … good party?'

A tipsy tear trickled down the side of Zara's nose, leaving a pale trail through the green eye-shadow. Shakily she wiped it away, transferring a green smudge to the back of her hand. 'There'sh something you should know, Deboah. Something not a lot of people know.' She gave a watery sniff.

A long pause.

'Yes?' I ventured.

Zara prised herself into an almost vertical position. 'Yesh, Deboah. I think you should know that ... that I, Zaza Poata-Bowne, am an abandoned woman.'

Like a marionette whose strings had been cut, she flopped dramatically onto the deck in a shuddering green heap. 'Chas has left me,' she wailed.

If Charles Mason had indeed loved and left her, it could prove useful to find out what was behind it all. She was in no state to make her own way back to the hotel, so with the help of one of the café's waiters I ladled her into a taxi. As it stuttered its way through the Funchal rush hour, she stared with vacant, glazed eyes at the grid-locked traffic.

Various approaches on the lines of, 'Anything I can do to help?' met with no response. We were nearing the hotel. There wasn't much time to winkle something out of her. Perhaps a direct approach would open the floodgates.

I put an arm round her. 'Something wrong between you and Charles, is there?'

Her shoulders shook in what I took to be a paroxysm of grief. I prepared myself for a torrent of tears, or a vengeful tirade on the lines of men are *shit*! But a high-pitched giggle ricocheted round the cab.

'Zara!' I gasped. 'You're not upset? I thought you said that Charles had ... had....' I tailed off, lost for words. 'Left you for another', seemed too prissy and 'dumped you', somehow too brutal.

'Caught him out, didn't I, Deboah?' She waggled an unsteady finger in my face. Another shoulder-heaving giggle. 'He thought I was a dim bird who couldn't spell.'

'Spell?' What on earth was she rambling on about?

Zara attempted to tap the side of her nose knowingly. After three near misses she stared morosely at the offending finger. 'He bet me that I couldn't spell my name.'

My mind raced, ranging over the possibilities – some kind of erotic game like strip poker, perhaps?

'Well, that was an easy one, wasn't it?' she laughed scornfully. 'But he cheated. Insisted I'd got it wrong. How can you make a mistake with you-ah own name? Za-wa Poat-a Bw....' She tailed off chewing her lip. 'Anyway ... he was laughing like a dwain until I asked him to spell the name of that flashy watch of his, the ... the ... Wo–Wo—'

'Rolex?' I offered.

'Yeah. Well, he wattled it off, W-o-l-e-x. So I said, "How come, then,

31

how come, then, that watch on your wist spells it with two l's?"' She collapsed in a glissando of alcohol-fuelled giggles.

'And he went off in a tiff, eh?' I said casually.

'He looked at me in a funny way and … and … pushed back his seat and went and sat at the bah with his back to me.' The giggles hiccupped into a series of snuffling sobs. 'He wouldn't speak to me again. Picked up a blonde and went off with the bitch.'

She raised a tear-stained face. 'I've blown it. Messed it all up! I should nev-ah have said that.'

I gave her a quick hug. 'It's not the end of the world, Zara. So he bought a fake watch to show off, and you caught him out. Embarrassing for him, but someone who can't laugh it off is not worth bothering about. He's either a conceited balloon or not what he seems.'

'Not what he seems?' Zara was staring at me, shocked into semi-sobriety. She lowered her voice to a whisper. '*What do you mean?*'

I blinked, taken aback by the intensity of her reaction. 'I mean he could be a conman, a gold-digger – after your money.' As soon as the words were out, I regretted them. It would be awkward if *she* started doing a Sherlock Holmes job on Mason. 'Only joking,' I added hastily.

Zara stared at me for a few moments longer, then slid down in the seat with her eyes closed.

I got no more out of her. She remained slumped and semi-comatose until we arrived at the hotel, where I managed to heave her out of the taxi and with the help of one of the staff, deposit her in her room.

CHAPTER THREE

Thanks to Zara Porter-Browne it was later than I'd planned when I arrived at police headquarters for the scheduled Monday morning meeting with the *comandante*. I'd left Gorgonzola, appetite restored, making herself quite at home on a cushioned seat on the veranda of the *casa*. I planned to use her to make some unobtrusive searches, but first I'd have to get the official go-ahead from The Ogre herself – and I had the feeling it wasn't going to be easy.

A constant worry was that one of my suspects might link me with the police. There were thirty steps up to the entrance of police HQ and it must have been on the unlucky thirteenth that I cannoned into a man who had come to a sudden stop.

'Sor—' I looked up to see Charles Mason's familiar designer stubble. 'Oh hello, Charles. Sorry, didn't see you. My mind was on other things. I'm on my way to sort out another holiday predicament, a lost passport crisis,' I said, thinking quickly. That should satisfactorily explain my presence. But why exactly was *he* here? *Cultivate each one individually. Everyone has his secrets.* I did some fishing. 'You've not lost *your* passport, I hope?'

Interestingly, he looked shifty, very shifty indeed. 'No, no, nothing as drastic as that. Just my watch. Should have seen to that loose link on the bracelet.'

'A Rolex, isn't it?' Now, how was he going to handle that?

Smoothly as it turned out. 'Well, yes, losing it *is* a bit of a blow.' The accompanying rueful grin was perfectly done. 'But to be honest, it's the sentimental value more than anything … my dead father....'

I was impressed. I really was. In a couple of sentences he'd managed to imply he lived a millionaire lifestyle in which a watch worth thousands of pounds was considered a minor trinket and at the same time he'd cast himself in the role of loving son who valued an object as a memento rather than for its monetary value. What's more, at a stroke he'd rid himself of the embarrassingly misspelled Rollex and by reporting the loss could claim the insurance money! I had to hand it to him. He certainly had ... what was the word ... *chutzpah.*

Charles was saying, '... on my way to ask if my watch has been handed in. But if it hasn't, I suppose I'll have to fill in some forms for the insurance. You couldn't help me with any translation problems, could you?'

Perhaps I'd get the chance to peel away some of those layers. I was fairly sure he was a con-artist rather than a drug dealer but ...

I led the way through the glass doors. 'The first thing to do is state your business to that officer over there and then you'll have to sit on one of these benches round the walls until you're called. The duty officer will speak some English, but I'll hang around.'

I wasn't going to leave without finding out what his game was, so took a seat, rummaged in my bag and flicked through a sheaf of papers, ostensibly taking little interest in the proceedings as he walked over to the dark oak desk behind which a grey-haired, bushy mous- tached officer was gazing into a computer monitor and giving an occasional one-fingered tap at the keyboard.

I watched him speak to the officer, then cross back across the expanse of marble floor to sit down beside me. I continued scribbling meaningless hieroglyphs against random paragraphs on the page I was studying.

I heard Mason mutter, 'There's a bit of all right,' and I looked up to see two skimpily clad girls, tourists by dress and behaviour, giggling behind their hands and eyeing him lustfully through the curtains of their long blonde hair.

On the bench to our right a stout woman was talking earnestly to a teenaged boy, probably her son, and an old man in a black suit was staring vacantly into space.

'Looks like you won't have to wait long, Charles. There's not much of a crime wave here, compared with big cities like London or New York.' I eyed him covertly. 'But there *are* some serious incidents – even the odd murder or two. Just the other day a body was found floating in the harbour.'

Charles Mason looked deeply unimpressed. 'I expect the guy fell over the edge of the quay when he was drunk.' He crinkled his eyes at the two girls.

Most people might assume that a body was male, so there was no significance in that. Certainly, the lack of reaction, lack of interest in a murder, was a trifle unusual. Of course, he could have already read about it in the Portuguese newspapers. After all, they had covered the story of the body in the harbour. But Mason didn't speak Portuguese – he'd just asked for my help with translating – or was that a double bluff?

Bushy Moustache had stopped tapping at his keyboard and was now beckoning Mason forward.

'You're in luck, Charles. You're getting preferential treatment. Losing a Rolex must have made quite an impression. I'll come over with you in case there are any difficulties when they take a statement.' This was going to be interesting.

'Er ...' A flick of his eyes betrayed his unease. 'I don't want to take up any more of your time, Debbie. When I spoke to the officer a few minutes ago, I made myself understood pretty well. He speaks quite good English, actually.'

So Mason was trying to get rid of me? Intriguing.

'Come on.' I bounced to my feet as if I hadn't heard. 'Can't keep him waiting or we'll be back at the end of the queue.'

For someone anxious to report a loss, Charles was displaying a curious reluctance to set things in motion.

'Er....' he mumbled again.

I flopped down beside him. 'Something wrong?'

'No, no ...' He shuffled his feet nervously. 'Well ... you know how it is.... Insurance companies are always trying to wriggle out of responsibility by saying that you've been negligent, so I spun a bit of a yarn – told him that I'd been mugged, that somebody had snatched the watch off my wrist.'

The Moustache beckoned again, more brusquely.

Sad to say, honesty would have to give way to expediency. Protecting an insurance company from a fraudster was of secondary importance to my investigations. I gave the self-styled mugging victim a conspiratorial wink. 'That's the only way to make sure insurance companies pay up.'

The old man in the black suit had levered himself to his feet and was shuffling sprily across to the desk. I eyed his retreating back. 'Come on. If we don't get a move on, that old man will beat us to it.'

And he did. His quick shuffle beat our smart walk by a couple of paces – it would have been too obvious a tactic to run. At the desk he launched into an interminable complaint about the rampages of a neighbour's dog among his chickens. This was received by the desk officer with much nodding of the head and a rapid tattoo of fingers on his keyboard. Strange, Bushy Moustache didn't look like the kind of guy who would tolerate queue jumping and, what's more, his typing skills seemed to have undergone a quantum leap in speed.

Curious, I edged round the right-angle of the desk and squinted at the monitor. The top third of the screen visible over Bushy Moustache's shoulder was full of assorted letters, numbers and symbols as his fingers hit random keys with machine-gun rapidity.

'Excuse me,' Mason said loudly, his public-school drawl edged with impatience.

The machine-gun rattle and the old man's quavering monologue continued unchecked, '... and that scumbag César Gonçalves just laughed like the hyena he is!' The old man's bristly grey chin quivered with unsuppressed rage.

Mason's 'Excuse *me*!' was repeated, this time at full volume. For added measure the flat of his hand smacked down on the desk with the crack of a pistol shot.

I jumped. The monitor went black as the officer's convulsed fingers hit several conflicting keys. The old man's stick clattered to the floor and he began to buckle slowly at the knees.

My own knees grew weak at the vision of the *comandante* leaning towards me over her desk spitting out the words, 'So, Sshmit. This is the second death for which I point the finger. I think you must explain.'

A wave of garlic engulfed me as the old man spluttered something drowned out by the heated altercation raging above us as Mason and Bushy Moustache shouted and waved fists at each other.

'... outrageous behaviour in a police station ...'

'... complain to your superior officer ...'

'... disturbing public order ...'

'... *every* right to expect ...'

The old man's fumbling fingers latched round the shaft of his stick. He heaved himself upward using the stick as a lever.

'Bloody interfering foreigner!' He poked his stick viciously into Mason's back. 'Gonçalves is paying you to prevent me making a formal complaint, eh?'

'See—' Charles half turned from eyeballing the minion of the law on the other side of the desk.

'You admit it!' With a scream of rage the old man brought his stick slashing down on the foreign mercenary's fingers splayed temptingly on the wooden surface.

Mason's howl of pain was followed seconds later by another sharp crack of the stick on the polished desktop.

'You heard that? He confessed!' The old man cackled triumphantly. '*Senhora*, you are my witness. And you, Raimundo Paulo,' – he swivelled towards Bushy Moustache – 'it is as a police officer that you hear him admit he is working for Gonçalves. That Gonçalves is behind it all. Arrest them both!'

'Let's just get out of here!' I hissed, hustling Charles past the sniggering police officer on duty at the front door. Taking hold of his arm, I shoved him none too gently outside.

'I can't think why that crazy old coot turned on me like that,' Mason whined. He skidded to a halt and half turned as if to rush back to continue the encounter.

I summoned up my reserves of charity – his purpled fingers did look extremely painful.

'Really, Charles, you brought it on yourself, pushing in front of the old man like that. He had just accused you of being in the pay of a thieving neighbour of his, and you, with rather unfortunate timing, shouted out what sounded to him like the Portuguese for "Yes, I am".' I tried to keep the laughter out of my voice.

He eyed his swollen fingers. 'I think the old buzzard's smashed them,' he moaned. 'Puts paid to the plans for tomorrow. I had it all set up to show Zara how to water ski without planks.'

I had to hand it to him again. You can't keep a conman down. There he was, bouncing back to latch on to another image-enhancing opportunity that couldn't be checked out.

'Hard luck, Charles. And I think you should let things cool down a bit. Report your missing watch tomorrow.'

He blew on his fingers. 'You're right, Debbie. Couldn't trust myself not to grab his walking stick and break it over his thick skull.'

'Well, I came here to see about a lost passport. I'd better get round to it. And what those fingers of yours need is ice. I'd nip along to the fish market, if I were you.'

I stood at the top of the steps and watched till his blond, gelled head disappeared round the corner. With Mason's luck, he'd plunge his fist through a heap of ice into the gaping jaws of a spiky-toothed espada fish.

I made my way back into the building. Before that meeting with the *comandante* I'd still have time to write a brief report on David Grant and Mason. Hopefully, that should soften up The Ogre before I revealed that, without consulting her, I'd brought in a new colleague from HMRC – and, worse still, that the new colleague was a cat. Back home, I was well used to reactions of disbelief and hilarity when instead of the expected sniffer dog, a sniffer cat got to work. But I'd the strong feeling that the *comandante* would take a dim view of this challenge to her authority and, far from being amused, would dismiss out of hand the whole concept of a sniffer cat.

When I entered her office, she was standing beside her desk rearranging the strelitzias in their vase. Whether by chance or design, an aggressive array of beaks was targeting the visitor's chair.

'Ah, Smith.' She tweaked a recalcitrant spike into submission. 'I hope you have made *some* progress in your investigations.' Her tone indicated that she had no hope, no hope at all, that I had, or ever would, come up with anything. She turned her attention back to the flowers, gave a nod of satisfaction and moved round the desk to sit in her chair.

I gave her my hastily compiled report. 'As you will see, *Comandante*, I've made some interesting discoveries about two of the suspects.'

She studied the sheet of paper, one hand motioning me to sit. In the silence I became aware of the muted roar of buses grinding up the narrow twisting road to the Botanic Gardens and the villages on the heights above.

I cleared my throat. 'As I've said, I think that as far as the death of Gomes is concerned, we can discount Charles Mason. However, Grant has behaved in a way that warrants further investigation.'

Overwrought Zara Porter-Browne, flamboyant artist Haxby and refined pensioner Winterton might also be worth investigating, but I'd keep that to myself. Concrete evidence was all that counted with the *comandante*. Intuition, conjecture and surmise were not words that featured in her vocabulary.

The blood-red fingernails drummed a brief tattoo on the desktop. 'So, the man Grant lied. Perhaps he was with a woman. You say that he tries to impress. Perhaps he was wishing to hide the fact that he slept late. Such a man would not wish to admit this. Are these not possibilities, Sshmit?' She leant back, eyebrows raised.

I nodded. She was right. I'd taken a dislike to him, so perhaps I was reading too much into what was nothing more than an image-saving fib.

She pushed the report across the desk towards me, a signal that it was not worth filing. Damn, I'd hoped I was on to something. Worse, I'd failed to soften her up for what I was about to say.

I got slowly to my feet. 'Er, there's something else, *Comandante*. I'm convinced that one or more of our suspects is implicated in the Gomes death. Revenue & Customs have already established that drug organizations make use of the Massaroco Hotel where he was a waiter. There's a strong possibility, therefore, that drugs are a factor in the murder of Gomes, so I've asked for an expert in drug detection to be sent out from England to assist me.'

'And this expert, he is so clever he can succeed when you have failed?' The eyebrows elevated themselves into a sceptical arch.

'Not he, she, *Comandante*.' Now was the time to disclose, to tell all, but I chickened out. I hurried on, 'My plan is to let her search the places these people hang out. She'll be able to detect any trace of drugs.'

With luck, The Ogre would be satisfied with that and then, if Gorgonzola came up trumps, the subsequent revelation that my new colleague was a cat wouldn't make the *comandante* blow her top. My luck was out.

'This woman, she has specialized equipment?'

'Er,' I floundered, 'er, smell. She detects the presence of drugs by smell.'

'I have not heard of such a machine. Tell me more about this wonderful device.' The *comandante* leant forward expectantly.

I racked my brain for a suitable smokescreen, but only dug myself in deeper. 'She doesn't use a machine. Her sense of smell is very highly developed. It's the same with a wine or fragrance expert. In English, we describe such a person as "a Nose".'

'Who is this lady? I must meet her.' She picked up a pen and held it poised over her desk diary.

I made a last ditch attempt to gain that extra moment in which there'd be a miraculous knock at the door, or a phone call to divert the *comandante*'s attention to some urgent case.

'She's known as G and er....' There was no way I was going to get out of this. I surrendered. 'And er ... she's a cat ...' I tailed off.

'*Cat? Cat*, Ssshmit?' Her face flushed. 'This is the strange English humour?' At the *hwack* of the flat of her hand on the polished surface of the desk, the strelitzias quivered in their vase, their steely grey beaks crossing and tangling as if some deadly skirmish had broken out.

'I can assure you, *Comandante*, that the cat is held in high regard by HMRC. Only last year, she was instrumental in—'

Hwack. 'Enough, Sshmit. I do not wish to hear more. I remind you, you have eighteen days left to solve this case.'

The two neat rows of perfectly matched teeth snapped shut. My audience with The Ogre was at an end.

CHAPTER FOUR

That afternoon found me perched on the high stool at the counter of the Massaroco's terrace bar sipping a leisurely coffee. A few couples were sitting around engrossed in newspapers, paperbacks, or travel guides of Madeira. Behind the bar, Márcio, the replacement for Luís, was standing half-asleep waiting for his shift to end and rubbing perfunctorily at the beer rings on the polished bar top, the sullen droop to his mouth evidence that he was not enjoying his work.

To the casual observer it might have seemed a repetition of the scene three days ago, but there were discrepancies, small changes as in a Spot the Difference competition. Celia in flowery smock, minus the chrome yellow sunhat, was pouring tea for Dorothy Winterton. David Grant, mobile phone now hidden in an accessible pocket but ready to be whipped out at the first beep of *Land of Hope and Glory*, was once again lazily propping up the far end of the bar. On the stool beside the jardinière of orchids where she and Charles had giggled together under the effect of the powerful Madeira *poncha*, Zara sat, this time alone, morosely sipping at a gaudy blue cocktail. Notably absent, of course, was Luís, his ready smile and bright eyes replaced by Márcio's downcast gaze and down-turned mouth.

I was feeling pretty gloomy myself, after that meeting with the *comandante*. Eighteen days was very little time in which to justify my presence by nailing Luís's murderer or proving the existence of a Massoroco-linked drug ring. At the moment I couldn't even be sure that Luís's death was tied up with a drug ring. Drug wars are usually waged in mean back streets away from the tourist eye, but whoever had silenced Luís had dumped his body in the busy working harbour.

Why? This was an angle I hadn't considered before. Was it to stop him speaking to me? It would mean my undercover role had been compromised, that I'd somehow given myself away. In that case I'd have to watch my back.... For the moment I should be safe enough. The last thing they would want was to have the police and security services buzzing round the hotel interrogating those connected with it.

I stirred my coffee thoughtfully. I could continue the slow process of 'peeling away the layers'. I had five suspects – four if I discounted Charles Mason – and that meant that I could devote less than five days to each of them. Barring a miracle and I didn't believe in those, I hadn't a hope of bringing things to a satisfactory conclusion before the *comandante* unceremoniously booted me out.

Or, if my cover had not been blown, I could fast-track my investigations by deliberately setting myself up as a target, just as a goat was staked out to lure the tiger to the hunter. I was as certain as I could be that those behind Luís's murder were part of a drug network. If they thought I was onto them, they'd take steps to remove me. And, hopefully, expose themselves.

The time factor made the latter course of action the only feasible one, but it had one huge, possibly fatal, drawback – the tiger often killed the goat. My first step must be to narrow the field of suspects. If I knew the direction the danger was coming from, I could take precautions, stacking the odds in my favour.

From the end of the bar the muted notes of *Land of Hope and Glory* rose above the hum of conversation. Grant put down his glass and launched into his phone-answering routine, 'Grant here ...' delivered at the usual full volume.

He was my prime suspect. If I could engineer a visit to that orchid farm of his, I'd let him give me the guided tour and, while oohing and aahing at the orchids, I'd suss out security measures in preparation for a little unofficial trespassing of my own. Of my own, but not quite *on* my own. I'd have Gorgonzola with me to sniff out the presence of drugs. If she found any, I'd bag my tiger.

The focus of my thoughts got off his stool and, phone clamped to ear, strode from bar to terrace doors and back shouting, '*Bloody hell*, what am I paying you for? Can't you buggers bloody well handle it on your own?' He snapped the phone shut with a final, 'I'll be up at the farm in fifteen minutes and if you're still arsing about, you'll be up shit creek.'

This strong language elicited a muttered 'Tut tut,' from Dorothy Winterton, a not so muttered, 'Well, *really!*' from Celia Haxby and a secret smile of satisfaction from me. He'd played right into my hands.

Now was the time to make my move. As he stormed towards me, I slipped off my stool. If Grant *was* behind Luís's death, by showing interest in the farm I was putting my head in the tiger's mouth, really upping the ante.

'Hi there, Dave. Did I hear you say you had an orchid farm? How absolutely *fascinating*. I'd just *love* it if you would show me round.'

Though it didn't appear to be the right moment to make the request, I was gambling on the fact that that kind of man wouldn't be able to resist a macho demonstration of kicking arse with his employees. I was right.

'Well now, Debs, I thought you'd never ask. Told you I was available twenty-four/seven, didn't I?' The slight but unmistakable emphasis on 'available' hinted that he had something other than murder in mind.

That, or he was a very good actor.

Located in the hills above Funchal town, the orchid farm was approached via steep, narrow, twisting roads. Funchal is a vertical city, not of skyscrapers, but of houses seeming to grow out of the roofs of those below, on hillsides that would be considered too steep for building in most European countries. As we left the hotel zone on the coast, modern blocks of multi-storeys gave way to shuttered old villas sleeping behind ornate wrought-iron gates and high stucco walls half-concealed in rampant greenery. Higher still, we looked down on the red pantile roofs of white bungalows scattered across the hillside. At an uncultivated grassy patch thickly spattered with yellow and red nasturtiums and the white trumpets of convolvulus, Grant braked to a halt.

'Great view from here. I always make a point of stopping.' He pressed a button and the window on my side slid smoothly down. 'Can you see, down in the harbour there?' Under the pretext of pointing out the tiny replica of Columbus's *Santa Maria*, he leant across me. One arm encircled my shoulders, the other pressed heavily on my breasts. I now realized that narrow twisting roads had one big advantage – Don Juans had to keep both hands on the wheel.

I've developed a technique for extricating myself from such unwelcome attentions – a subtle version of what I believe in Scotland is called The Glasgow Kiss, a vicious and devastating technique of street fighting involving a sudden ramming of the head into an opponent's face.

'Really, where?' I leant forward and flicked my head sideways, with gratifying results.

'*A-uh.*' Both arms were smartly removed.

'Oh, I'm so sorry. I didn't mean…. Oh dear, was that your *nose?*' A somewhat redundant question as both his hands were clasped to that facial feature.

A muffled, 'My fault, clumsy of me. Just pass me a tissue from the glove compartment….' A drop of blood trickled from behind the hands.

I twittered apologies and proffered a succession of tissues while he dabbed at what could only be termed a self-inflicted injury.

This little episode did nothing to improve his temper. It flared up five minutes later at the electronically operated gates of the orchid farm. *Beeeeeeep*. A furious blast on the horn was followed two seconds later by another strident *BEEEEEEEEEEEP* that bounced its way round the surrounding hills and valleys.

'*Christ*, where is everybody? He jabbed at the horn again. 'Have the buggers fallen asleep over the bloody CCTV screen?'

That was interesting. Orchids are ten-a-penny in Madeira, beautiful, but not rare – or worth their weight in gold. Nobody was going to bother to raid the place and load a van with pots of orchids. There'd be the difficulty of selling them on, shipping them off the island without detection in a place where everybody knows everybody else and everybody else's business. So, what *was* he protecting? Why did he need to know who was at his gates?

The gates swung silently open. We shot through and bumped along a cobbled drive curving left through a tunnel of dark-leaved trees and bushes. I blinked in the sudden glare of sunlight as we drove out of the gloom and screeched to a halt in front of an old cottage with clumps of grass and houseleeks growing out of its faded pantiles. Through its open door I could see a computer and a fax machine. The adjoining open-sided concrete shed held only a stack of flat-pack cardboard boxes covering one end of a battered galvanized metal table and bins of discarded flower stems and heads. A line of wheeled trolley-carts contained strap-leaved plants in black plastic pots.

I must say that I was a trifle disappointed. I'd somehow expected a showy display of orchids. On my arrival in Madeira, as part of the standard familiarization procedure at the start of a new mission, I'd visited Jardim Orchídea, a commercial orchid nursery. To draw in the visitor the sales area at the entrance had offered a tempting display of orchids and a stand of air plants, their flower spikes like red and yellow flames licking up from their pots. I'd spent a fascinating hour wandering through a mass display of orchids of every kind and colour. Tall-stemmed cymbidiums (I read the label) carpeted the ground in peach, pink, terracotta and cream. Exquisite yellow, orange, or white orchids clung to artificial-bark trees draped with Spanish moss. In one tree, a waterfall of white blossom tumbled down from a crevice and, from another, a spectacular blue orchid dangled long spaghetti-like roots.

But there was nothing like that here, no trees with dainty orchids roosting on their branches like exotic birds, no colourful massed cymbidiums, no cobweb draperies of Spanish moss.

'Gosh, this isn't *at all* like Jardim Orchídea,' I said somewhat tactlessly, considering the state of his temper. 'Where are all the flowers?'

Grant stopped dabbing his nose long enough to grind out, 'This is a working farm, not a poofy flower shop, my girl.' He flung himself out, slamming the door with a force that made the windows rattle, and strode across to the cottage-cum-office.

Oh dear, off to a bad start. I got out and stood irresolutely beside the car listening to Grant spluttering profanities at increasing volume. Offensive to the ears, but while he was thus engaged it gave me the chance to have a little snoop around. I wandered casually over to the shed, sizing up the office door as I passed. That door was fairly new and of solid modern construction, certainly not of the same vintage as the cottage. Interestingly, in addition to the usual mortise lock, there were another two, top and bottom. Under the eaves, a shiny red burglar alarm box and CCTV cameras stood guard. Supplier and client records can, of course, be valuable, irreplaceable, but it all seemed a bit excessive. Was commercial espionage such a threat in the orchid business? Was he merely protecting his computer from industrial espionage?

Or, was it a clever distraction from the real treasure house? If there's a locked drawer, the general assumption is that there are valuables inside. The best way to keep something under wraps is to conceal it among ordinary objects that nobody would look at twice. I had a feeling that if I was going to find evidence of narcotics, it would not be in that heavily fortified office, but somewhere else on the farm. And that somewhere else was definitely not the packing shed. Any criminal activity would take place elsewhere, well out of view of workers who might talk out of turn.

An overhead pulley system ran the length of the metal table. I put up my hand and gave the cable a tentative chug.

'That carries the individual flower stems to the packers.' Grant was standing behind me.

I swung round. Busy with all those thoughts and theories, I hadn't noticed that he'd got tired of inflicting verbal bloody noses on his minions. As if I had nothing else on my mind, I said, 'I'd love to see this in action. When do the packers come back from their break?'

'You're too late. They finished a couple of hours ago.' He saw my surprise and added, 'Everything must be packed and sent off by midday.'

'So that's why you were at the market at six,' I said.

There was a short pause, both of us busy with our own thoughts. Was he thinking about what he'd *really* been up to?

'That's me, early to rise, early to bed.' His eyes roved slowly over me.

A shout of, 'The vents are open now, boss,' from the doorway at the far end of the shed distracted Grant, sparing me from what he was inevitably about to propose – a jolly romp in that early bed of his.

'Open now, are they? That's three bloody hours too late.' He set off at a pace that had me trotting to keep up. 'The flower spikes will be well and truly open by now. And it's going to hit the bastards' wage packets. That's for sure.'

I dodged round a trolley-cart that had been left in the middle of the floor. 'What's gone wrong, Dave?'

He didn't slacken his pace. 'The lazy buggers didn't check that the vents had opened in greenhouse number four. One thing cymbidiums *don't* like is heat. And if they're forming their spikes, that's next season's flowers done for.'

A narrow dirt alleyway separated the packing shed from a terraced row of six huge greenhouses, each door crudely painted with a white number. Outside house number four, a pony-tailed man and a skinny youth in grubby T-shirt and shorts were shifting nervously from foot to foot waiting for the axe to fall.

'Christ, the temperature's sky high! The moisture's bloody well running down the glass.' Grant strode forward and slid open the green-house door. Hot humid air engulfed us. 'Don't just stand there, you cretins. Create a through-draught. Stir your arses and open the door at the other end.' As the men scuttled past him, he planted a kick on the said arses.

I hadn't expected the greenhouse to be so big, about the length of a football pitch, at a rough guess. Rows and rows of cymbidiums, a sea of yellow, pink, and maroon, above strap-like green leaves stretched into the distance. Here was no attempt to prettify for the public with artificial bark branches. Practical metal staging and black plastic pots were the order of the day.

While he charged up and down the rows examining the state of the flower spikes, I strolled casually towards the back of the greenhouse, stopping now and then to admire a particularly large and colourful bloom.

'Do you mind if I take a photo of this one, Dave?' I called. 'It's such a wonderful shade of green. I've never seen a flower that colour.'

'Fine by me, Debs,' he sounded pre-occupied. 'We don't keep things under wraps on this orchid farm.'

I glanced in his direction. He was peering closely at a white-flowered plant, paying no attention to me. I raised the camera, positioned a stem and two flower heads artistically on the screen and pressed the button. If Grant took an unwelcome interest in my photographic activity, it would be something to show him. A general shot carefully featured the two employees who had staggered in with an enormous fan and were manhandling it to point at an angle across the greenhouse. I'd email it to London. Criminal records might dig up something.

Behind them through the open doorway was a flat-roofed low building with no visible windows. If I was correct in my theory that the office dripping with security gadgets was a clever decoy to lure the inquisitive and distract attention from somewhere else, this just might be that somewhere else.

Grant was making his way towards me carrying the white-flowered cymbidium. Even at a distance I could see damaged brown areas on the petals. I'd ask him some innocent questions, then slip in a loaded one, like a bowler sending the batsman some deceptively easy balls and then delivering a googly. His reaction to that loaded question might tell me a lot.

I gestured towards the sea of flowers. 'I was just wondering how you increase your stock. Besides buying in, I mean. Do you grow from seed or take cuttings?'

His smile faded. Had I irritated him by betraying my ignorance of orchid propagation? To show him I wasn't totally ignorant, I rattled on, 'When I went round Jardim Orchídea I saw a laboratory for growing new orchids in test tubes. You can look through a window and see all the equipment – microscopes, ultra-violet lights, that sort of thing. Do you have anything like that, Dave?'

Behind me a loud vibrating hum was followed by a blast of cool air as the fan started up. It seemed to startle Grant too, for he dropped the pot of cymbidiums he was carrying. He stood there scowling down at the precious specimen, at the snapped-off flower stems and chunks of bark scattered across the floor. It was as if I'd bowled the googly and uprooted the stumps.

'Oh dear,' I cried, rushing forward, 'that must have been – er, must be – a valuable plant.' I crouched down and attempted to gather up the broken stems. 'I shouldn't have been asking you all these questions and taking your mind off what you were doing.'

He took a deep breath, pulling himself together with a visible effort. 'Not your fault, Debs. Nothing you said. Those bloody ham-fisted layabouts nearly toppled the fan onto that bench of orchids.' He grabbed the empty pot and hurled it at Pony-tail's head. 'Don't just stand there, you lazy bastards. Get a brush and sweep up this mess.'

As the employees took the opportunity to beat a strategic retreat, I got to my feet, not quite sure what to do with my sorry bouquet.

'Er, what will I do with these?'

Grant stared at me, his mind elsewhere, then with a brusque, 'Just throw them on the floor. They're no use to me,' he turned away. 'Keep them. Stick them in a vase. Do what you bloody well like with them.'

Something had struck a raw nerve, but I couldn't figure out what it was.

'C'mon, I've got to get back to Funchal.' He walked briskly back through the greenhouse.

I took a last look at that nondescript, windowless building framed in the doorway at the rear. That, not the office with its high-tech security, would be my objective when I paid the orchid farm a second visit. And when I came, it would be with Gorgonzola.

On the drive back to Funchal, Grant was uncharacteristically silent, unnervingly so. Where was the chat-up routine, where the yawn-making anecdotes of one-upmanship, the endless tales of how he had scored over business rivals? Was he still brooding over whatever had upset him in the greenhouse?

I certainly was. I didn't for one minute believe that his outburst had been provoked by his employees' clumsiness with the fan. *Was* it something I'd said? I'd brought up once again the name of the rival nursery, Jardim Orchídea. Was it just a case of business jealousy? He'd certainly been a bit touchy earlier when I'd made that innocent comparison between his place and the Jardim. 'Poofy flower shop', he'd called it. But if it *wasn't* simply a case of warring businesses.... I leant my head against the headrest and thought about it....

'Where do you want me to drop you? It's the second time I've asked.' The irritation in his voice was unmistakable.

I jolted awake. 'Sorry, must have been day-dreaming. Anywhere near the market will do. I need to buy some fruit and vegetables before it closes.' And I did. One of the cardinal rules of undercover work is never to let your guard drop. You must behave as if the enemy has you under surveillance 24/7.

At this time of day the market was practically deserted, only a handful of tourists were wandering among the stalls. I made some purchases, then crossed the road to the commercial centre where I could lose myself among the early-evening shoppers crowding the arcades and filling the cafés. I strolled into the building – and out by the back entrance. When I was sure I wasn't being followed, I made my way to the police station, entering by an unobtrusive side door. I'd jot down some notes on the orchid farm and Grant's behaviour while it was still fresh in my mind. It might also be worth asking my police colleagues if they knew of any ill-feeling between the Jardim's owners and Grant.

The windows of my cubby-hole of an office face south. When I arrive in the morning, I usually make a point of opening the window and closing the louvred shutters, but today I hadn't been in at all and the heat had built up. In an action replay of Grant's measures for fast-cooling his cymbidium house, I flung the door and window wide open and for a few minutes leant on the sill gazing over the tumble of pantiled roofs and narrow alleys. On a rooftop clothes line, a green apron and faded blue trousers flapped in the stiff breeze blowing from the harbour; a couple of pigeons squatting on a nearby gutter were crooning love-notes to each other, and from the lane below the window drifted up the *click click* of hurrying heels on the cobbles.

I returned to my desk and was just finishing a rough sketch of the layout of the orchid farm, outlining the windowless building in red, when I noticed a closely typed sheet of paper lying on the floor between my desk and the window, blown off my desk by the artificial gale I'd created. I gave it a cursory glance as I scooped it up. It was a summary of the pathologist's post-mortem report on Luís Gomes, translated into English for my benefit. Scrawled across the top of the report in the *comandante*'s aggressively spiky writing was, *Explain, Smith!!*

Explain? Explain what? My eyes raced down the page ...

CAUSE OF DEATH:
Single stab wound in the back ... long, narrow instrument, possibly a fish or meat skewer ... Penetration of the heart ...

TIME OF DEATH:
Post-mortem changes in the body ... extent of rigor mortis ... examination of corneal fluid ... Estimated time of death not earlier than 0800 hours, not later than 1100 hours on Friday April 7.

I was puzzled. There was nothing out of the ordinary in the report. Nothing that would account for the *comandante* blowing her top as signified by that peremptory *Explain, Smith!!*

It was true that over the past month I had done little right in her eyes, and now she seemed to be blaming me for whatever it was that had been found at the post-mortem.

I read the report again, this time more slowly. If I had to go knocking at her office door asking *her* to explain, she'd take it as further clear evidence of my incompetence.

I was only on the third reading of the report that the import of the final sentence sank in. *Estimated time of death not earlier than 0800 hours, not later than 1100 hours on Friday April 7.*

Not *later* than 1100 hours ... Stunned, I stared at the words in disbelief. When Luís had whispered to me, 'Meet me *três á tarde* at the Beerhouse', he was already dead!

CHAPTER FIVE

'No, *senhora*, there is no doubt at all. This man cannot have been dead less than five hours. All our tests confirm it.' Dr Palmeira's tone was sharp. Clearly the pathologist was impatient to end the conversation and get on with his next grisly dissection. 'Now, if you will excuse me....' He turned and walked away.

There *must* be some explanation. At eleven o'clock Luís Gomes had been very much alive. At four in the afternoon I had been *sure* it was the eyes of Luís Gomes that had stared sightlessly up into mine from the bottom of the rescue boat, as sure of that as Dr Palmeira was of his conclusion that he'd died not *later* than eleven in the morning. Assuming he was correct about the time of death, the only possible explanation must be that the dead man was *not* Luís. I stared after the pathologist.... When the report had come into police HQ with his name on it, I had just accepted it, hadn't given it another thought.

Before Palmeira could disappear into his clinical white-tiled world, I called after him, 'One last question, doctor. Who made the formal identification?'

Not bothering to turn round, he called over his shoulder, 'Ask at reception, *senhora*. The information is there.'

It was. Initial identification of the body had been from a credit card bearing Luís's name and address. Formal identification had been made, not by the manager of the hotel, but by the closest of relatives, his mother. There was nothing for it but to do some gentle probing. Luís's mother would have to be asked some delicate questions. That was why a couple of hours later, Gorgonzola and I were driving up to the mountain village of Boa Morte situated in the range of hills round Funchal that end abruptly at Cabo Girão, one of Europe's tallest sea cliffs.

'A case of mistaken identity, eh, Gorgonzola? Has to be.' I could think of no other explanation for that time discrepancy.

There was no reply. Strapped into her harness, she was resting her paws on the window and staring down wistfully at the red roofs of the fishing village of Câmara de Lobos and the grey sea far, far below.

'Still smelling the fish, G? If I'm right, there's definitely something fishy going on here and if drugs are at the bottom of it, you'll soon nose them out, won't you?'

A loud purr signified assent – though that could have had something to do with the word 'fish'.

I swerved to avoid a man walking up the road carrying a crate of cabbages on his shoulder, a reminder that such a narrow twisting road demanded my full attention. Pondering over why a mother might fail to identify her own son had to be put on hold.

Every inch of the almost vertical hillside was stepped with terraces of dark green interspersed with lighter green and the red-brown of bare earth. Across the valley a waterfall tumbled in a thin white line down a series of cliff faces plummeting finally into the depths of a *barranco*.

Peeeeeeeeep. The loud blast of a horn gave a second's advance warning before a local bus careered towards me round the blind corner ahead, edging past with a loud hiss of compressed air from its brakes. Hairpin bend after hairpin bend, the road clung to the mountainside, narrowing as it climbed towards the top of the ridge of hills clothed in pine, eucalyptus, and a layer of dark-grey cloud.

'Should have brought your raincoat, G,' I said, as a scatter of drops bounced heavily off the bonnet, leaving their mark in the dust. 'Luckily I've got mine.'

A flurry of rain hit the windscreen. I switched on the wipers and peered through the streaming glass at a signpost. *Levada do Norte, Boa Morte*. I turned into the road indicated, changing down into second gear for the hill ahead.

Five minutes later I drew to a halt at the crossroads that seemed to be the heart of the straggling village. Boa Morte translated as Good Death, but it hadn't been a good death for the man they'd fished out of Funchal harbour. The misty drizzle that had replaced the torrential rain lent a suitably funereal air to the place. Droplets of water trickled like tears down the face of the statue of *Nossa Senhora da Boa Morte* gazing across the deserted street from her wall shrine of discoloured green and blue tiles.

The only sign of life was the open door of the one public building, a little bar-cum-shop. I'd been given no specific address for Luís's mother. I'd ask for directions in there. As my eyes adjusted to the gloom I could make out a long low wooden counter and the dull gleam of bottles on shelves.

A voice spoke softly from the shadows. '*Bom dia.*'

'I was wondering if you could tell me—'

A man rose from the stool behind the counter. 'If it is the *levada* you want, *senhora*—'

My turn to interrupt. 'No, no, I am looking for the house of Senhora Gomes.'

He rubbed his bristly chin. 'The name is common here.'

'It is the *senhora* whose son died four days ago.'

A silence. From the gloom came the sharp *click click click* of rosary beads.

'Senhora Carmella Gomes has her house on the *levada*, but it is not a good time to visit the poor lady.'

It was a struggle to understand the thick local accent, but his meaning was clear. He did not want me to call upon Senhora Gomes.

I chose my words carefully. 'Of course, *senhor*. I would not wish to trouble the lady at such a time, but I spoke with Luís a few hours before he died, and ...' I let the sentence trail away. The inference that she'd want to hear what I had to say sank into the silence.

Click Click Click Click. The worry beads metronomed into action once more.

I waited. Any more pressure would be counter-productive and end in a point-blank refusal to divulge the information.

After subjecting his grey bristles to another going over, he seemed to come to a decision. 'You take the road going up the hill. When you reach the *levada*, turn left.' A machine-gun rattle of the beads. 'You'll find the *senhora*'s house half a mile along the *levada*, after the tunnel.'

He sank back onto his stool. As I left the bar, the beads clicked into action once again.

A weak shaft of sunlight was shining into the watchful eyes of *Nossa Senhora da Boa Morte*. The low cloud had moved on from the mountain tops, but the cloud of grump over Gorgonzola's head was decidedly black. She hated being left in the car when there was a world out there to explore. Placatory titbit of a crunchy cat biscuit administered, I drove slowly up the road that the barman had indicated and parked on a flat patch of ground next to the *levada*.

The Levada do Norte is part of the old irrigation system that brings down water from the interior mountain range to the coastal plain. Alongside the channel ran the narrow maintenance path used by walkers and hikers. Wearing her working collar, G strolled ahead of me on the beaten earth track beside the narrow concrete channel. The tip of her tail twitched as she investigated clumps of strap-leaved agapanthus, the patches of clear-yellow oxalis and wild purple pea that edged the path. Around us the mountain slopes were clothed in pine and silvery eucalyptus arrowing their pencil-thin trunks to a blue sky scattered with clouds. The only sounds were the scuff of my shoes on the hard earth of the path and the distant bark of a dog.

Fifteen minutes or so along the *levada* and with perhaps quarter of a mile to go before I would reach the tunnel, an alcove shrine to the Virgin was built into the wall of a house. In her role of Our Lady of Sorrows she gazed mournfully back at me reminding me of the delicacy of the forthcoming interview. To speak to a mother grieving over the sudden death of a son was a difficult enough task, but how was I going to suggest to Senhora Gomes that her son might not in fact be dead? I wasn't looking forward to that conversation.

I tickled the back of Gorgonzola's ears as she sat on the wall grooming her fur. 'C'mon, G, we'd better be moving.'

Obediently she gave a last lick at her paw, stretched lazily, and jumped down, not onto the path but into the garden.

Yip yip yip. A small brown dog shot from under an almond tree frothy with blossom and leapt forward tugging at its chain. With a provocative twitch of her tail, G stalked slowly past, just out of reach. Before she could embarrass me further by bringing out the owner, I hurried on along the *levada*, knowing that having made her point, she would follow.

A volley of barking pursued us past a second house with its lichened pantiled roof level with the *levada* path. Beneath an apple tree in pink bud, a washing line of faded blue jeans, yellow T-shirt, assorted socks and a cotton bedsheet drooped soggily, as wet, or wetter, than when first hung out.

A gust of wind sent a scatter of withered eucalyptus leaves into the silently flowing water of the *levada*. They kept pace with me as I followed the concrete channel that hugged the rock face in a lazy curve across the wooded mountainside. Up to now the path had been broad and level with a wide border of low bushes and long grass acting as a natural safety barrier against the sheer drop to the valley hundreds of metres below, but when I rounded a jutting shoulder of rock, although the path was still broad, it had lost that comforting buffer of vegetation. I've a good head for heights, so it did not trouble me unduly. What did, was the bulge of rock face overhanging the water channel. The path tapered away to practically nothing. Two hundred metres beyond the bulge, I could see the dark mouth of the tunnel, but to get there I'd have to edge past the overhang on a ledge barely the width of a kitchen shelf.

I stopped. The directions of Worry-bead Man in Boa Morte had been precise. *You take the road going up the hill. When you reach the* levada, *turn left.* Could I have got it wrong? After all, his accent had been difficult to understand. No, there was no way I would have mixed up *esquerda,* left, with *direita,* right. And he'd definitely said I'd find the house half a mile along the *levada, after* the tunnel. Well, I'd turned left, and I'd found the tunnel, but no sane person would contemplate continuing along such a path. Certainly not Senhora Gomes, a middle-aged housewife with her carrier bags of shopping.

Gorgonzola brushed past me. For her, the tiny ledge held no terrors. Moth-eaten tail held aloft, she was moving confidently forward, as graceful as a fashion model gliding along the catwalk sporting an avant-garde fur accessory.

'Come back, G,' I called. 'Somebody's being playing silly buggers with us.' It was clear that Worry-bead Man had not *wanted* me to find Senhora Gomes's house. The question was why? *Had* it been merely because he didn't want a grieving mother disturbed? Well, there was no way of telling, and there was nothing for it now but to retrace my steps.

As we neared the house with the chained dog, I produced G's harness.

'For cats who can't be trusted, G,' I said. She had the grace to look guilty as I clipped on the lead.

I'd trot past the house at a speed that would keep her from straying from the straight and narrow. Best laid plans and all that.

An old woman dressed from head to toe in black was leaning on the gate. '*Bom dia, senhora.*'

I returned the greeting, casting a surreptitious look over her shoulder for the chained dog. Gorgonzola could withstand only so much temptation. 'Nothing less than perfect behaviour, G,' I muttered.

The woman clutched at my arm and peered at me short-sightedly. 'The *senhora* must take care. This *levada* is not good to walk a dog. Near to the tunnel it is very dangerous. Only last week, two tourists were killed when they fell from the path.' Turning towards the Virgin nestled in the alcove, she made the sign of the cross.

'*Obrigada,* thank you for the warning, *senhora.* I think I took the wrong turning. I was looking for the house of Carmella Gomes. Perhaps you can tell me if it is along this way?'

'Yes, *senhora.* Carmella's house is on the *levada.*' Her hand clutched again at my sleeve, as with her right she made another slow sign of the cross. 'May Our Lady of Sorrows, who knows what it is to lose a son, bring comfort in her hour of darkness.'

I muttered something appropriate and gave a warning tug at the lead as Gorgonzola gathered herself in preparation to jump up onto the wall, the perfect vantage point to survey enemy territory.

Now was the chance to gain more information. Women of all ages and nationalities love nothing more than a good gossip.

'He was a good son to the poor lady?'

'Ah, *senhora,* that is where we do not understand the ways of God.' She crossed herself again. 'The son who brings dishonour to the name of Gomes lives; the son who was an angel to his mother dies. The Lord gives and the Lord takes. Only Our Lady understands.'

'Perhaps the son whom God has spared is young and foolish, but will now mend his ways,' I said.

'If it were only so.' A heavy sigh followed another energetic signing of the cross. 'Roberto is her first born.' Though there was no one in sight along the *levada,* she lowered her voice to a whisper. 'Alas, that one is a slave to the evil powder, *senhora.* The young today are—'

A violent tug pulled the lead from my fingers as G took the opportunity to put into operation a plan of her own. A leap and a scrabble, and she was sitting on the wall ready to taunt the enemy.

'Down, G.' I made a grab at the trailing lead.

When there were no retaliatory barks from the other side of the wall, I relaxed. The dog must be asleep.

'*Senhora,*' I said, 'can you tell me how far—?'

I never did get an answer to my question for a loud provocative *purrrrr* from G triggered a strident *yip yip yip yip yip* and frenzied rattling of chain from the other side of the wall, making further conversation impossible. G and I beat a hasty retreat along the *levada.*

'That was really naughty, G,' I scolded. 'If it hadn't been for that little interruption of yours, I might have learned more about Roberto Gomes.'

A twitch of the tail and a wide yawn made it clear that she was unrepentant. The message was plain: a cat has to do what a cat has to do.

I arrived back at the road that led down to Boa Morte. Here, Worrybead Man had told me to turn left. This time I turned right, and fifteen minutes walk along the *levada*, brought me to a small cottage. Nailed to the gate was a wooden board with the name *Gomes* in faded black lettering. At first sight the little house appeared unoccupied, curtains tightly closed, no smoke spiralling out of the chimney, no sign of life whatsoever. Senhora Gomes must have gone to stay with a relative.

For some minutes I stood on the path with my hand on the gate. My journey had been a waste of time. I'd half-turned to make my way back along the *levada*, when out of the corner of my eye I glimpsed an infinitesimal movement of a curtain. Somebody was at home after all. I pushed open the gate.

I suppose you might describe the garden as a sort of Mediterranean potager: blue firework-bursts of agapanthus heads, purple spears of gladioli, white arum trumpets as smooth as silk, and a pink rose, exotic for Madeira, mingling happily with the rough foliage of cabbages and potatoes.

I hadn't yet decided how I was going to handle the difficult meeting with Luís's mother. I'd just have to play it by ear. I unclipped G's lead, stuffed the harness in my bag, and replaced it with her working collar.

'You know what to do,' I said.

With a pert waggle of her rear that signified, 'You're talking to a pro', she threaded her way through a clump of arum lilies. If Luís's brother had stashed any drugs, she'd soon nose them out.

The shadow of a cloud flitted across the sunlit path, dulling the glint of upturned green bottles buried neck-down in the red earth. Perhaps Luís had collected those empty bottles from the bar to use as an artistic decorative edging. An ancient pine, devoid of needles except for its topmost branches, twisted arthritic limbs low over the pantiled roof, its huge grey cones black against the sky like a huddle of roosting birds.

'Senhora Gomes,' I called. Again the curtain twitched. 'Senhora Gomes,' I called again.

I heard the rattle of a key in the lock, and the door opened a cautious few centimetres.

'Who is it? What do you want?' The voice was wary.

'I worked beside your son at the hotel.' This was only a slight exaggeration. 'I have something to tell you.' What that was, I had no idea.

I hoped inspiration would strike if I managed to draw her into conversation.

The door swung open. Against the gloom of the interior, her funereal clothes rendered her almost invisible. A pale disembodied face, eyes red with weeping, appeared to float in the darkness. For a moment she said nothing. Then she stepped back and beckoned me in.

She closed the door behind me. I heard the sound of the key being turned. In a country where people do not normally lock their doors, it was a sign that Senhora Gomes was afraid of visitors. As I stood letting my eyes become accustomed to the gloom, she brushed past me and threw open the window shutters. Light flooded in, revealing a sparsely furnished kitchen-living room: a sink with a single plate and cup on the draining board, and above it, two shelves displaying a row of earthenware plates and cups. Four wicker-seated chairs were set round a heavy wooden table. The only other furniture in the room was a low cupboard. On it stood a vase of arum lilies, a black-framed photograph of her dead son – and, startling alien anachronism in a setting reminiscent of a Brueghel interior, a modern telephone, no doubt provided by Roberto. In the drug world speedy communication is essential.

She pulled out a chair and motioned me to take another. The woman was younger than I expected. Thick black hair, as yet without a trace of grey, was swept back from an oval face and secured with a black ribbon. On her lap her work-roughened hands kneaded a sodden handkerchief.

'It is hard for a mother to lose a son,' I said.

When she made no reply, I reached for the black-framed photograph and set it down on the table between us. 'Never to see him again....'

I let the silence grow.

While she dabbed at her swollen eyes with the tiny square of cloth, I reached over again and picked up another framed picture standing half-hidden by the vase of flowers. It could have been a photo of the same man. But it wasn't.

The resemblance was striking, but my training in facial recognition enabled me to pinpoint slight differences: the shape of an earlobe, the distance between the eyes, the shape of the lips – things that would have gone unnoticed by most. With the two photos side by side, it was easy.

She was watching me, fear in her eyes.

'It is harder still, *senhora*, when that son is her first-born,' I said gently. I held up the black-framed picture. 'This is not Luís.' I waited for her reaction.

Her hand flew to her mouth.

'And I can prove it.'

An animal wail that lifted the hairs on the back of my neck filled the small room.

'My son is dead,' she sobbed.

I held her gaze. 'It is as I thought. Luís was in danger because he was going to speak to the police. If the killers think he is dead, he will be safe.'

'Who are you?' she whispered.

'A friend of Luís. I wish to help him, if you'll let me, *senhora*.'

She sat there, eyes wide, hand still pressed to mouth. For some minutes neither of us spoke. Through the open window the chime of a clock striking the hour drifted faintly up from the valley below. I waited.

'Who–are–you?' the words sank into the heavy silence like pebbles into a still pool.

'My job is to fight drug crime.' I took her hand. 'You must help me find the men who killed Roberto – before they find Luís.'

Apart from a sharp intake of breath, she made no response.

'Believe me, *senhora*, Luís is in great danger. These men are ruthless. Roberto is beyond your help, Luís is not.'

'I don't know what you mean.' Her face flushed. 'My Roberto was – is – a good boy. I will hear nothing bad against him. *Nothing*, do you hear? It is Luís who is in his grave.' She jumped up with such force that her chair toppled backwards with a crash. 'I must ask you to go now and leave a mother to her grief.'

The instinct to protect the reputation of her dead son was blinding her to the danger Luís was in. Slowly I rose to my feet. I'd gone too far, overplayed my hand.

She ran over to the door and flung it open. 'Go, *senhora*!'

I made one last attempt. 'If you hear from Luís' – I pointed at the telephone – 'tell him—'

'How can I hear anything from the grave, *senhora*? You must not come again.'

There was nothing else I could do. To prolong my stay, would be a gross intrusion. With a sigh I stepped out onto the path.

At that moment of defeat I felt the receiver in my pocket vibrate. It was picking up the low crooning purr from Gorgonzola, the signal she had been trained to give when she detected drugs. I pulled it out of my pocket and studied the readout. Close, very close, five metres away. I turned till the flashing location indicator pulsed red, directing me to the source. There could be no mistake, G and the drugs were somewhere inside the house.

'Roberto kept bad company, Senhora Gomes. And this' – I held up the receiver – 'proves it.'

Before she could block my way, I brushed past her and re-entered the house. The door of the adjoining room was slightly ajar. From inside came the faint rumble of G's crooning purr.

'Let me show you,' I said, and pushed open the door.

Apart from a couple of gold-framed religious prints hanging on the wall, this room was as sparsely furnished as the kitchen-living room. A brass double bed filled most of it, leaving space only for an armoire wardrobe and the most amazing three-tier metal ring washstand. Above the white porcelain bowl with blue floral design, the metal looped ornately round to clasp a porcelain-framed oval mirror, two curved tendrils branching off to form perfect towel hooks. The second tier held a small soap dish, and on the bottom ring stood a matching water jug in a bowl.

On top of the wardrobe crouched a smugly purring Gorgonzola.

'Where are you going? What do you think you're d—?' At the sight of the scruffy cat making itself at home in her bedroom, Senhora Gomes's protests terminated in a small scream.

'This animal has been trained to detect drugs, *senhora*.' I stepped over to the wardrobe. 'Move over, G,' I said.

She leapt lightly onto the bed and I reached up and lifted down the suitcase. Judging by its weight, I – or rather G – had made quite a find, ten kilos perhaps. I opened the lid, watching Senhora Gomes as I did so. The blood drained from her face at the sight of the neat packages lined up inside. Eyes wide, she stared at the case like a terrified rabbit mesmerized by a predatory stoat.

'*Nao, Roberto, nao.*' It was a cry of despair, a cry of anguish that no one could fake.

I sat her down on the bed and put an arm round her shaking shoulders. 'On the day that those men killed Roberto, Luís was going to tell me something.' I pulled her round to look at me. 'I have to speak to him, *senhora*. He is in grave danger. When you see him, if he phones you, tell him he can leave a message for me at the Massaroco Hotel. I am Senhora Smith. He knows when I will be there.'

I could only hope that *this* assignation with Luís would be more successful than the last.

CHAPTER SIX

Late that afternoon I sat in my cupboard of an office at Police HQ, staring at the battered green suitcase on my desk, trying to decide what to do. I should, of course, hand it in to the *comandante* with a report, but I was reluctant to do so. Undoubtedly her response would not be subtle. She'd order a Shock-and-Awe armed raid on the Gomes house. Poor Senhora Gomes would be bundled into a police car and hauled off for questioning. Luís would go to ground, and with him, any hope of solving the case.

The blades of the ceiling fan moved slowly overhead, barely stirring the heavy air. Out in the corridor a door slammed. I came to a decision. Pulling open a drawer, I rummaged till I found an evidence label. I filled in location and date and attached it to the suitcase together with my report. Then I shoved the whole lot into the narrow gap between the filing cabinet and the wall. I'd bring it to the *comandante*'s attention at a time when it wouldn't throw a spanner in the works.

Satisfied that the suitcase and its contents would be quite safe, I switched off the fan and closed the door behind me. It was time to head off to my little gingerbread house and relax.

Gorgonzola welcomed me back by twining herself affectionately round my legs as I walked up the path. I made up a rum *poncha* with a slug of orange juice, then G and I climbed the wooden stairs to the little balcony with its screening curtain of wisteria. From here I could look out over the busy main road and the pavements of strolling pedestrians to the broad sweep of Funchal Bay. I sat on the wicker rocking chair sipping the *poncha* and reviewing the day's events. Eyes closed, G lay on my knee drooling and twitching, carried away in some feline dream.

I was half asleep too when the blare of car horns brought me sharply awake. At first I wasn't going to disturb G's slumber over something silly like a prohibited U-turn on the road, but curiosity got the better of me.

'Sorry about this, G.' I lifted her off my lap and deposited her on a chair.

Sure enough, a car was guiltily straightening itself up from a U-turn. I was just about to sit down again, when I saw the spikily gelled blond hair of Charles Mason. He was walking quickly along the far pavement in the direction of town. The body language, the way he brushed past the pedestrians, almost elbowing them out of his path, showed he was a man with a mission. And fifty metres behind was Zara Porter-Browne. Dark glasses hid her eyes, but the large floppy hat hanging low over her face didn't quite conceal those emerald green locks. When Mason stopped to allow a car out of a hotel driveway, she darted behind one of the thick-trunked eucalyptus trees lining the pavement. When he hurried on, she came out from her hiding place and followed at a discreet distance. Interesting.

'Life's full of little surprises, eh, Gorgonzola?' I said, and thought-fully resumed my lazy rocking.

Next morning I decided G and I would pay a visit to Celia Haxby – or rather to her room at the Massaroco Hotel. I knew she wouldn't be there as she was touring the cellars of Blandy's Wine Lodge. I reckoned I had about an hour and a half before there was any danger of her returning.

'An ideal opportunity, G, to have a sniff around, don't you think?' I fetched her working collar and dangled it in front of her.

She stretched, yawned, and sat up. A few minutes later we were speeding along the Estrada Monumental. At the hotel I parked under the shade of a spreading kapok tree, and pulled out the hated cat-carrier from the boot.

'Box time, I'm afraid, G.' I held the door open invitingly, keeping my fingers crossed that she wouldn't create too much of a fuss. The working collar did the trick. Duty was Duty. With a loud *miaow* signi-fying, 'I hope you appreciate I'm only doing this because I want to,' she got in.

I left her in the car and made a quick reconnoitre through the foyer. The key to room 316 was lying in its pigeonhole behind the reception desk. The coast was clear. I wasn't going to risk a face-to-face encounter with Dorothy Winterton or even Haxby herself. The fact that she'd left her key at reception was no guarantee that she had *actually* gone on the trip to Blandy's so, cat-carrier in hand, I slipped through the swing doors to the service stairs. I make it a practice not to use a lift in hotels or apartments unless it's absolutely necessary.

When I search a room, it's not a quick flip through the contents and out. It's essential to leave everything exactly as found. Ninety minutes would soon slip by. Therefore I didn't pause to listen to raised voices as I passed the service door to the second floor. What stopped me in my tracks was Zara Porter-Browne's high-pitched trilling laugh. It cut through the metal door as cleanly as the hot flame of an oxyacetylene torch through steel plate. I nipped back and eased the door open a fraction.

'... and you didn't count on me following you to that restaurant last night, did you, Chas? Never once looked back. Too intent on making it with your next meal ticket, were you?'

'I won't tell you again, Browne. Get out of my way. I'm warning you!'

'Or what, Mr Ro-ll-ex? Another soaring trill of laughter. 'Spaghetti, *tee hee hee*, hanging from your ears, tomato sauce dribbling down your face and off the end of your nose! Spoilt your cosy *tête-à-tête* with little Miss Moneybags, did I? I can't wait, Chas, to put those shots on *You Tube.' Tee hee – ow*!

'You silly *bitch.*'

'You're hurting me, Chas. Ow! You'll break my arm! *Ow!*'

I'd have to do something. I put the cat carrier down and prepared to walk casually in on them.

Charles's response to her cries was a mocking laugh. 'This is nothing to what I'll do if you mess—' His yelp of pain told me that Zara was in no need of rescue.

'I'll be watching you, Chas. Try your tricks on anybody else and you know what to expect.' The *tap tap tap tap* of high-heeled sandals receded unhurriedly along the corridor.

I picked up the cat carrier and continued up the service stairs. 'No need to worry about her. She can look after herself – just like you, G.'

I turned my thoughts back to the task in hand: the search of Haxby's room. Instinct told me Victoria Haxby with her loud paintings and her equally loud ego was up to no good. Instinct is something I never ignore.

I pushed open the service door on the third floor. The corridor was deserted. I stepped smartly along to 316 and tapped on the door. You can't afford to take anything for granted in my line of work. I counted to twenty and knocked again, excuse at the ready. No reply. I inserted my electronic picklock and I was in.

Once we were safely inside, I opened the carrier and let Gorgonzola explore. I'd expected *some* sign of painterly activity, but was surprised to see a whole row of pictures stacked in twos leaning against the wall opposite the bed. I'd seen the speed with which Haxby had covered a canvas in splodges of paint, but it was astonishing to find that in the five days she'd been in Madeira she had completed no fewer than six paintings. I flicked through them.

The first one, of the 'splodge and smear' school, brought to mind the artist Howard Hodgson. 'Pleasing and possibly mood evoking, these colours, eh, G?'

She sat down in front the picture, head on one side. After a few moments' consideration of the orange, yellow, green and aubergine splashes, she yawned dismissively.

'Not up to *your* standard, is it? You could have produced one of these in five minutes.'

G was one of the rare 'cats that paint'. On four notable occasions in the past, she had shown herself to be equally artistic. Another yawn and she wandered over to give a once-over to something more interesting, Haxby's gaudy multi-coloured smock hanging over the back of a chair.

Behind the Jackson Pollock look-alike picture was that spectacularly awful Gaugin-cum-Van Gogh I had seen her working on in the garden. I carefully replaced both paintings as I'd found them and turned to the next stack. A scene of fishing boats drawn up on a foreshore was probably the fruits of those visits to Câmara de Lobos.

Behind that picture was a sombre study in muddy greens and greys of rolling hills. I picked it up and studied it. Haxby couldn't have set her easel in front of this sort of landscape in Madeira.... There were enough views here to keep any artist busy, so why would she...? Anything that breaks an expected pattern, I file away carefully for future reference.

Still life studies formed the third stack. One, very small, was a realistic and quite pleasing composition depicting a giant teacup towering pinkly over a slab of raw fish and assorted unidentifiable objects. The other was, in my eyes, a rather childish drawing with poor perspective, the sort of thing that gives Art a bad name: two vases of flowers and a goblet appeared to hover over a yellow table on which lay, in weird combination, an apple, a rose and a banana.

I stood back and surveyed the stacks of paintings. This conveyor-belt production implied that there must be a market for them.

'Whatever turns you on, eh, G?' I said, looking to see what she was up to.

Having finished an unproductive recce of the room, and now bored with the proceedings, she had turned her attention to the portable easel propped in a corner near the window and was standing, front legs braced on the wood. Another couple of seconds and she'd be clawing vigorously at that expensive piece of equipment.

'No, Gorgonzola.' The intended nail filing was converted to a swipe at an imaginary fly.

Ugly scratch marks would hardly go unnoticed by Haxby on her return – they'd be a sure giveaway that somebody had been in the room. I could visualize all too clearly the interrogation of the maid, indignant protestations, the summoning of the manager ... Just the knowledge that there had been an intruder would be damage enough. Haxby wouldn't have to find out who it had been.

'That was *really* bad of you, G,' I said reproachfully.

She must have thought so too, for she crept guiltily into the cat-carrier without any of the usual fuss. It was while I was bending down securing its door that I spotted the corner of a leaflet lodged between the chest of drawers and the wardrobe. Another of my rules is never to leave a promising stone unturned – or a piece of paper unread. I fished it out. It was merely a pricelist of artists' works, the sort of thing that private art galleries provide for prospective buyers at an exhibition. Well, can't win them all. I slipped it back where I'd found it.

Mind occupied with the near-disaster of the damaged easel, I stepped out into the corridor. And only just avoided bumping into Dorothy Winterton on her way to her room on the same floor.

Her startled, 'Oh!' synchronized with my gasp of, 'Sorry, I didn't—'

In a reflex action I swung round, concealing the cat-carrier with my body and pulled the door shut, at the same time calling out, 'OK, Celia, I'll see to that and let you know tomorrow.' With a nod and a smile to Mrs Winterton, I headed back along the corridor.

There'd be time to deliver G to the gingerbread house before I nipped back to the hotel for my office hour. It was while I was driving along the Estrada Monumental that an unwelcome thought occurred to me. By addressing that departing remark to the absent Celia I'd probably increased the chances of Dorothy Winterton bringing up the subject of my visit at one of their tea-and-cake sessions. I had taken a calculated risk. Perhaps I'd just succeeded in drawing unwelcome attention to myself....

CHAPTER SEVEN

I hadn't bargained for a traffic snarl-up on the road to the hotel, so I walked into the Mimosa Bar for my office hour a bit later than planned. It was already quite crowded with late-morning snackers or early lunchers. I took up my position near the counter-bar, ready to give advice or deal with problems, but today nobody was waiting to consult me. At the opposite side of the room Zara Porter-Browne sat hunched and brooding over a long drink. She was shooting malevolent glances in the direction of the terrace where Charles Mason had joined Dorothy Winterton for afternoon tea. A charming smile and easy laugh are tools of the conman's trade and he was employing them to the full with total disregard of the threatened repercussions from Zara.

He was certainly not the type to socialize with lonely elderly females, chivalry being a concept foreign to his understanding. That made two of us wondering what he was up to. I made it my business to find out. From my briefcase I selected a leaflet on the lava caves at São Vicente and wandered casually in their direction. Keeping my back turned to Dorothy and Charles, I stopped at a nearby table ostensibly to chat with the couple sitting there. They had been a little apprehensive about taking a trip on the Monte toboggan – a high-backed wicker bench on sledge runners. Two men in traditional whites and straw boater hats steer this flimsy carriage down a twisting narrow road into the centre of Funchal, braking the headlong rush by the friction of their boots. As George launched into an enthusiastic account of how they had careered down the steep tarmac road meeting on-coming cars and trucks, I nodded and smiled at appropriate intervals. My real interest, however, was in the conversation going on at the table behind me....

'Really?' Dorothy sounded more than a bit bored. She wasn't going to be the easy pushover that Charles had no doubt envisaged. 'Well, I've not got any spare cash to invest.'

'That's just it, you get ninety per cent return.' The sincerity in Charles's voice was calculated to reassure and smooth away any doubts. 'You see, the secret is—' The rest of what he said was drowned out by a re-enactment of the scariest bit of the toboggan ride, complete with Susan's mini-scream and George's white-knuckle grip of the table edge.

If I lingered a bit longer, I could eavesdrop a bit more, so I spread out the São Vicente cave leaflet in front of them. 'After all that excitement, the excursion to these caves may seem a bit tame, but I can certainly recommend it. You'll find them a very interesting experience. It's not just a walk through caves, you see. There are entertaining effects like a make-believe journey to the earth's core and a river of lava, and illustrations of the famous volcanic eruptions at Pompeii and Krakatoa.'

Behind me Dorothy was saying, 'I *am* a bit of a wine connoisseur as you guessed, and that *does* sound as if it has interesting possibilities. But ...'

'You just can't lose.' The confidence in Charles's voice would have convinced the most swithering Doubting Thomas. 'There's always more demand than supply for reliably fine Bordeaux wines like Château Lafitte. But I don't have to tell *you* that.'

George was saying, 'Sounds OK. We'll let you know when we want to go.'

I couldn't prolong my conversation with George and Susan any longer. I made my way back to my seat pondering whether I should warn Dorothy about Charles and his little schemes. I didn't like the thought of such a vulnerable elderly lady falling victim to a glib conman's scam.

Zara was slumped at her table, still nursing a drink, still glowering in the direction of the deliberately provocative Charles. As I watched, she slammed down the empty glass, shoved back her chair and made her way somewhat unsteadily to the bar. After she'd made two unsuccessful attempts to clamber up onto a high stool, I came to her rescue.

'Awkward things, bar stools, aren't they?' I said, heaving her up onto the seat.

Ignoring me, she slurred. 'How 'bout 'nother *poncha*-n-orange, Mar-Marshio?'

'I don't think you—' I began, but I needn't have tried to intervene. Márcio instantly adopted the barman's ostrich-head-in-sand manoeuvre for avoiding a tricky situation. Keeping his gaze firmly averted from Zara, he developed an intense interest in the glass he was polishing, holding it up and examining it for microscopic specks or smears.

Zara gazed blearily at him for a few moments, swaying gently. Suddenly she toppled sideways. I made a grab for her, but she pushed me away.

'Don't fuss, Deboah. I'm pefekly capa-bib-le of taking off my shandal.' She reached down and whipped it off.

Whap whap whap. Her shoe-assault on the bar top had no effect on Márcio, but was certainly a conversation-stopper for the rest of those in the Mimosa Bar. Silence fell and all heads turned.

'They've run out of *poncha*, Zara,' I shouted above the *thwacks*. 'How about a coffee instead?'

She abandoned her sandal in mid-whap and turned to stare at me. 'Wha-at?'

'Two black coffees, Márcio – large,' I called.

Deafness miraculously cured, he busied himself at the espresso machine at the far end of the bar. He slid two cups of black coffee across the counter. I put one in Zara's unresisting hands, and the other one in front of her. She buried her nose in the cup. I waited patiently.

Eventually I broke the silence. 'I can see you're a bit upset about something, Zara,' I said, feeling my way carefully. 'Want to talk about it?'

Her eyes brimmed with tears. 'I thought I had it made, gave him thousands of euros – a deposit for a pad for us. Then I saw that bloody watch … I knew then he was no good. But it was too late….' She took a gulp of coffee. 'What a nerve he's got. Even filed an insurance claim when he said he'd lost the bloody thing. He's wearing that piece of rubbish now.' A muffled, 'The guy's a prick!' drifted out from behind a curtain of green hair.

I looked across the room. Mason's sales pitch was in full flow. With each expansive gesture, his cuff slipped back to reveal what at this distance did indeed seem to be the maligned 'Rollex'.

After a moment she sighed, shook back the screen of hair, and picked up the cup. Her gaze followed mine. 'The little shit! One day he'll get what's coming to him.'

I tried a few sympathetic noises and gentle probing, but got nothing else out of her.

Coffee cups drained to the last dregs, she muttered a vague, 'Thanks', and wandered off morosely without a backward glance at Charles and his new companion. I'd just have to wait and see if the fall-out from her feud with Charles would help or hinder my investigations.

The message came as I was stuffing papers into my briefcase at the end of my office hour.

'Phone call for you, *senhora*.' Márcio held up the receiver and motioned me to come behind the bar.

I'd asked Luís to contact me, but this morning's search of Celia's room, speculation about conman Charles's motives for befriending Dorothy Winterton, and Zara's recent antics had pushed that to the back of my mind. So it took a second or two to register what the voice at the other end of the line was saying.

'Senhora Smith?' The whisper was barely audible.

'Yes, who is it?'

'You spoke to my mother yesterday.'

Luís.

'I must meet you, *senhora*.'

'Yes, of course,' I said tone casual, and smiled for the benefit of anyone that might be taking too close an interest.

'We meet in Monte Gardens at five fifteen, just before they close the gates.'

The garden covered a huge area so we'd have to rendezvous at a particular spot. 'Where do you suggest we meet?'

'At the big lake. *Senhora*, I must go now, the....' His words became an indecipherable mutter.

'Just a moment, L—' I stopped myself just in time from saying his name. 'Where exactly—?' But a click told me that he'd hung up.

Though outwardly calm, as I gathered up my papers my heart was racing. This could be the breakthrough I so desperately needed. I glanced at my watch. It was now quarter past one. That gave me plenty of time to go back to Police HQ, write up my report on today's events and make the rendezvous.

I could have taken the cable-car up to Monte but Comandante Figueira's only too predictable response to that expense would have been to snap, 'What is this nonsense, Sshmit? My officers do not behave like tourists, spending many euros on luxury travel. I refuse to sanction such extravagance.' The next second I'd see the offending expense chit brusquely stamped with 'Claim denied!'

So that left the public bus – crowded and inconveniently timed for my rendezvous – or my own car. I didn't have to think twice: I'd need the car. After all, I couldn't tell where I might be going after the rendezvous in Monte Gardens.

Before long I was regretting my decision. The heavy traffic and the steeply twisting narrow road, barely wide enough to enable two cars to pass, made a mockery of the road sign wishing *Boa Viagem*. If I'd taken the bus, instead of having to keep my mind on the driving, I could have dozed, let my mind wander, or read a newspaper all the way up to Monte.

While I waited in a tailback, the result of a fiendishly noisy municipal refuse truck edging its way teeth-grittingly slowly past a couple of parked cars, I got the chance to speculate about what Luís might say to me. Revenge would be uppermost in his mind. He'd be ready to tell me all he knew or suspected, nothing held back. Where would the trail lead? 'Everyone has his secrets', the *comandante* had said. 'Peel away each layer like an onion.' Well, I'd unpeeled a few layers here and there, and not come up with much. My best bet so far seemed to be David Grant and that nondescript, windowless building at the rear of those greenhouses of his....

The car in front lurched into life. I switched my attention back to the road, and ten minutes later the name on the bus stop sign changed to Monte, an indication that I hadn't far to go. In spite of the traffic hold-ups, I was early. I'd have time for a leisurely stroll through the themed gardens as I made my way to the lake.

I nudged into a parking space underneath the huge plane tree in Largo da Fonte square. Everything depended on Luís making the rendezvous. He was our only lead, and the *comandante* was expecting me to report back on the meeting. But if once again he failed to turn up....

I locked the car, and set off along the cobbled lane past the picturesque grey and white church. At the foot of its steps a few straw-hatted toboggan men were lounging, waiting for custom beside the wicker sledges, though most had given up for the day. I had expected no queues at the ticket booth so close to closing time, but when I rounded the corner to the entrance I was dismayed to find the ticket kiosk besieged by a mob of excited cruise passengers on a specially organized evening visit. At the slow rate the tickets were being dispensed....

'Excuse me.' I pushed politely at a broad back clad in a hideously patterned shirt.

'Wait your turn, buster.' He didn't turn round.

I gave a gentle tug at the awful shirt. 'I'm sorry. I'm in a hurry. Can you just let me—'

'We're all in a hurry. Something wrong with your ears?' The red neck bulging over the collar deepened in colour. 'Stand in line.' He shuffled sideways to block my attempt to sidle past. Short of felling him with a blow to the back of the knee, there was nothing I could do to jump the queue.

Five minutes passed ... eight ... ten.... Now I'd have to hurry through the garden to make it in time. A nervous Luís would wait only so long. If I missed him, the *comandante*'s sibilants would once again scythe through the air with the swish of scimitar blades. 'Luís Gomes was our best lead. And you have, as you English say, blowed it. You are *useless*! Utterly useless, Sshmit!'

At last I reached the ticket window, slapped down a euro note that more than covered the entrance fee and made my way through the gate. The cruise group were clustered on the entrance terrace, wandering round the ancient gnarled olive trees and giant terracotta jars. I hurried past them and walked briskly down into the ravine, an enclosed world where railings and pillars of flyover bridges slashed scarlet red through the mingled greens of ferns, laurels and palms. Tightly furled fronds of giant ferns like elaborately engraved bishops' crosiers showered me with drops of moisture as I brushed past; hidden birds peeped and twittered; water trickled and gurgled.

The garden seemed to have swallowed up all other visitors, and I risked breaking into a run, the thud of my feet on the path loud in my ears. At last I caught my first glimpse of the sparkle of water from the lake. The rendezvous was only a couple of minutes away.

A few minutes later I leant on the railing of the viewpoint terrace to catch my breath and scan the shores of the lake fifteen metres below. 'At the big lake ...' Luís had said, and rung off without being more specific. A tiny island linked to the shore by an ornamental bridge held only tree ferns and a neat little terracotta-roofed swan house. No one was pacing the reed-fringed edge. No one was making a show of feeding the couple of swans. I was only five minutes late. Surely he would have waited for me.

The obvious place for him to lurk was the grandiose tower on the stone bulwark bulging out into the lake with its double row of water-spouts protruding like cannon from a half-moon battery. He wouldn't want to draw attention to himself pacing round the lake, so that's where I'd find him.

I was wrong. Nobody was there. I had to face the fact that either he hadn't waited for me, or it was another no-show as had happened at the Beerhouse – without the discovery of the body floating in the water, of course. That triggered a disturbing thought: if he had been followed here, could Luís have met the same fate as Roberto? I steeled myself to crane out over the waterspouts to peer into the depths of the lake.

No dark eyes stared up at me from beneath the surface. The only occupant of the lake was a swan, the wind ruffling its feathers as it glided serenely towards me, neck outstretched in anticipation of a morsel of bread.

And then I saw him. I'd been concentrating on the lake and hadn't noticed him on a stone platform a mere 200 metres away, on the same high level as myself. He was sitting on a metal seat with his back to me watching an impressive cascade that gushed in a smooth pewter curtain down into the dark waters. A thin spiral of tobacco smoke drifted up in the still air. As I watched, he rose to his feet, took a final puff, and threw the stub of his cigarette over the railing into the lake.

'*Luís!*' I shouted, and see-sawed an arm wildly to attract his attention.

Even as I did so, I knew there wasn't a chance of him hearing me above the roar of the water. He glanced at his watch and stood for a moment, hands resting on the railing, looking down across the garden at the Bay of Funchal far below.

'*Luís!*' I screamed again, and willed him to look in my direction, then let my arm drop to my side. I was wasting precious time.

He straightened and began to walk away.

I turned and raced back through the arched doorway of the tower. It took barely thirty seconds to reach the broad walkway, and another thirty seconds to race along it, but when I rounded the shallow curve that hid the cascade and Luís from view, he'd gone. The seat was empty. In those sixty seconds I'd lost him.

I could see along the walkway as far as the white bulk of the old hotel, but there was nobody on that path either. The gloomy interior of the grotto under the platform would make an ideal place for a discreet rendezvous, the thunder of falling water ensuring that there could be no eavesdropper to any conversation. That's where he'd be. At the top of the steps down to the grotto, I hesitated. He might have run to catch one of the buses that passed the lower gate. Which way should I go? *Which?* Every moment lessened my chances of catching him up.

If I messed up now, there'd be no way of retrieving the situation. In the report I'd written before setting off for Monte, I'd informed the *comandante* that I was going to meet Luís and that I was confident that he would give me vital information. Yes, if I messed things up now, it would be the perfect excuse for her to send me packing with 'Adeus, Sshmit!' ringing in my ears....

If I made for the lower gate and he wasn't there, there was still the chance that he might still be waiting in the grotto. That decided me. I turned to go. Lying under the seat was a booklet of matches bearing the distinctive logo of the Massaroco Hotel. I bent down, picked it up and with a slightly shaking hand, flipped open the cover. He'd left a message for me. *Stand near the cascade. I'll see you from below. L.*

I should have stopped to think that there was something odd about him leaving the message where I would have little chance of finding it. But I didn't. With the waterfall of water roaring out at my feet, I stood at the railing scanning the shore, trying to pick him out. He couldn't be far away. Down below, a group of the cruise passengers and a guide were gathered round a tall pottery vase. I spotted the boor in the hideously patterned shirt posing for a photo on the sill of an old stone window. He seemed to be staring straight up at me.

Guiltily I turned away, and that saved my life. The numbing blow, intended for the back of my head, fell instead on my shoulder, paralysing my arm. My attacker had planned it well. The noise of the water had concealed the rush of footsteps behind me. Stunned with pain and shock, I collapsed across the railing. Hands grabbed my legs and heaved me headfirst into the thundering waterspout of the cascade.

CHAPTER EIGHT

Falling ... falling ... mouth open in a silent scream....

But by throwing me in headfirst, my would-be murderer had miscalculated, for he'd put me into a dive, a position that would give me a chance of surviving unscathed. It's not the sort of situation you'll find in the Department's self-defence manual, but instinctively my left hand grabbed my paralysed right arm and formed a protective V over my head. I hit the water like a tyro high diver. Four points on the judges' scorecard, I'd say.

Neither had my assailant taken into account the depth of the lake at this point. Down, down I went till my fingertips touched mud. A few metres shallower and I'd have broken my neck. When I surfaced spluttering and blinking water out of my eyes, the cavalry, in the form of half a dozen of the cruise passengers led by the boor in the hideous shirt, were running towards me along the edge of the lake. I managed an awkward splashy sidestroke towards him with my good arm.

He reached out to pull me to the shore. 'You were mugged, lady. I saw it all,' he yelled.

A few moments later I stood dripping on the bank, shivering with cold and shock. Just before my knees buckled, someone wrapped a coat round my shoulders and helped me to a bench. I sat hunched and dazed while dissenting voices clashed and bickered over my head.

'She's awfully pale. Lay her down.'

'Keep her walking.'

'Call the police!'

'No, an ambulance.'

'The police'll want to speak to her first, and get a statement.'

'Who saw it? What did he look like?'

'A tall, thin guy with a beard. I'd be able to pick him out again.'

'I've got twenty-twenty vision. I'm telling you, definitely a small guy with a moustache.'

I put an end to it all by fainting dead away.

Later that evening, a solicitous Gorgonzola on my knee, I sat on the veranda of my little gingerbread house in the Estrada Monumental recuperating with a strong cup of tea. Amid the pinpricks of light on the hills high above Funchal I was just able to make out the floodlit façade of the church of *Nossa Senhora* pinpointing the position of Monte Gardens and the scene of the attempt on my life.

'I was more than lucky to escape with only a badly bruised shoulder, eh, G?'

Her rough tongue rasped my hand in sympathetic agreement.

'Explain, Sshmit!' Comandante Figuera's fierce glance managed to encompass both the sling on my injured arm and Senhora Gomes's battered green suitcase with its stash of heroin, now lying open on her desk. When I'd stowed it carefully away in my office on Tuesday afternoon, I'd been confident that no one would be poking around and it would be safe enough there till I decided how to deal with it. Which just shows that I should have gone by my rule never to take anything for granted.

A blood-red fingernail flicked the evidence label with its tell-tale location and date. 'This, Sshmit, was *not* in yesterday's report.'

Stirred by a gust of warm air from the half-open window, the strelitzias arranged themselves in a muttering Greek chorus of condemnation.

'No, but you see—'

'What I see, Sshmit, is this.' She passed the account of my meeting with the *senhora* slowly across my vision, the matador teasing the bull with his cape just before he readies his sword for the kill. 'And this.' Her hand rested accusingly on the bags of heroin. 'But I did not see them till I found them myself. The head, Justinia Figueira, did not know what the hand, Deborah Sshmit, was doing.'

In the vase the Greek chorus swung into action again, foretelling doom.

'Well, as I – er – mentioned in Tuesday's report, Luís Gomes contacted me to arrange a meeting, and I thought it would be better if....' I stumbled to a halt, unnerved by her unblinking stare.

'Let me make it clear, Sshmit. *You* feed *me* the information. *I*, Justinia Figueira, do the thinking.'

'Yes, *Comandante*,' I said meekly, in the hope that a gentle answer would turn away wrath.

In this case it didn't. For another five minutes she read the riot act, employing an astounding range of English vocabulary, never repeating herself once.

'So, Sshmit, you understand me, I think.' She leant back in her chair. 'And now that we have, as you say, cleared the air, tell me what Gomes said to you at this meeting. What did you learn?'

'Er, nothing, *Comandante*. I have to admit it was all a set-up, a trap. Someone tried to kill me.'

There was no reaction of shock-horror, only a mildly raised eyebrow. She already knew about the incident in Monte Garden. The cat had been playing with the mouse. And that was why she'd made no enquiry as to why my arm was in a sling.

She jabbed an accusatory finger in my direction. 'I will tell you what you are thinking, Sshmit. You are thinking, how was it that the so-clever *comandante* found this suitcase that I so very foolishly concealed from her.' A statement, not a question.

She was a mind-reader. 'Yes, *comandante*.'

Making no attempt to conceal a little smile of satisfaction, she slid open a drawer, and produced the department's machine for recording interviews. With the triumphant air of a magician pulling a very large rabbit out of a very small hat, she switched it on.

A few seconds of the standard preliminaries established place, date, and time, then, 'Comandante Justinia Figueira interviewing Senhora Carmella Gomes.'

She'd interviewed Senhora Gomes yesterday evening. At the sheer unexpectedness of it I sank onto the hard wooden chair in front of her desk, hitherto pointedly un-offered as clear indication that I was being carpeted.

She ran the tape forward. 'I think you'll find this of particular interest.'

She stabbed *Play*.

'... and when I opened the door,' a tremulous Senhora Gomes was saying, 'two men shoved me back into the room, and pushed me into a chair. One shouted at me, "Old woman, where is the suitcase?" I was too frightened to speak. The other man went through to my bedroom.

I heard terrible crashes. Then he appeared in the doorway and said, "Everything in there is smashed, and if you don't tell us where it is, we'll start in here as well". I said, "What suitcase? I know nothing about a suitcase". And the man who had been in the bedroom swung his hand along both shelves and swept all my plates and cups onto the floor. All of them. All in pieces on the floor.' For a few revolutions of the tape there was only the sound of sobbing. Then, 'Still I said nothing. The man who was standing threateningly over me, snatched up Roberto's picture. I gave a cry. It's the only thing I have left to remember my Roberto. "This'll make her talk", he said. And he dropped it on the floor. "If you don't tell us right now, you old bitch, this picture goes under my foot".'

The burst of hysterical sobbing as she relived the moment choked me up. Even the *comandante* must have been affected, for she pressed the button to stop the tape. The sound of children's carefree laughter filtered in from the street outside.

She broke the silence in the room. 'The *senhora* could resist no longer. She told them that a Senhora Smith from the Massaroco Hotel had taken the suitcase.'

Another silence fell as I considered the implications, the fall-out. Had Senhora Gomes mentioned that lady's cat? *This animal has been trained to detect drugs*, senhora. I recalled my words with dismay.

'*Comandante*,' I said slowly, 'did the *senhora* tell them anything else? Did she tell them that my cat found the suitcase?'

'She did not say, and I did not ask because I did not know myself – until I read the report, the report you did not give to me.' She held my gaze to underline the point. 'But she did say that she had worried all night about your safety because she had let it slip that you wanted to contact her son. And that is why she came to the police. And that is why I went along to your office to warn you that your cover has been – how do you say it – shot?'

'Blown,' I supplied, my thoughts grim. Since the body had been found in the harbour, I'd let the hope grow that my arranged meeting with Luís had no connection with the murder, and that nobody had overheard the *Meet me in the Beerhouse on the harbour at* três á tarde. *I tell you something then*. I had begun to convince myself it had just been an unfortunate coincidence that Luís had decided to go to ground the very same afternoon. But whether or not this line of thought had been correct was of no consequence now. My cover had definitely been blown. And if the gang now knew about Gorgonzola, her life would be in danger too.

Comandante Figuera was saying, '... evidence tag caught my eye, and when I pulled the suitcase out from its *hiding place*,' she couldn't resist the dig, 'I read the report you attached. But it was too late to warn you that your rendezvous with Gomes might be a trickery, that there might be ...' –she searched for the word – 'that there might be a skulduggery. You must take great care, my dear Deborah.'

Her use of my first name sent a chill down my spine. That, more than anything else, made me realize the danger I was in.

After leaving the *comandante* I made my way to the Massaroco Hotel for my office hour. My little group of clients were bound to ask how I came to have my arm in a sling. Bearing in mind that one or more of them might very well know the answer in advance, I couldn't afford to have too much of a discrepancy between what had happened and what I chose to tell them. Of course, anyone who was in cahoots with my attacker would know my reason for being at Monte, but a truthful, if edited, version of the event would keep them thinking that I didn't suspect any of my clientele of being involved.

'What *have* you done to yourself?' Head on one side, Celia Haxby studied me with a frown of irritation. 'I took you at your word when you said you wanted to see a professional artist at work, so I'd pencilled you in to drive me to those quaint little triangular houses at Santana this afternoon. I was *depending* on you.' From somewhere in the depths of her smock, she produced an appointment diary, crossly flicked through the pages and with a dramatic black line disposed of the services of Deborah J. Smith.

Dorothy Winterton put down her cup. 'That's not very sympathetic of you, Celia. We should be asking how it happened.' She patted my good hand. 'Did you trip on those lethal pavements in town, dear? All bumps and dips. You must be careful. Keep your eyes on the ground. Those jacaranda trees are lovely when they're in flower, but roots and mosaic pavements just don't mix. Only the other day, Celia nearly—'

'Really, Dorothy, she doesn't want to know about things that never happened. *Of course*, I'm sympathetic.'

'Well, how *did* you hurt your arm, Deborah?' Dorothy seemed to be determined to find out.

'Actually, I was mugged in Monte Gardens.' I studied audience reaction. Nothing but surprise and shock. 'Although I don't remember much about it,' I added carefully. 'Somebody hit me and pushed me into the lake.'

Dorothy picked up her cup with a trembling hand. 'Oh dear, oh dear, and I thought Madeira was such a safe place. I wouldn't have come here otherwise.' A quick gulp of tea, and the cup clattered back into the saucer. 'And to think Celia and I were actually planning to go there later this week. Dear, oh dear.'

Celia leaned forward, eager for details. 'Did you see who did it? Did you get a description for the police?'

'Well, no, it was all so sudden.' And that was the truth. It could have been the man I'd thought was Luís, but it could equally well have been somebody else who'd been lurking in the shrubs behind the cascade terrace. At the time I'd not been in a fit state to question anybody and, as it had turned out, the eyewitnesses couldn't even agree whether my assailant had been clean-shaven or not.

'Really, Celia! She hasn't got eyes in the back of her head! How could she possibly see who did it when he crept up from behind!'

Was Dorothy just taking it for granted, as anyone might, that the attacker had approached from behind? Or had that been an incriminating slip?

'No need to be sarky, Dot.' Celia closed her diary with a petulant snap.

'*Dorothy*, Celia. Not Dot. You know I *hate* when you call me that.'

The Flamboyant Artist flounced the folds of her smock in a dismissive 'up yours' gesture. 'Returning to the subject. Your shoulder's not broken, is it, Deborah?'

At the sight of an arm in a sling, most people jump to the conclusion that it's the *arm* that's been injured. Was I reading too much into this?

'It's only bruised. I was really lucky,' I said. 'It's a nuisance more than anything, because that means—'

'Ooh, Deborah, what *have* you done to yourself?'

I looked up to see Zara standing in the doorway.

'Mugged. She was *mugged*.' Celia's ample bosom heaved in indignation. 'In broad daylight, too.'

'Daylight or dark, mugged is mugged!' Zara dragged a chair across from another table. 'Tell me more.'

And I had to go through it all again.

She soaked up the account of my misfortune with the blotting paper intensity of an avid reader of tabloid blood and gore. 'Wowee! You certainly don't expect that sort of thing to happen here. In London, now, let me tell you ...' Zara launched into a dark tale of misadventure and mayhem. '... and there I was, lying bleeding in the gutter, and—' She paused dramatically.

Dorothy didn't wait for the climax. The noisy rattle of the teaspoon in her cup shattered the tension. 'Yes, well. Isn't it time you were getting back to that young man of yours? Where is he, anyway?'

Knocked off her stride, Zara took a moment to react. Her face flushed. 'If *you* don't know, *I* certainly don't. I thought he might be with *you*.' She pushed back her chair and stalked angrily away.

'Temper, temper.' With a hint of a smile, Dorothy Winterton laid down her teaspoon.

'Uppity young madam! Well done, Dorothy.' The Flamboyant Artist and the Colonel's Widow clinked congratulatory cups. I had not been the only one to see that Mason's sudden interest in cultivating Dorothy's company had put Zara's nose out of joint.

I made my excuses. If I could catch David Grant, it might be instructive to see *his* reaction to my arm in a sling. When there was no sign of him in his usual place at the bar, I went out to the terrace on the chance that he might be outside. He and Mason were sitting at a table in the shade of one of the striped parasols. The cluster of empty beer bottles indicated that they'd been there for some time.

As I approached, Grant set down his empty glass. 'Yes, I'll have another one, Chaz. So you really think there's money in wine?'

'Yes, Dave, *en primeur*'s a dead cert, believe me. If you play your cards right.' Mason leant back lazily. 'Buying vintage, still in the cask, can give huge profits – nearly ninety per cent after only five years.'

So Charles Mason was trying his investment scam again. Onto a loser this time, though. I doubted he'd get much joy out of a hard-boiled character like Grant.

'Hi there, guys,' I said.

'Geez, Deborah, you've been in the wars, haven't you!' Mason's surprise seemed genuine.

Grant didn't say anything, merely rubbed reflectively at his nose, possibly remembering the Glasgow Kiss incident. While I recounted my sorry tale, I studied their expressions but could come to no conclusion.

'And that's all I can tell you,' I finished. 'This sling's more an inconvenience than anything else.'

'Where did you say it happened – at the cascade overlooking the lake, was it?' Grant chewed reflectively on a toothpick.

I nodded. *Had* the word 'cascade' somehow slipped into my carefully worded account? I couldn't remember.

'Lucky escape, then. That's quite a height to fall. What I'd like to know is—' The muffled strains of *Land of Hope and Glory* floated up from the briefcase resting against the table leg. 'Excuse me. Back to work.' Grant got up and wandered away, phone to ear.

Like a fisherman who has been playing a fish for hours only to have it slip the hook, Mason slumped back in his seat despondently. Muttering to himself and casting black looks at the array of empty glasses, he pulled out his wallet.

Curious to see if I could provoke a reaction, I said chattily, 'Not that I want to intrude into personal matters, but I couldn't help noticing that you and Zara seem to have had a bit of a bust-up.'

'None of your business.' Pushing away the table, he jumped to his feet and stormed off.

The array of beer glasses rocked. Two teetered, and before I could grab them, smashed on the ground. I stared after him. I'd got my reaction, but what had upset him – my mention of Zara, or Grant's obvious lack of interest in the wine scam? I stirred the pieces of broken glass with my foot. Whatever it was, he'd just managed an effective way of leaving without paying. I sighed. It looked like it would be me who was footing the bill for Mason and Grant's drinking spree.

Twenty euros poorer, I made my way to the taxi rank outside the hotel. I was in a bit of a black mood myself at having to rely on taxis because of my injured shoulder. Altogether it had been a most unsatisfactory morning.

I wouldn't have noticed the metallic-green car nosing its way out of the car-park fifty metres down the road if it hadn't been for the road-rage blast on its horn as it tried to force its way into the traffic. The passenger was wearing a distinctive floppy yellow hat. There could be only one like that ... I peered out of the taxi's back window. I was right. Celia Haxby was gesticulating rudely through the windscreen at a jaywalker tourist wearing the equally distinctive headgear of an ear-flapped woollen Madeira hat. She'd obviously managed to persuade someone to take my place and drive her to Santana. Her day, at least, was proving more satisfactory than mine.

The taxi driver tilted his head and eyed me in the mirror. 'Where does the *senhora* wish to go?'

'Estrada—' I started, looking forward to a recuperative afternoon nap on my veranda.

The metallic-green car was passing me just a metre away. And the *driver* was none other than Dorothy Winterton. Less than a week ago when we'd discussed car rental, she'd been quite adamant that peace of mind was her priority and had most definitely decided to get about by taxi or chauffeur-driven transport. Anyone can have a change of mind ... Nevertheless....

The taxi engine revved impatiently. 'Where you want to go, *senhora?*'

I stared after the car and came to a decision. 'I've to catch up with my friends at Estrada...or was it Rua...? Oh, there are my friends – in that green car. Follow it, will you?' Thanks to the heavy traffic of central Funchal there'd be little danger of Dorothy realizing that she was being followed. Besides, taxis have a camouflage of their own.

With a *vroom* and a *zoom* the taxi forced its way into the traffic. Dorothy and Celia's car was still in sight. As I'd expected, the volume of traffic defeated even the taxi driver's aggressive manoeuvres and we remained a comfortable distance behind. The green car headed down the Rua Carvalho and soon it became obvious that it was making for the port. When it turned onto the quay at the Lion Rock, I leant forward.

'Just drop me here, *senhor*, it'll save your time, and I'll catch my friends up at the shipping office.'

The old fortification on the Lion Rock would be an ideal vantage point to see and not be seen. I climbed the short flight of stairs to the top as the taxi sped away. From the little terrace I had a bird's eye view of the harbour, the quay below and the green car drawn up near the ticket kiosk. The car doors opened and Dorothy and Celia made their way across to the kiosk. After a few minutes' conversation at the window, they returned to the car, drove back along the quay, and headed towards the centre of town.

It took only a few minutes to descend the steps of Lion Rock and make my way to the kiosk. Positioned in front of it was a large notice in English and Portuguese giving details of the ferry service to the island of Porto Santo.

Daily except Wednesdays. Departs Funchal 0800.

Departs Porto Santo 1800. Journey Time 2 hours 40 minutes.

If Dorothy and Celia had purchased tickets to Porto Santo, I'd have to find out which day they were going.

'Yes, *senhora*, how can I help?' The ticket clerk was looking at me enquiringly.

'I was just deciding which day to visit Porto Santo....' I pretended to give it some thought. 'I'd quite like to go the same day as my friend, the lady with the large yellow hat.' I made a wide circular motion with my hand to indicate its ridiculous dimensions. I pretended to consult my diary. 'She's going on Saturday, isn't she?'

The ticket clerk shook his head, 'No, *senhora*, she has taken a ticket for next week, *terça-feira*, Tuesday.'

'Tuesday? Oh well, I'll book for Tuesday too,' I said and raked in my purse for the cash.

'You wish tourist class, like your friend, or first class?'

I paused in my raking and considered the pros and cons for a moment. They'd catch sight of me sooner or later, but the later the better. 'First class, please,' I said, and handed over the money in full knowledge that this hard-to-explain item in my expense account would be an extravagance that wouldn't escape the eagle eye of the *comandante*. 'Do you think the police department in Madeira are *millionaires*, Sshmit?' she'd snap and reject the claim with a stroke of her pen.

I stuffed the ticket into my bag. What now? I'd walk into town, do some shopping, have something to drink at one of the outdoor cafés. The sunshine was warm, the purple bougainvillea spilt spectacularly down the cliff beneath the old Quinta Vigia and I wandered along feeling rather pleased with myself. 'Pretty damn clever of you, DJ, to find out what that pair were up to,' I thought smugly.

A familiar voice made me jump. 'You were right, Celia. It *is* Deborah.'

I swung round. The green car I had last seen heading towards the centre of town had drawn up at the kerb. Dorothy and Celia were peering at me from the open window. They must have turned left at the marina and doubled back via the Rua Carvalho. Could they have spotted me getting out of the taxi at Lion Rock, and suspicious that I'd been following them, were they now checking up?

'Oh hello, Dorothy,' I said, mind racing through plausible answers to awkward questions.

Dorothy leant her elbow on the edge of the window. 'Well, what are you up to, then?' The tone was light.

Celia's smile was friendly. 'Why didn't you tell us back at the hotel that you were coming this way? We could have given you a lift.'

If Dorothy and Celia *had* seen me at the kiosk, and I lied about it.... Honesty is the best policy, lies have a nasty way of tripping you up.

I moved over to the car. 'I've been to book a ticket to Porto Santo. Never been there, I'm afraid, and it's high time I paid the place a visit.'

Dorothy took off her sunglasses and polished them. 'So you'll be going on—' Tone casual, eyes sharp.

I supplied the information. 'Tuesday of next week.'

Just audible was Celia's low mutter. 'Of course, that's her day off.'

I added, 'I've decided to treat myself, splash out and travel first class. It's only ten euros more, after all, and includes a meal each way.'

'That does seem *quite* a bargain.' From the frosty look Celia shot at Dorothy, I surmised that Dorothy's penny-pinching had prevailed when it had come to purchasing their cheaper tickets.

I waited for them to tell me that they too were going to Porto Santo, had already booked their tickets. They didn't. Of course, that might have a totally innocent explanation – they might genuinely want their own company, be anxious that I might impose myself on them by tagging along with them wherever they went.

But if they *were* up to something, had I done enough to make our joint trip to Porto Santo seem a mere coincidence? To give them something else to think about, I asked an awkward question of my own.

I patted the roof of the car. 'So you've decided to take the plunge and have a go at driving, after all. Good for you, Dorothy. You were a bit nervous about it, weren't you?'

Her eyes flickered, 'Well, I—'

Celia leant eagerly across. 'Driving in Madeira's not bothered her at all. Yesterday when we drove down all those hair-raising zigzags to the Nun's Valley, you didn't bat an eyelid, did you, Dot? And—'

'Shut up, Celia.' A thunderous look. 'How many times have I told you not to call me that?' She revved the engine. 'Must love you and leave you, Deborah. We've got things to do.'

I watched them drive off. Less than two weeks ago, she had gone out of her way to cultivate the image of nervous driver. Yet, if Celia was to be believed, Dorothy had taken in her stride hairpins and sheer drops that could turn even confident drivers into nervous wrecks. It seemed I'd just peeled away another of the *comandante*'s onion-layers. But what exactly had I found?

CHAPTER NINE

A t 10 p.m. that evening I was making final preparations for my clandestine raid on Grant's orchid laboratory.

'That shed at the orchid farm is worth investigating, don't you think, G?'

She inspected a paw noncommittally.

I took my arm out of the sling and wriggled my injured shoulder experimentally – painful, but not unbearably so. I'd have the use of both hands if needed, and the rest of the time I could put my hand inside my buttoned jacket or trouser pocket to take the weight off the joint.

Gorgonzola watched expectantly as I sat down on the bed to lace up my rubber-soled boots. My all black, disappear-into-the-night outfit was the sign that an expedition was on the cards. She was particularly fond of night expeditions with all their exciting sounds and smells, tantalizing, though forbidden, of course, till duty had been done. But after that … she sheathed and unsheathed her claws in anticipation.

At odd moments in the last few days I'd been mulling over that incident at the farm when Grant had flown into a rage over the dropped pot of cymbidiums. I was increasingly convinced that he'd dropped the plant because he'd been startled by something I'd said. I couldn't recall my exact words, but laboratory and orchid propagation had definitely featured.

'Why would those words provoke such a reaction from a commercial orchid grower, tell me that, G?'

She scratched her ear, and thought it over.

I buckled her working collar round her neck. 'Of course, you weren't with me the other day, but there's a good chance that the building at the rear of the greenhouses is his laboratory, and we'll have to find out why he's so touchy about it. Unpeel another layer of onion, eh?' I unzipped the rucksack and held it open invitingly. 'Your carriage awaits, G.'

I'd accustomed her to transportation by soft-lined rucksack as being less obtrusive than the hated cat-carrier in certain situations, and the lure of a comfortable, warm, dark nest ensured I'd never had any difficulty getting her into it. I swung it from my good hand by its straps. 'You're getting heavy, G. Maybe I should think about putting you on a diet.'

A low rumble from the rucksack signified the occupant's contemptuous rejection of this suggestion.

I closed the front door behind me and together we waited in the darkness of the garden for the car that was coming to pick us up. Under the palm trees the ghostly white trumpets of the Madonna lilies loomed eerily, their cloying scent heavy in the still air. Beyond the garden, the intermittent hum of passing traffic exaggerated the silence around me.

A surge of adrenalin made my heart beat faster as I reviewed my plan. What if dogs guarded the building at night? What if I walked through an invisible electronic ray and triggered an alarm? If he *was* manufacturing heroin or crack cocaine in that innocuous-looking building, Grant or his henchmen would be prepared to kill to safeguard his secret. Gorgonzola and DJ Smith might very well end up floating in Funchal harbour like Roberto Gomes.

The same thought had crossed the mind of the *comandante*. I'd found a message waiting for me when I returned from my trip to the Porto Santo Line's office.

We cannot have London asking why one of their officers has been found dead on the so beautiful island of Madeira. Bad for tourism, eh? I'd thought sourly. *Therefore, I am assigning someone to look after you, watch the back, I think it is called. Since for the next four days you will not be able to drive, I have placed a car at your disposal.* It was signed *Justinia Figueira*.

Thoughtful of her, but I suspected that her ulterior motive was to put a mole in place to report my movements back to her. She certainly wouldn't approve of tonight's plans, and I didn't intend to tell her in advance. No doubt she would find out soon enough as I had no option but to make use of the police driver. A waiting taxi in that remote spot close to midnight would be as good as putting up a neon sign *Breaking and Entering in Progress*.

Gorgonzola stirred restively in the rucksack at my feet as night sounds filtered through the traffic noise. Her head emerged, ears tuned in like radar dishes swivelling to track tantalizing rustlings among the fallen camellia leaves.

'Duty first, G,' I said firmly, pulling the zip closed over her shoulders so that there would be no chance of her giving in to temptation. 'Won't be long now.'

From the direction of Funchal came the sound of an approaching car and the noisy clatter of a loose exhaust. It rattled closer … passed by … and receded. Silence surged back.

'There should be a law against it,' I muttered. 'Disturbing the peace with a fiendish noise like that.'

I resumed my contemplation of the twinkling lights on the hills above Funchal Bay. Somewhere up there in one of the patches of darkness was the orchid farm's shed with its secrets. From along the road came a faint *clang clank clang clank clang clank*. It was that wreck of a car again. *Clang clank clang clank clang clank*. I gritted my teeth. I willed it to pass by. Only it didn't. The din reached a crescendo. Where were the traffic police when you wanted them? In front of my rusty gates, it turned out.

The dark shape of a small car materialized on the far side of the railings and shuddered to a halt with the long-drawn-out sigh of a departing soul. Silence descended as if a soundproof door had slammed shut.

From the driver's open window, a hoarse voice said softly, '*Olá, inglesa*. The Ogre sends your transport.'

Hell's bells! Not content with saddling me with a spy in the cab, the *comandante* had also inflicted a clapped out vehicle that would track my movements over the whole of Funchal.

I shouldered the rucksack and crossed the garden to the cobbled driveway. All I could make out of the speaker was a white shirt and the pale blob of a face shadowed by a large black hat of the homburg type. I stooped to peer in the window. Beneath the hat was the familiar bushy moustache last seen when Mason tried to report his 'stolen' 'Rollex'.

'Raimundo Paulo Ribeiro at your service.' A cloud of cheap tobacco engulfed me.

I disguised my instinctive recoil as a lunge for the rear door handle.

'I think we've already met,' I said. 'Last Monday, in the public waiting room at Police HQ. One of my clients was reporting a lost watch.'

The moustache twitched. 'Ah yes, the *senhor* who so enraged my uncle, old João.'

With the excuse of, 'I'll just get into the back seat. I've got a cat here in my bag,' I clambered in and felt for the seat belt.

'*No funciona*, not working,' said silhouette. 'You not need it. I, Raimundo Ribeiro, am expert driver.'

The engine exploded into life in a series of backfires. Faintly above the *clang clank clang clank* I heard, 'I take you to your destination, *senhora*.'

With a jolt that snapped my head back against the worn upholstery and toppled the rucksack, we kangarooed into motion along the Estrada Monumental.

G's *yoooowl* of protest blended with my shriek, 'But I haven't told you where—'

'*No problema*. You tell me, we go.' The shout just carried above the din.

I righted the rucksack and leant forward. 'The Englishman Grant's orchid farm,' I bellowed at the back of his head. 'It's up—'

I just caught the response, 'I know. I know. For thirty years I am traffic *polícial*. Sometimes when there is sickness, or I anger Comandante Figueira, I have to work at the desk, but it is not something I like.'

I sank back against the seat. Everything has its flipside. At least I didn't have to make conversation. During the journey I would be able to concentrate on possible stratagems for breaking and entering.

Not a hope. My mind dulled by the awful din found it impossible to do anything except worry about the attention we would be attracting. After several nick-of-time rescues of the rucksack as we hurtled round the numerous hairpin bends, horn blaring, it was all too much for G. Each time we were subjected to one of those violent changes of direction, the rucksack pulsated with rage, threatening to gyrate its way across the back seat. I grabbed the bag and hugged it tightly to me, whispering soothing words to the occupant and attempting a rendition of the Spanish *madrelena* music that usually worked as a magic charm to soothe her. Like the Portuguese *fado*, it has its devoted followers. G was one of them. To anyone not brought up in the tradition of that ethnic music, however, it can seem a tuneless cacophony.

'*Aa-ee-aaa*,' I moaned in her ear. As I gained confidence and my *aa-ees* and *aa-oos* soared and swooped, the rucksack vibrations gradually subsided. The mound of her head sank lower and lower into the comforting dark of the rucksack. The *madrelena* had worked its charm again.

Only a tuft of red hair remained visible. I let rip with a particularly fine soaring note. My yowl cut through the air like a lone wolf baying at the full moon. We screeched to a halt. Raimundo switched off the engine and in the sudden silence his narrowed eyes studied me in the rear view mirror.

'The cat she is a lover of Portuguese *fado* music,' I said, laughing to hide my embarrassment. I quickly changed the subject. 'Have we—?' I just managed to bite back 'broken down' and change it to 'Have we arrived?'

'Yes, *senhora*.' He switched off the headlights.

A blackness that seemed almost solid pressed against the glass. I lowered the window and peered into the darkness looking for even a pale glimmer of the orchid farm sign that marked the opening to the driveway. 'This is the orchid farm?'

A chuckle came from the front seat. 'I stop a little way before the farm, *senhora*. I think you want to make the *private* entrance.'

I didn't try to keep the exasperation out of my voice. 'Well yes, that *was* the plan, but we seem to have advertised our presence a bit more than I intended.' The rucksack heaved and G's furious face glared accusingly at Raimundo.

'Two angry ladies, eh!' the white-shirted shoulder shook with mirth. 'There is no problem, *senhora*. No one has noticed our arrival. In this car I am invisible.' He twisted round in his seat. 'Everyone has heard the noise of this engine many times. Their ears no longer hear it.'

'But what if—'

'What if someone comes and says, "What are you doing here, Raimundo?" I am right? That is your question?'

I nodded.

'I look at the engine, I curse and swear and kick the car. They think that old Raimundo has broken down again. If they offer to help, I tell them I am waiting for the garage truck. They go away. They forget they have seen me. So you see, *senhora, no problema.*'

I climbed out of the car, feeling for the rucksack, but it edged out of reach as Gorgonzola's shoulders heaved and one paw scrabbled to get a grip on the opening. Another heave of the shoulders exerted pressure against the zip.

'You'll get your chance to explore when we get near that storeroom of Grant's.' Hard-heartedly I stuffed her back in. 'Too many temptations out there.' I closed the rucksack and slung it onto my good shoulder.

Raimundo flung open the driver's door as if about to join me on my expedition, then slammed it shut again. 'The Ogre say, "Do not let that one out of your sight, Ribeiro. I wish to know everything she does".' One eye closed in what I could have sworn was a conspiratorial wink. 'But I think it is better that you tell me everything when you return.' He produced a cigarette from his shirt pocket, and stuck it in his mouth. 'Someone has to remain here in case there is need for a quick speed-away, yes?'

I tried to make amends for my earlier irritation. 'Yes, it is better that I tell you things when I return. We make a good team, Raimundo. I've no idea how long I will be. Could be an hour, could be two.'

Fifty metres up the road, I glanced back. The only evidence that the car was there was the glowing red tip of Raimundo's cigarette.

On my previous visit with Grant I'd noted a dirt track running roughly in the direction of where I judged the greenhouses and the mysterious building to be. On checking it out on the aerial survey map, obtained courtesy of the police department, I saw that the track curved in a circle close to the grey rectangles of the greenhouses and the dark rectangle of the shed, before continuing to an abandoned forestry clearing. On the map the narrow strip separating track from shed was fuzzy and indistinct. I could be faced with an electric fence or impenetrable thorny hedge – or anything. I wouldn't know till I got there.

First things first. I had to find the over-grown entrance to the track. That wasn't going to be easy with no moon to provide even the faintest light. I began picking my way uphill. After about five minutes my irritation with Raimundo returned. What the hell had he meant by 'a little way' before the farm?

In the end, I found the track by chance. I'd stopped to listen for sounds that could mean somebody else on the prowl, and stood, eyes closed in concentration, ears straining. Only the *sshhh* of the wind in the trees, a faint hum of traffic on the motorway far below, the smell of damp earth.

I peered into the darkness at the side of the road wishing for G's night vision, and took another tentative step forward. On that first visit I'd noted that the track began beside a patch of white Arum lilies and wild garlic growing in a nearby ditch. Now, the pungent smell of crushed garlic rose from the ground at my feet. I risked a quick flash of the pencil torch. In the beam, over to the right, was my marker patch of arum lilies. First obstacle overcome, all I had to do now was follow the track.

It took *a lot* longer than I'd expected to pick my way over the rutted surface and emerge cautiously from the belt of trees. From this point, scrubby bushes struggled for life in a tangle of tall grass on either side of the dirt road. A short distance ahead, glass glimmered greyly in the faint light from the now rising moon. If I left the track as it approached the end of the greenhouses, I'd be close to that mysterious building with its secrets.

When I was level with the last of the glasshouses, I stepped off the track and waded through the tangle of grass and scrub towards the black rectangle of the building I'd dubbed 'the laboratory'. In front of me was a rusty chain-link fence. I hooked my fingers in its links, tilted my head back and assessed it for climbability. Four metres high, I estimated, with no possibility of a toehold. *Shit.* I hadn't brought wire-cutters. In the hope that there might a padlocked gate, I made my way along the fence. Picklocks are something I always carry with me. But in the strengthening moonlight I could see that the fence ran on uninterrupted by a gate. I stared through it at the concrete wall of the 'laboratory'. So near but yet so far. Stymied.

If I made my way back to the road and the main entrance, I'd be faced with electronically operated gates and the cameras at the cottage-office. Even if there wasn't a security guard to raise the alarm, there'd be a filmed record of my visit. I pondered my next move. The chain-link fence was the only option, as in keeping with the shed's lowly status, there were no such CCTV cameras covering it. But without wire-cutters....

The rucksack on my back heaved. Paws scrabbled none too gently. Gorgonzola had had enough of inactivity.

I put the rucksack on the ground. 'OK, G, head only. I'm not letting you out.' I pulled open the zip a few centimetres.

Like an underground missile leaving its silo when the doors slide open, G launched herself skyward. Caught off balance, struggling to stay on my feet, I clutched at the chain mesh. Pain stabbed through my shoulder. G had made a neat four-point landing at the base of the fence. I made a grab for her. Too late.

On the principle that she might as well be hung for a sheep as for a lamb – or for the feline equivalent, a blackbird as for a sparrow – she made a bolt for it and shot through a rabbit-sized hole in the mesh at the base of the fence.

'Come *here*,' I hissed.

She scratched at one ear, then the other, signifying the onset of deafness.

'At *once*,' I said through gritted teeth.

She stared at me, pupils wide, as if trying in vain to read my lips, then began a meticulous brush-wash of her face with her foreleg.

'If I could get through that hole, G, I'd— I'd be on the other side of the fence,' I finished slowly.

I knelt down and scraped at the earth. It was soft and crumbly, and there was already a gap of several centimetres between mesh and soil ... so if I managed to scoop out a shallow depression, I'd be able to wriggle under the wire. Unfortunately, another omission from tonight's breaking and entering kit was a collapsible spade. I rummaged through the outer pockets of my rucksack and came up with a knife and a plastic bottle of water. If I cut up the bottle to make a scoop.... No sooner thought than done.

The earth shifted easily and when I reckoned that the depth and width of the hole were sufficient, I pushed the rucksack under the wire. Now to squeeze myself after it. I dug in both elbows, ignored the pain in my shoulder and began to wriggle through. For several heart-stopping moments, when only my head and shoulders were on the other side, it seemed that I'd misjudged. I clawed at the long grass trying to pull my body forward. After several attempts I gave up, exhausted.

No doubt about it, I was stuck. I lay still, damp grass tickling my nostrils, red earth smearing my cheeks, trying to keep calm, trying to block out of what would happen when I was discovered by Grant's men once daylight came.

G's rough tongue licked my ear. That was enough to steady me. I took a deep breath, arched my back, rammed my toes into the ground, and *heaved*. I was through.

I lay there for a moment, biting back the pain, trembling with relief, then gathered up the rucksack. G twined herself round my legs, purring softly, consumed, I'd like to think, by guilt.

'No use being sorry after the event,' I murmured not too sharply.

After all, without her I wouldn't have found the hole, so I had her to thank for getting to the other side of the fence.

I stood listening for any indication that my presence had been detected. G's body tensed against my legs, her ears pricked as she tuned into faint rustlings in the long grass. I pulled her lead out of my pocket and clipped it on.

'Yield not to temptation, for yielding is *sin*,' I whispered, giving the lead a sharp tug.

We made a slow circuit of the windowless building, checking the far side, unseen on my previous visit, for alarms, wires, floodlights. Nothing. The only entry point was the door. Shielding the lock with my body, I risked a quick flash of my torch. My heart sank. I'd been expecting a keyhole padlock, one that my picklocks could deal with, no matter how intricate. But this was a four-number combination type. My only hope was that repetition breeds carelessness – often it's just the middle two numbers that are moved up or down one or two positions. I held the pen torch between my teeth so that the beam played on the figures 1246. I pushed the middle two numbers anti-clockwise one position and tried the hasp. No luck. I pushed them anti-clockwise again, on the off-chance that Grant had flicked the numbers twice for 'security'. I tugged at the hasp once more. Still no luck. There wasn't time to work through all the numbers. This time I'd try moving clockwise from 1246, but if that didn't work, I'd have to call it a day. I flicked the tumblers once and pulled, twice and pulled. It didn't open. I'd failed.

I tugged at the hasp in frustration and detected a slight movement. There was just the chance that one of the tumblers was slightly out of line. I turned it back a fraction. *Success*. I swung the hasp sideways, lifted the padlock from its metal hoop and eased open the door.

As the door cleared the frame, a thin line of light seeped through the widening gap. *Someone was in there.* I froze, then relaxed. The padlocked door was a sure sign that there *couldn't* be anyone working inside. I stepped quickly in, yanked Gorgonzola after me and shut the door. If anybody had seen the light and came to investigate, I was trapped.

My first reaction was disappointment. The shed was merely a horticultural lab. Suspended from the ceiling by short chains, powerful fluorescent tubes with intensifying reflectors shone down on metal shelving containing rows of glass jam jars. Out of each white plastic lid sprouted a blob of blue cotton wool. I lifted up a jar for a closer look. Tiny plantlets, probably orchids of some kind, jostled for growing space in a greyish jelly.

Behind me a small refrigerator hummed into life, the sound startlingly loud in the enclosed space. I put down the jar, opened the fridge door and peered inside. Lidded specimen tubes filled every shelf. I unscrewed one and tipped out the contents. On my palm lay a tiny glass phial full of microscopic seeds. I returned it to its container and sent G off on a sniff-around while I had a closer look at a filtered-air cabinet of the type I'd seen at the Jardim Orchidea. In it was a cotton mask such as surgeons use, and a few jam jars, some empty, some lidded, containing a couple of centimetres of the jelly substance. On one end of the adjoining bench, a honeycomb of closed tubes rotated almost imperceptibly in a strange circular machine. The other end of the bench was fitted up as a mini kitchen with a pressure cooker, a blender, a hot water urn and an electric ring. Next to these were more jam jars, a bottle of bleach and a pair of green kitchen gloves.

With a soft thump Gorgonzola landed beside the kitchen gloves. There'd been no croon that signified a drug find.

I tickled behind her ears. 'No luck, eh.'

No luck for me either. I took a last look round. The building was a laboratory, all right, but it looked as if all Grant was up to was propagating his orchids. It had been a complete waste of time.

I clipped on G's lead in case she took it into her head to go AWOL again, flicked round the padlock tumblers, and we trotted back to the fence. I tied the lead to my ankle while I spent a minute or two deepening the hole, then squeezed under the mesh.

'Your turn now, G,' I said and rolled over, expecting her to stroll through the DJ-sized gap.

She stood stiff-legged and mutinous, with clearly no intention of moving.

'Come *on*.' I tugged sharply at the lead.

Her response was to stick her rear in the air, brace her forelegs and narrow her eyes.

'What's got into you?' I hissed. '*Why* are you behaving like that? No, you can't investigate all these intriguing sounds and smells. OK, I know you've had a nightmare car journey. OK, you've been put on a lead and set a boringly simple task. But we can't risk being here *any* longer.'

None so deaf as those who don't want to hear.

Then, I'm ashamed to admit, stress got the better of me. A mighty tug of the lead dragged G under the fence by *force majeure*. With one quick movement I bundled her into the depths of the rucksack and zipped it firmly closed. Before I started back, I filled in the hole as best I could and camouflaged the disturbed soil by uprooting a large clump of grass and dumping it on top. That would have to do.

While I'd been gone, Raimundo had been assiduously working his way through his endless supply of evil-smelling cigarettes, filling the car with noxious fumes. As soon as I flung myself onto the back seat and pulled the door closed behind me, he gunned the engine into ear-shattering life.

He twisted round. 'Mission accomplished, *senhora*?'

'Yes and no.' I coughed as the smoke caught at my lungs.

'The *comandante*, she will ask me, "Ribeiro, where did she go? What did she do?" so we must please the *comandante*, eh? You must tell me what you want her to know. Heh, heh, heh.'

I gave him a carefully edited account of my night's work. '… but I didn't find anything that would interest the *policía*. Only rows of orchid plants,' I finished.

'She will be disappointed,' he shouted above the din. 'That is when we tiptoe on the eggs.'

He spun the wheel in a tight U-turn of the getaway-type much favoured in American movies. The car lurched as a front wheel mounted the low bank separating the road from a water-filled ditch. He didn't seem to notice.

As we jolted back onto the road and clang-clanked our way down towards Funchal, I reviewed my actions from the moment I'd entered the lab … I'd left no trace that anyone had been inside the building, put everything I'd touched back in its place, taken care to flick round those padlock combination numbers exactly twice. Yes, I was confident I'd covered my tracks.

Then came a disquieting thought: I had turned those tumblers *anticlockwise*, hadn't I? Well, it wasn't important. Grant himself wouldn't be sure which way he'd turned them. I settled back against the upholstery.

CHAPTER TEN

Celia Haxby picked up the leaflet on the table. 'This looks interesting. The meaning of *orquestra* is clear enough, but what exactly is a *bandolin*?'

'That's Portuguese for mandolin,' I said. 'A mandolin concert's held most Fridays in the English Church. The musicians are very young, some of them barely teenagers.'

She turned to Dorothy. 'Shall we give it a go then? We aren't doing anything else on Friday night, are we?'

Furrowed brow and pursed lips signalled the answer. 'I'm not in favour of these amateur affairs, Celia. Just because children are involved, we're supposed to suspend all our critical faculties. Fifteen euros are fifteen euros.'

'Old skinflint,' Zara muttered under her breath.

'I've already got one booking for tonight,' I said hastily. I flipped open my organizer. 'Charles has bought a ticket. This will be the last concert for some time, because they're off on tour round Europe.'

'Well, that settles it.' Celia delved for her purse in a newly purchased ethnic tote bag.

At the mention of Charles's name Zara's eyes had narrowed. She sipped at her smoothie and studied Dorothy thoughtfully.

Celia counted out her euros. 'Why don't the two of us make a night of it, Dorothy? Concert first, then dinner in the Old Town.'

After a moment's hesitation Dorothy nodded slowly. 'We-ell, I suppose dining out would be a change from hotel food. But if the concert's nothing to write home about, the meal's on you.'

I noted down their names. 'That's another two, then,' I said, but not quite loudly enough to cover up Zara's, 'Grumpy old bat!'

'That's *quite* uncalled for!' Dorothy snapped. 'The less I see of you the better, young woman!'

Zara reached into her skimpy shorts and produced a twenty euro note. 'That's just too bad 'cos I'm coming too.'

Celia rolled her eyes. 'Youth nowadays! They should be—'

'I'll be there,' I broke in. 'I'm sure we'll all enjoy it. All the seats are unreserved. I'll order a taxi to pick you up early so that you'll arrive just before the doors open.'

I hadn't originally intended to go to the concert, but I couldn't miss the chance to study these intriguing undercurrents. For instance, I was sure Zara had spent her euros solely in a desire to keep tabs on Charles Mason. And it was obvious that Charles's sole interest in Dorothy Winterton was to charm that old lady into buying into his latest scam.

Rain had been threatening all day. Now the fine drizzle had turned to a heavy downpour. Already water was coursing its way in a mini torrent along the gutters. I shrugged deeper into my raincoat, and quickened my step. I'd set off early to ensure I was in place to meet the taxi at the church door and hand out the tickets. The English Church was to be found in a maze of narrow streets lined with picturesquely distressed two-storey houses, the pavements so narrow that two people couldn't pass.

I turned off Rua da Carreira into a cobbled cul-de-sac. On my right, behind a high wall topped by railings entwined with a thick old vine, lay the extensive grounds of the English Church. The brass plate inscribed *The Parsonage*, the pillared portico of the church entrance, the neo-classical Georgian dome of the church itself, all evidence that English residents of Madeira in the past had done their best to make this corner of a foreign field a piece of Home.

Though it was forty minutes before the concert was due to begin and the doors had not yet opened, taxis were already queuing to drop off their passengers. I joined the huddle of those sheltering from the rain under the spreading branches of the giant kapok tree in front of the church and looked round for my little group, but there was no sign of Celia and the others by the time the doors opened at 8.30 and the crowd surged in. At 8.45, they still hadn't appeared: there was little chance now of finding five seats together. In fact, it would suit my plans perfectly if they arrived really late, as then we'd be assigned the overflow chairs at the very back. In the jostle for the seats I had a hunch that Charles would manoeuvre himself next to Dorothy. That would undoubtedly precipitate an interesting reaction. When tempers are lost, tongues are unguarded; some onion layers might well be unpeeled. And if I could narrow the field by eliminating Mason and/or Porter-Browne from my list of suspects....

Five minutes before the start of the concert, the flow of arrivals had slowed to a trickle. The persistent rain was beginning to penetrate the thick canopy of the kapok tree, several large drips finding their mark on the back of my neck. A small group turned in at the gates. One of them was holding up an extra large multi-coloured umbrella of the sort much favoured by golfers. I stepped out of the semi-shelter provided by the kapok tree and peered through the dark and the rain.

'Not so fast! Slow down, for Christ's sake,' wailed a bedraggled figure trailing behind the others. Unmistakably Zara. She was tottering along on impossibly high heels that could have been designer-made to catch and skid on the wet cobbles.

'You've only yourself to blame with those silly shoes.' Celia's voice issued from beneath an enveloping oilskin slicker.

Seemingly oblivious to his soaked shoulders, Charles was holding the umbrella in a chivalrous and totally unnecessary gesture over Dorothy Winterton's old-fashioned transparent raincoat and hood.

'Ah, there you are, Deborah. I'm afraid we're a *lot* later than you suggested. Put it down to young madam here.' She glowered in the direction of Zara's limping figure.

'The sodding taxi stopped miles away. And then *someone*,' – Zara shot a vicious look at Dorothy – '*someone* said they knew a shortcut that turned out to be a dead end and— *Aaaagh*.'

Charles had tilted the umbrella, sending a cold douche down her neck. 'Well she got us here, didn't she?' he snapped. 'Which is better than you did, dragging along behind us whining and moaning. And anyway, *who* kept the taxi waiting at the hotel?'

Things were going according to plan. And now that the doors were about to close, those overflow chairs at the back of the church were sure to be ours.

'Never mind, you're here now.' I ushered them into the porch, and handed over the tickets.

'Quickly please.' The girl at the ticket table held open the side door. 'The concert begins. These seats here.' The girl indicated five cane-seated chairs lined up behind the wooden pews. Perfect.

Celia surged along the row to the end seat, then hesitated. 'These chairs are a *leetle* miniscule, not at all comfortable for normal people, though they might suit a stick insect.' She glanced sideways at Zara.

'Stand, if you like, Celia.' Dorothy settled herself on the next seat.

Zara hesitated. Decision made, she stepped forward, and with a smirk claimed the seat next to Dorothy.

Charles pushed past me. 'Hey, I wanted to—'

'I'll take the end seat,' I said, leaving him no choice but to sit next to Zara. I had the feeling that it was only a matter of time before pent-up resentments exploded. They might sit out the concert in glowering silence, but if I kept the party together afterwards, I'd see results.

An air of expectancy rippled through the audience as the orchestra filed in and took their places. The conductor raised his arms in a signal of readiness, the faces of the young musicians tensed in anticipation. Zara Porter-Browne studied her coral-pink fingernails and yawned.

'Manners!' Dorothy dug her elbow hard into the culprit's ribs.

Charles sniggered.

The loud thrumming chords of *In a Persian Market* filled the church. Impervious to Dorothy's frowns and disapproving looks, Ms Porter-Browne yawned and sighed throughout the highly polished performance. Charles Mason didn't seem to be enjoying the concert either. Sideways glances, furrowed brow and the couple of seconds delay in joining in the appreciative applause after each item on the programme, showed that his thoughts were elsewhere. Things were simmering nicely. It would all come to a head when we walked back together through that maze of narrow streets.

We were amongst the first out when the concert ended. The rain, though not as persistent, was still heavy enough for umbrella and rain-coats. Zara had neither, and almost immediately my plan started to unravel.

'I'm going to bag myself a taxi,' she whined, and stepped out from under the shelter of the porch.

To keep the group together I'd have to act now. 'Hold on a minute, Zara,' I put a restraining hand on her arm. 'You won't get one. The taxis out in the street will all be pre-booked. You can share my rain-coat.' I turned to the others. 'I suggest we all walk down to the *avenida* near Blandy's Wine Lodge. It'll take less than ten minutes and we'll be sure to get a taxi there.'

Celia adjusted the hood of her oilskin. 'Well, count *us* out. One of those pre-booked taxis outside will be ours. I had a word with the driver when he dropped us. We're going to have dinner in the Old Town…. Dinner's on you, Dorothy,' floated back as they set off towards the gates.

At a stroke I'd lost two of the group, but I consoled myself that there was still the chance of Charles and Zara having a blazing row. All it needed was a little spark, and I was sure I could provide that. In the event, however, I didn't have to.

With Charles and his umbrella in the lead we came out of the gates and turned left into the cul-de-sac, lit only by the occasional globe lamp on a wall-bracket. The distinctive Haxby silhouette was making its way down the line of parked yellow taxis interrogating each driver with a booming, 'Taxi for Haxby and Winterton?' Dorothy, hunched in her clear plastic raincoat, trailed behind radiating impatience and complaining querulously, 'If you'd made a note of the number, Celia, we'd be on our way to the restaurant by now, instead of getting drenched. I'm going back to the church. There'll be a phone there.'

She swung round and cannoned into Zara and me. Joined like Siamese twins under the protection of my raincoat, we performed an awkward little dance and just managed to keep our feet.

Zara lost her temper. 'Watch what you're doing, you crazy cow!'

I had to admire how Charles swiftly turned the occasion to his advantage. As Dorothy staggered and almost fell, he steadied her and said smoothly, 'Can I offer you my arm, Mrs Winterton?'

Zara's face contorted with rage. 'You're always sucking up to her, you prick. You strung *me* along when you thought I was an heiress, but I saw through you. All that talk about wine's as fake as that so-called Rolex of yours. C'mon, Debs. Let's go.' She moved off dragging me after her. 'You're only after the old bag's money,' she yelled over her shoulder.

This dramatic storming-off was somewhat marred by a sideways lurch and a sharp cry as her spiky heels skidded on the wet cobbles. Gripping the raincoat, I stumbled after her. As we left the cul-de-sac I glanced back. People were now streaming out of the church gates, filling the narrow street, threading their way between the parked taxis. All I could see of Charles was the multi-coloured umbrella forcing its way after us through the crowd.

We turned into the narrow Rua dos Aranhas, more a lane than a street. With its peeling stuccoed walls, dilapidated shutters and gridded windows it was a decrepit survivor of old Funchal. The rain, the soft golden glow from the Victorian-style lamps, the cobbles, the tiny shops, the storeyed houses – we could have been in the England of Dickens. Zara, oblivious to ambience, was treating me to a vicious character assassination of conman Charles. I made the appropriate noises and listened with half an ear, hoping to tune in on something that would help me to come to a decision about Mason. Conman, yes, but was dealing in drugs another of his little enterprises?

'Hey, hold on a minute.' The shout came from behind.

Recognizing Charles's voice, I slowed down, Zara speeded up. As we tussled to retain our due share of the raincoat, he caught up.

'Right, you bitch. Take back what you said about me, or—'

'Or what?' Zara sneered. 'You'll sue me?'

Fifty metres away, headlights sent shadows flitting across the shuttered façades as a car turned into the street.

As Charles advanced towards her, I tugged hard at the raincoat. 'Car coming. We'd better keep in.'

The twin beams caught us. I tugged again at the raincoat and Zara allowed herself to be pulled towards a doorway.

'Look out, Charles!' I shouted.

He showed no sign of moving, didn't seem to hear me. He was glaring at Zara. 'Sue you? I'll—'

But he never completed the sentence. Afterwards I pieced together the sequence of events, but at the time it was a confusion of scrambled images and sensations: in my ears the roar of an accelerating engine, a woman's scream; the multi-coloured umbrella soaring into the air like an exotic bird in flight; a vicious blow to my back that sent me staggering forward into the path of the car; a sickening stab of pain shooting through my injured shoulder as I slammed onto the cobbles.

I might have blacked out for a moment, for the next thing I was aware of was a heavy weight pinning down my legs and a babble of English and Portuguese voices.

'It didn't stop! It didn't stop!'

'I've phoned for an ambulance.'

'This one's dead.'

Who was dead? Where was I? Couldn't remember, couldn't remember. For a confused moment I was back in Monte Gardens. I forced my eyes open … glistening cobbles and a forest of legs. Not Monte Gardens, then.

Trousered knees knelt on the wet road and a moustachioed face loomed close to mine. 'Don't try to move, *senhora*, in case there are injuries. The ambulance will soon be here.' Someone patted my hand reassuringly.

The weight on my legs shifted and a shaky voice that I only just recognized as Zara's wobbled, 'Somebody pushed me ... somebody pushed me ... somebody pushed me,' as if the gramophone needle had stuck on an old vinyl record.

A woman's voice, authoritative, professional, 'You must stay calm, *senhora*.'

'Calm, *calm*?' Zara's voice rose to a shriek. 'You expect me to be calm when someone's just tried to *murder* me! I was pushed, I tell you. I was *pushed*!' Hysterical sobs rendered the rest of her words unintelligible.

That violent shove between my shoulders ... I saw again in the stark illumination of the headlights, Charles Mason holding aloft the umbrella in a ghastly imitation of the Jack Vettriano's painting *The Singing Butler*.

'*This one's dead.*' Not Zara. Mason? The wail of sirens, at first so faint that they'd barely registered, was now loud, very loud. The forest of legs shuffled out of my field of vision to be replaced by two pairs of navy trousers tucked into military-style leather boots. Blue strobes flickered on the green-shuttered façades of the houses on the other side of the street, colour-washing the pale plaster. Gentle hands eased me onto a stretcher and carried me to the waiting ambulance. As the stretcher tilted, I caught a glimpse of a still form sprawled on the cobbles. A limp hand stuck out from underneath the covering sheet. Circling the wrist was the metal strap of an expensive-looking watch, its face starred and crazed.

CHAPTER ELEVEN

'Somebody wanted me dead, and if Charles Mason hadn't been with me, he would still be alive. I feel responsible. I—' The catch in my voice took me by surprise. I trailed to a halt. I hadn't even liked the slick conman who preyed on vulnerable females. But burnt into my memory was the image of the still form, the broken watch. I swallowed hard.

The *comandante* stared at me thoughtfully. 'Like that cat of yours, it seems you have the nine lives. You have received no serious injury. But you are in shock and must not blame yourself. You were not the driver of the car.' Long red fingernails drummed a tattoo on the desk. 'Have you considered that perhaps this Charles Mason had played the confidence trick once too often and his victim decided to eliminate him, to take him out?' She seized one of the flowers and whipped it out of its vase. 'This is the rotten apple, the bad egg hiding under the cover of its so beautiful companions.' I hadn't noticed before, but this flamboyant orange and blue crest had withered to brown shrivelled tufts standing up at a rakish angle in a dishevelled Mohican hairdo. 'You see, my dear Sshmit, when something is intolerable, it has to be disposed of.' *Crack. Crack.* The snapped-off head and two pieces of stalk vanished into the waste bin beneath her desk. 'Now, Sshmit,' – she dusted one palm off against the other – 'just, perhaps, you and that silly girl were attacked to create a smoke-screen, lead us up the garden path, as you say. Yes, what we have to consider is, who among your little group of suspects might have wanted to get rid of Mason?'

'Porter-Browne couldn't possibly know that Mason would be in position for a hit-and-run "accident", and she was almost a victim herself, so that leaves Grant, Haxby and Winterton,' I said, 'but I don't *really* think any them would go as far as to—'

'Ah, Sshmit, too much thinking, that is your trouble.' Frowning, she rearranged the remaining blooms, inspecting each closely for signs of possible deterioration. 'To expose the rotten heart of a fruit, you must peel off the unblemished skin and cut down to the canker. Yes, my dear Sshmit, you must act. How, I leave to you.'

Towards the back of the garden, half-hidden from the road, there's a ramshackle trellised arbour, a favourite retreat for Gorgonzola and myself on a hot day. I stroked her soft fur and mulled over my latest interview with the *comandante*. 'It's all very well, G, but thinking *is* important, isn't it? How *can* I act if I haven't thought it all out first?'

Her moth-eaten tail swished a drowsy agreement.

'Which of us was the *intended* target, G? Me, Zara, or Charles?' That car had made no attempt to avoid Charles, though he must have been clearly visible in the headlights; somebody had definitely shoved *me* into its path; and Zara too – I heard again those screams of, 'I was pushed, I tell you. I was *pushed*!'

Yes, who was the intended target? If I could figure that one out, I could perhaps set a trap that would expose the 'rotten heart under the unblemished skin' as the *comandante* had so picturesquely put it.

Assuming that she was right and Mason *was* the target, who would want him dead? I'd seen him try out his wine scam on David Grant and get the brush-off, but there'd been no animosity on Grant's part, only boredom. No motive there.

Could Dorothy Winterton have wanted him dead? Mason *had* pestered her on several occasions. She'd appeared to be listening intently, so intently, in fact, that at the time I'd thought about stepping in to save her from a financial mugging. But even if, privately, she thought he was a boring pest, she'd hardly go as far as organizing an attempt on his life. There *were* one or two things about her that didn't add up, but as for her being a cold-blooded murderer....

Celia Haxby had a motive. She didn't have much time for Charles, had made her dislike plain on several occasions, but dislike doesn't normally lead to murder.

I'd originally ruled out Zara as being behind the hit-and-run, on the grounds that she was a fellow victim of attempted murder. But she had motives enough – anger, resentment, revenge. Her screams had been convincing – but was it all just a clever act? Now, *that* was a thought. I'd been deliberately pushed into the path of that car, no doubt about that. But had *she*? We only had her word for it. Eyewitness accounts of the incident had been so conflicting as to be totally unreliable, and all had focused on the car's impact with Mason.

'Am I on the right trail, G?'

There was no help from that quarter. G's furry sides rose and fell in sleepy rhythm. I detected something very like a snore. Stretched out on the soft cushion, G's legs twitched in pursuit of dream prey.

I continued with that train of thought. Nobody, but nobody, had come forward to say they'd seen *either* of us being pushed into the path of the car, though some eyewitnesses had reported a rowdy gang of youths barging their way down the street. So Zara *could* have organized Mason's death. Had I been expendable, the attack on me a convenient smokescreen giving credence to her story?

But what if I had indeed been the target? I thought back to that night – the darkness, the rain, Zara and I sharing the same raincoat – from behind it would have been impossible to distinguish who was who ... so Zara *could* have been pushed. She could very well be speaking the truth. I was back to where I'd started.

G, too, seemed to be having her problems. Once again her body quivered, her paws lunging in hot pursuit of a rapidly escaping victim.

It was all very well for the *comandante* to wave her hand with the flourish of a conjuror about to produce a rabbit out of a hat. She had demanded that I track down the culprit, but how, just how, was I to set a trap that would expose the bad egg, the rotten apple in the barrel? Grant, Winterton, Haxby, Porter-Browne – there was no hard evidence against any of them, yet one, I was sure, had masterminded Charles Mason's death. I stared at the clump of Madonna lilies, at the crystalline texture of their unblemished white petals and eased my stiff shoulder into a more comfortable position against a cushion.

Clang clank clang clank clang clank. Faint but familiar, *clang clank clang clank clang clank*. A blue light strobed through the tangle of magnolias, camellias and other greenery that obscured my view of the road. With a screech of brakes, what could only be Raimundo's wreck of a car pulled up across the driveway. Silence descended as the hideous metallic clatter ceased. The blue light was still flashing as the *eeeeeee* of the driver's door being wrestled open was followed by a *thwunk* as it banged shut.

Alarmed by these indications of an emergency, I carefully lifted recumbent Gorgonzola off my knee and rose to my feet as Raimundo burst into view and panted to a halt in front of me. This surprising flurry of activity from someone so laid-back could only mean there'd been a major development. Luís dead? Mason's murderer arrested?

'I–hhh–I–hhh—' The seriously unfit Ribeiro struggled for breath. 'I–hhh–have to tell you—'

I waited impatiently for enlightenment.

He drew a deep breath. '*Senhora*, I have to tell you that—' A hacking smoker's cough engulfed the rest of the sentence.

Disturbed from her slumbers, G opened a disapproving eye. Mystified, I watched as he fumbled for his handcuffs and whipped them from his belt.

'I have to make an arrest of a dangerous female criminal, *senhora*.' He struggled to suppress another bout of coughing.

So there *had* been a major development. At last, a breakthrough. Who was about to be arrested – Haxby, Winterton or Porter-Browne?

'Who is it? Where is she? Let's go.' In my excitement the words tumbled out.

Raimundo Ribeiro pulled himself up to his full one metre seventy. 'She is here, she is *you*, Deborah Smith. Heh, heh, heh.' He brandished the handcuffs.

I stared at him, not quite taking it in, then sat down heavily on the arbour seat. Just in time, Gorgonzola took hasty evasive action, streaking off to claw her way up the wisteria to the safety of the veranda.

The handcuffs clinked as they swung slowly to and fro in front of my eyes. 'Heh, heh, heh. Your accomplice has made her escape, I see.'

'*I'm* under arrest? But, but, but …'

He grinned, 'But I think we not be needing these.' He tucked the handcuffs back into his belt, extracted a pen and notebook from his top pocket and flicked through the pages. 'Comandante Figueira said, "Ribeiro, bring in the *inglesa*. There has been an accusation".'

'Accusation? What accusation?' I squawked.

He scribbled in his notebook. 'Now, *senhora*, I read out what I am writing. *When arrested on suspicion of breaking into the premises of Senhor David Grant, Exotic Flower Importer & Exporter, the suspect said nothing.*' Several horizontal strokes heavily underlined the last word. One eyelid drooped in a slow exaggerated wink.

So not only had the break-in been discovered, the identity of the perpetrator was known. This latest evidence of my incompetence must have infuriated the *comandante*, especially as she'd have to think of a way of getting me off the hook. Even more disturbing was the thought that the easiest way out for the *comandante* would be for her to send me straight home to England. Afterwards, she'd inform Grant that I'd got wind of my impending arrest and fled the country.

Raimundo snapped shut the notebook. 'Come, *senhora*. The more the *comandante* waits, the angrier she will be.' He wagged a roguish finger. 'She is a woman who does not like to be kept waiting, eh?'

I followed him to the car. At the gates I looked back. Like the Cheshire Cat in *Alice in Wonderland*, Gorgonzola's disembodied face was peering out from among the racemes of purple-blue wisteria. But she wasn't grinning.

'The back seat for prisoners! Heh, heh, heh.' Raimundo slammed the door shut and got behind the wheel, but didn't start the engine.

We sat there, blue strobe light flashing, while passers-by cast curious glances into the car. All sense of urgency seemed to have evaporated. He fished for his battered pack of cigarettes, selected one and took a long slow drag.

'Like Senhor Holmes your famous English detective, I know how the guilty one is thinking, *inglesa*. You are thinking how does Senhor Grant come to know about our – your little excursion to his orchid farm.' He pursed his lips and exhaled. A perfect smoke ring drifted upwards and hung between us.

I nodded. That was exactly what I was wondering. I was sure nobody had seen me as I crawled under the fence and worked on the lock of the hut door. Had perhaps an electronic ray in the hut activated a remote alarm? No, someone would have come rushing to investigate, and they hadn't. That left a hidden CCTV camera linked to a tape, but a tape only reviewed every few days.

'There was a hidden camera?' I said.

'*Sim*, you are correct.' His shoulders drooped a little, like a boy whose childish riddle has been too quickly guessed. 'It takes the pictures of you and the cat in a place where you should not be. Senhor Grant shouts on the telephone at Comandante Figueira. She is not pleased. And she is not pleased now, if I keep her waiting.' He flicked a switch, and siren howling, blue light flashing, we hightailed it into town.

The interview with the *comandante* went badly. As I'd surmised, my sin of omission – the failure to take precautions against the possibility of a hidden camera – was a hanging offence.

'Sshmit, I *despair*.' She brought the flat of her hand down on the desk with such force that the strelitzias on her desk trembled and quivered as if their heads too were waiting for the chop. 'If you *must* go breaking and entering, to hide your face is the most elementary of precautions. Even the most recently recruited undercover officer knows *that*.'

She was right. My halting explanation seemed lame even to my own ears. A face-concealing balaclava was indeed an integral part of my all black, disappear-into-the-night outfit. Yet I hadn't been wearing it in my prowl around the hut. Hot and sweating after my struggles to get under the fence, I'd pulled it off and stuffed it in my pocket. With no one around, wearing it had seemed a pointless discomfort. But now I was paying for that fatal lapse in security.

'This morning I advised you against too much of the thinking, but it seems' – she glared at me with narrowed eyes – 'that on occasions, Sshmit, you do not do enough of the thinking. Senhor Grant has influential friends and is making a lot of trouble. I remind you, that until Officer Ribeiro reported back, I had no knowledge of your visit to the *senhor*'s place. To be frank, Sshmit, I would not have wanted to know. Though once I had been informed, I said to myself, "If the end justifies the means, Justinia, you can conveniently forget what Ribeiro has just told you".'

For a long moment there was silence.

'But did the end justify the means? *No*. Did you discover evidence of criminal activity? No. All you found was little plants. *Plants*, I say.'

'But, *Comandante*,' I ventured in a last ditch attempt to avert the inevitable, '*why* does he have all that security? He doesn't need high fences, special locks, and CCTV cameras to protect plants. Not in Madeira, anyway. The man's got something to hide. And if I—'

'Enough, Sshmit!' With the crack of a pistol shot, the flat of her hand smacked down once again on the desktop. The strelitzias shifted uneasily in their vase, their sharp beaks swinging towards me like the rifle barrels of a firing squad. 'After the Gomes murder I gave you the ultimatum. You had twenty-one days to solve the case.' She strode over to the wall-planner and stabbed a blood-red fingernail on day 25. 'In ten days you leave the country. I can delay proceedings, stall Senhor Grant only till then. Ten days, Sshmit.'

When the door of the *comandante*'s office closed behind me, I was astonished to note that barely fifteen minutes had passed. I went in search of Ribeiro to ask him for a lift home. His wreck of a car would be a bit of a hell-ride, but cadging a lift was my only option since the *comandante*'s summons had been so peremptory that I'd been carried off with no cash in my pockets to buy a bus ticket. I found him in the entrance hall as I'd expected, but he wasn't slouched on a bench puffing away on one of his vile cigarettes, he was behind the desk at the public counter.

I waited in the small queue till it was my turn. '*Olá*, Raimundo, I didn't expect to find you here.'

No response.

I tried a little cough to attract his attention. 'Standing in for a sick colleague again, are you? I was hoping you'd be able to give me a lift home.'

He didn't meet my eye. 'Alas, *senhora*, that will not be possible.' One finger tapped slowly and randomly over the keyboard. 'It was not *quite* accurate when I said I am taken off the traffic to work behind the desk when someone is sick.' A furious burst of typing conjured up *Uff4orm,b.@.c.;lhjsjjzlkf.* 'Alas, *senhora*, you are not the only one who has brought on their head the anger of The Ogre.' *;k;k;, hdhh; ;skzkjk' 'dfmbzlb;x .dzjih* appeared on the computer screen.

'But why is she angry with *you*?' I said indignantly. 'What have *you* done?'

'Guilt by association, *senhora*,' he said grimly. A vicious two-fingered stab downward, and on the monitor blossomed blue, the Microsoft Windows' Screen of Death.

'Oh dear, buggered,' I said, and unsure whether his muttered oaths were directed at myself or the *comandante*, beat a hasty retreat.

The long hot walk back to the house on the Estrada Monumental gave me plenty of opportunity to ponder over what to do next. The only conclusion I reached was that time was running out.

'I'm back, G,' I called, as I walked up the drive.

No familiar gingery face peered out from the racemes of wisteria twining round the veranda.

I advanced up the path. 'Wake up, lazybones.'

The arbour was empty, the only sign that she'd ever been there, the long indentation in a cushion. I smiled to myself. Hide-and-seek was one of her subtle ways of letting me know I'd fallen from grace. Raimundo's noisy arrival in the middle of her power nap, added to my abrupt departure, would have been more than enough to precipitate a little bout of huffiness.

I wandered round the garden, peered up into tangles of palm fronds, poked under the magnolia and camellia bushes, parted the luxuriant fronds of ferns. Not a sign of her. Could she have scaled the thorny-trunked kapok? I tilted back my head and scanned the canopy of the giant tree. No cat crouched on a branch among the cotton wool pods.

Playing possum on the veranda, that's where she'd be. I felt in my pocket for the house keys, then remembered that in the flurry of my departure I'd completely forgotten to take them. Fortunately I'd also forgotten to lock the front door.

'Tsk, tsk,' I muttered.

I let myself into the house and tiptoed up the stairs. The louvred doors to the veranda were standing ajar.

I pulled them open. 'OK, G, game's up!'

I'd been so sure that I'd find her stretched out on one of the chairs, that for a moment I couldn't take in that she wasn't there. I craned over the rail. No twitching wisteria foliage, no cat. It was then I felt the first stirrings of unease.

I stood gripping the rail, gazing out over the sunlit bay of Funchal. Away to the right, just visible, was Cabo Girão, and beyond, the hazy blue mountains where I'd gone to seek out Senhora Gomes at Boa Morte – Senhora Gomes who had revealed to two men that the English lady's cat had found the suitcase they were seeking.

They couldn't have— They couldn't have—! I turned back into the room, crossed it at a run, and raced down the stairs. I knew with a leaden certainty that G's vanishing act was no game. Mouth dry, I stood in the hall.

'Gorgonzola, where are you?' I whispered.

Stolen, *killed*.

In the silence, from the kitchen came a faint sound. I let my breath out in a long sigh of relief. I'd worked myself up into a frenzy for nothing!

'Snacking again, G? If you get too fat, I'll have to put you on a diet!'

Hchaahch. The sound came again, louder. *Hchaahch*. The retch, the rasp, the choke of a cat being sick. Very sick. In two strides I'd reached the half-open door. I flung it wide and stopped dead. Trails of vomit and diarrhoea led to the dark space under the old kitchen dresser. *Hchaahch*. Again, that awful retching. I dropped to my knees and peered underneath. Gorgonzola was crouched in the gloom, a shivering mound of ginger fur, eyes closed, mouth slavering.

Poison. I'd seen similar symptoms in a police dog that had eaten meat doctored with some toxic substance. It had suffered horribly and died within a few hours. I reached in, grabbed her by the scruff of the neck and hauled her out. With shaking hands I wrapped her in a towel. What was the right thing to do? Dilute the poison by spooning some water into her? Induce more vomiting? Or would that be entirely the wrong treatment? Panic paralysed any rational thought.

I closed my eyes and took several deep breaths. *Phone a vet.* One arm cradled G as I fumbled for the phone book and scrabbled through the pages. *T ... U ... V ... Veterinário* There were several. Senhor Jorge Ramos, Senhor Carlos Sousa, Senhor Artur Spinosa ... I stabbed in the number of the nearest surgery, and bent my head to murmur soothing words in G's ear while I listened to interminable ringing at the other end of the line.

Click. The answering machine activated. *The surgery is closed at the moment. Surgery hours are 9 a.m. till 2 p.m., and 5 p.m. till 8. Anyone requiring urgent advice, should phone the emergency number.* A rapid fire, instantly forgettable, nine-figure mobile number followed.

Another hour to wait before the surgery opened. I slammed down the receiver. Should I redial and attempt to note down that emergency number, or phone another vet? I stroked G's head and tried to come to a decision. Her body jerked in violent spasm. That decided me. To phone another vet would only be wasting precious time – all of them would have similar hours, so I'd just hear a series of answering machines.

With my free hand I dragged up a chair and collapsed onto it. I gently positioned G on her side on my lap, and punched in the numbers again. It took me two attempts to jot down the emergency number in full. Mouth dry, I waited to be connected.

'Spinosa speaking. There is a veterinary emergency?'

'*Sim, senhor.* My cat has been poisoned.' My voice cracked. 'I have just come into the kitchen and found her vomiting. There is much diarrhoea. And ... and I....' The sentence ended in a strangled sob.

'Compose yourself, *senhora*, for the cat's sake. I will do what I can to help you.' The calm voice radiated reassurance. 'You say you found her in the kitchen. Now tell me, could she have eaten something harmful there?'

In my panic I hadn't given a thought to what could have caused these symptoms.

'Something harmful?' I echoed.

114

'Spilt powders or liquids, *senhora.*'

'No, there's nothing like that. There's only her food bowl.'

'And that contains?' The voice betrayed no hint of impatience.

I gathered up the swaddled G and went over to examine the bowl. I expected to see the remnants of the substantial lunch that she'd polished off before that postprandial session in the arbour. Cats always leave a little something of their meal to come back to, something to ward off that imaginary pang of imminent starvation, so there were indeed flakes of fish and crumbs of biscuit.

'Just what's left of the fish that I—' There *was* something else in the bowl, something *I* hadn't put there. Something that shouldn't have been there.

'Yes, *senhora?*'

'Well,' I said, 'she's been eating fish, but there are a couple of what look like hard, black seeds. I don't know how *they* got into her bowl.'

'Large, black and shiny? Bring the bowl with you, so that I can confirm what I suspect is the toxin.'

The bundle in my arms shuddered and twitched, the prelude to spewing up more fishy vomit. I fought down rising bile and coped with the whole stomach-churning episode without adding my own contribution to the contents of the plastic box I had in readiness.

'She's just been very sick,' I reported.

'The cat, she has vomited again? That is good. Now you must make her swallow water, as much water as you can, a little at a time on a small spoon by gently lifting her lip. I will stay on the line while you do this.'

I did my shaky best to follow the vet's instructions and managed to spoon a few drops into G, but I had to call a halt as she became more and more distressed. I laid her down on the worktop and picked up the phone again.

'She took some water, but not very much.'

'You are doing well. Now see if she will take some milk. That will coat the intestines and slow absorption of any toxin.'

'I don't know if I can do that. She's very distressed and seems much weaker.' The tears welled up in my eyes.

'Then I think you should call a taxi and bring your cat here immediately. Do not attempt to drive here yourself. That would not be wise. Keep her warm and her head low. Courage, *senhora.* I will be at the surgery to meet you.'

*

The next few hours were the longest of my life – that frantic dash to the surgery, the traumatic handing over of Gorgonzola, the interminable waiting.... When they had carried G off, I sat on a chair in the empty reception room listening to the loud *tick tick tick* of an old-fashioned wall clock, as infinitesimally slowly the large black hands kicked their way round the Roman numerals on the dial.

At last the *tap tap tap* of footsteps in the corridor roused me from my gloomy thoughts. The door swung open and a tall, slim girl in whites poked her head round.

'Senhor Spinosa has identified the plant seed in the cat's bowl. Toxicity depends on how many the cat swallowed. He will have a better idea in an hour or two how she is responding to the treatment.' The door closed softly behind her.

Plant seeds in her food bowl.... Nothing with seeds like that grew in the garden, so somebody had pre-planned this, come to the house, watched and waited till they saw me leave. Then they'd gained entry by forcing a window or climbing up to the balcony-veranda, or picking the front door lock— But they wouldn't have had to do *any* of these things. I myself had made it easy for them. I'd gone off in such a hurry with Raimundo that I'd left the front door unlocked. I tried unsuccessfully to comfort myself that they'd have got into the house somehow.

In sombre accompaniment to my thoughts the clock ticked on....

Drug dealing had to be behind this. The men who had paid that visit to Senhora Gomes knew about Gorgonzola and her talent for sniffing out drugs, though I didn't have a clue as to the identity of the shadowy figure who had sent them. Luís was the only definite lead I had, so it was more important than ever that I make contact with him. And how was I going to do that? I stared at the black hands of the clock, and found no answer.

At last the door opened. As Senhor Spinosa crossed the room towards me, I tried to read his face. No reassuring 'Everything's going to be all right' smile. But equally, no evasive sliding away of the eyes, the telltale sign that G's condition was deteriorating. I swallowed hard and rose to meet him.

'Senhora Smith, I have to tell you that the toxin in the seeds is highly irritant and can be fatal. While I am not able to predict the outcome with certainty, I hope that with supportive care, your cat may make a full recovery.'

I subsided back onto the chair, weak with relief that G still had a chance.

He was saying, 'We have hydrated her to counteract the diarrhoea, and now we must wait.'

'How long before you can…?'

He pursed his lips. 'Any deterioration will occur in the next few hours. Tomorrow we will know the outcome. Until then she is in the hands of God.'

In the taxi home I was consumed by a deep smouldering rage, a rage directed at the shadowy figure whose plan it had been to put the deadly seeds in G's bowl. Was it a vindictive act of revenge because she had detected the drugs at Senhora Gomes's house? Or did they fear that she would sniff out a more incriminating cache, one that would point a finger at the identity of that shadowy figure?

I let myself into a house that no longer felt like home. Without G, there was an emptiness, an absence. Whether Gorgonzola lived or died, I now had more than a professional interest in tracking down the man who ran this drug cartel. As far as I was concerned, it had become a crusade. *My* revenge for this attack on Gorgonzola would be to track him down and bring him and his organization to justice.

No time like the present. Firmly putting aside any inclination to huddle in a chair and weep, I flicked through the telephone book till I found Senhora Gomes's number. She answered on the second ring. Had she been expecting a call, perhaps from Luís?

I spoke quickly. I must get my message across before she put down the phone. 'Senhora, I am the *inglesa* whose cat found the suitcase.' I heard the quick intake of breath. 'When we met, I warned you Luís was in grave danger. If you want to save him, you must get him to contact me *immediately*. It is essential that I speak to him tonight. My house is the old house on the Estrada Monumental, next to the big kapok tree. If he wishes to telephone, my number is …' I repeated it twice. 'I will wait for his call till midnight.'

On the other end of the line there was silence, then a *click* as the phone was put down. All I could do was wait – and hope.

woke with a start, momentarily disorientated, pins and needles in my arm, hip numb. After a quick snack in lieu of an evening meal – the afternoon's events had deprived me of all appetite – I'd sat on the veranda waiting for Luís to get in touch. I must have dozed off while gazing at the lights twinkling on the hills above Funchal, for a glance at my watch showed it was now a few minutes after two in the morning.

Luís hadn't phoned.

Neither had the vet. 'I'll phone you at nine tomorrow when the surgery opens,' he'd told me, 'unless there is news before that.' There'd been no need for him to spell it out. Any news before morning would be bad news.

Ftk ftk ftk. A moth was fluttering and dashing itself against the dim bulb of the veranda light. I eased myself upright from an awkward slouch in the wicker chair. I'd played my best card in that phone call to Senhora Gomes, gambled and failed. What was I to do now? Nothing came to mind. I rose stiffly to my feet and flicked off the switch.

I sat there in the faint light of the stars and the crescent moon staring out over the bay. With the failure of Luís to contact me, that line of investigation had petered out. Little chance now of turning up a new lead in the nine days left before the *comandante* presented me with my economy class air ticket.

The tired brain is an inefficient problem-solver. Six hours' sleep, and things might seem a bit brighter. When I woke up, my subconscious might just have come up with a solution. Faced with a seemingly insurmountable problem, I'm a believer in going to bed and giving the brain free rein.

Things didn't turn out quite like that. First of all, try as I might, I couldn't get to sleep. Eyes closed, I lay in bed but instead of drifting gently into the arms of Morpheus, my head was a swirl of thoughts. In desperation I tried all the recognized techniques – slow, deep breaths, relaxation of the muscles starting at the feet and working up to the neck, visualization of tranquil scenes, counting sheep – nothing worked.

More wide-awake than ever, I stared up at the ceiling. Normally falling asleep is no problem, no problem at all: I can cat-nap on planes, trains, and buses, had even on occasion been prodded awake at concerts and lectures. Why didn't I try a few lines of that soporific poem, *Song of the Lotus Eaters*? It might do the trick. How did it go? I closed my eyes and trawled my memory ...

... thro' the moss the ivies creep ...
And from the craggy ledge the poppy hangs in sleep ...

I dragged the words out as slowly as I could.

... And ... from ... the ... cra-ggy ... le-dge ... the ... po-ppy ...
hangs ... in ... sle-ep ...

No use. The poppy might be drowsy, but *I* definitely wasn't.
Perhaps the line, *ti-red eye-lids on ti-red eye-s....*
My eyelids *were* heavy and my eyes certainly were tired, but my mind was a whirling kaleidoscope of disturbing images: handcuffs dangling from Raimundo's nicotine-stained fingers; a trail of vomit leading to the darkness under the kitchen cupboard; G's body lying limply in my arms, her frightened eyes staring up at me....

To sleep, perchance to dream.... Did I *really* want to sleep? Anything was better than uncontrollable dreams. In one movement I sat up and threw aside the bedclothes. I'd listen to a CD, read a book, or brush up my Portuguese. I swung my legs over the side of the bed and pulled on a light sweatshirt and jeans. A glass of *poncha* wouldn't go amiss either. Yes, I'd sit in the wicker chair on the balcony-veranda and pass those long hours until dawn broke over the eastern headland of Funchal Bay.

I switched on the table lamp on the veranda then settled myself comfortably in the rocking chair with a copy of *Madeira and Porto Santo* and the promised glass of *poncha* within easy reach. There'd be no harm in doing a little homework. Dorothy and Celia's purpose in taking the ferry to Porto Santo on Tuesday might be entirely above board, but if it wasn't ... I might be clutching at straws, but at least it was a possible lead.

I thumbed through the pages. *Four miles of unspoilt golden beach....* That was one up on Madeira's concrete lidos, fine as some of them were. *Horse-carts with canopies and curtains....* Picturesque enough to justify Celia toting along her canvas and brushes. Perhaps that was all this jaunt of theirs was – a totally innocent painting trip, its end result the effortless reduction of golden sand and invitingly blue sea into a hideously garish daub.

I took an appreciative sip of the *poncha* and idly turned a page in the guidebook. Apart from a small Columbus museum and a seventeenth-century church, the main tourist attraction of Porto Santo was the excellent beach, also claimed to have therapeutic properties in the treatment of varicose veins, arthritis, aches and pains.... *The sufferer is buried up to the neck in the sand....* Though my shoulder wasn't bothering me as much as it had, perhaps I'd give the sand treatment a go. That, of course, would have to take second place to tracking Dorothy and Celia's movements – even if all they were up to was murder by paintbrush. Porto Santo was a very small island so following them would be easy. There was one big problem: by trailing after them everything, I would draw attention to myself. I reached for the glass of *poncha* and took another sip. I'd have to work that one out when I got there.

For the moment I was content to lean back against the cushions and rock slowly to and fro, the only sounds the rhythmic creaking of the chair, the soft sigh of a lone car passing by on the road below, the rustle of the night breeze in the leaves of the wisteria. Relaxed, and at last drowsy, I drifted towards sleep.... By the sound of it, the wind was getting up ... the rustle of leaves was more lively now ... the wisteria seemed to be taking a bit of a battering. Must be in for a storm ... my eyelids slowly closed....

'*Merda.*'

The muttered oath from somewhere just below the level of the veranda shocked me wide-awake. Momentarily powerless to move, I stared at the shaking stem of wisteria, thick as a man's wrist, which twined and twisted in a stranglehold round the railings of the veranda. There could be no doubt about it – someone was using the network of branches as a makeshift ladder.

On the outermost fringe of the warm pool of light cast by the table lamp my eye caught a movement, just where the edge of the veranda plunged down into darkness. Fingers scrabbled for a hold, gripped, knuckles whitened. Agent James Bond 007, weapon aimed, would have been out of his seat, stamping down on those fingers in a nanosecond. Agent Smith, HM Revenue & Customs, just sat there like a tailor's dummy, mouth agape.

A leather-jacketed arm hooked itself round a railing, a white blob of a face rose out of the darkness like a phantom from a grave. I screamed. I'd intended a blood-curling, mega-decibel scream that would ricochet round the hillsides bringing aid and succour in the form of the entire garrison of Police HQ. The reality was a pathetic squawked *aaaarkh* that wouldn't have startled a sleeping bird from its roost in the neighbouring kapok tree.

'Do not have fear, *senhora*,' whispered a voice I recognized.

'Luís?' The surge of relief had the curious effect of making me want to giggle.

'I get your message, *senhora*, but I am afraid to use the telephone. Ears might be listening. I see light on veranda and so I come.'

As he prepared to heave himself up over the rail, my training at last reasserted itself. I leant forward and switched off the lamp. My night visitor must remain part of the night.

'I think we have a lot to tell each other,' I said, and ushered him inside, beyond the range of prying eyes. Behind closed curtains in the kitchen I plied him with coffee and brought him up to date on events.

'As you may have guessed by now, Luís, my job involves a bit more than being client liaison rep for Agência de Viagens Madeira. I am working with your Drug Enforcement Agency to bring to justice those evil men who killed your brother. You loved your brother and want revenge. Is this not so?'

He stared into his coffee, saying nothing, but the involuntary white-knuckle grip on the mug gave me the answer.

'When you set up that meeting at the Beerhouse on the harbour, you were going to tell me—?'

I stopped. I'd suddenly realized that I might have got it all wrong. At that time he'd no idea that I was anything other than a travel rep, so why would he have passed on to me any information about a drug ring he'd stumbled on? In our discreet coffee-time conversations we had gossiped about guests and their peccadilloes, not serious crimes like murder and robbery. But if I'd jumped to the wrong conclusion, so it seemed, had someone else. Perhaps *all* that Luís had been going to impart was a juicy bit of gossip about one of the guests then present in the coffee-bar, something the guest concerned might overhear. Had something so simple, so ordinary, set in motion a murderous train of events? I might have been on the wrong track from the beginning, but it didn't alter the fact that *somebody* in that little group had a secret they were prepared to kill for.

Luís was still staring into his mug of coffee.

To get him talking, I asked again, 'Just what was so important that you asked me to meet you at the Beerhouse?'

He looked up and sighed. '*Senhora….*' He stopped.

I reached up to the shelf for the liqueur bottle and added a generous slug to both our mugs. It had the desired effect.

'I've been wondering what it was you wanted to tell me,' I said. 'All I know is that your brother was killed and you disappeared. I think you are hiding because Roberto told you something that puts your life in danger. Is that not so?'

His reply was a barely perceptible nod of the head.

'That is why I needed to contact you, Luís. We must track down those men before there is more killing. What is it you know that might cost you your life?'

He avoided my eyes. I could just make out the muttered words, 'Now they just look for me. If they know I have spoken to the *polícia*, I have great fear also for my mother.'

'Neither you or your mother will be safe until these criminals are brought to justice.' I put my hand on his. 'I can make a phone call now, and your mother and yourself will be taken to a safe house, a place of safety where they will not find you.'

He pulled his hand free. 'A safe place? You do not understand, *senhora*. Nowhere on this small island is there a safe place for enemies of the drug criminals.'

'The safe place can be anywhere of your choice. It can be in England.' I let that sink in. 'It is your only chance, Luís,' I said softly. 'The *only* chance, for as you say, there is no place that is safe in Madeira for you – or your mother.'

'I must think, *senhora*.' He pushed back his chair, made to get up, then slumped back down and sat head in hands, staring at the worn wooden floor as if trying to memorize the pattern of the grain.

I let the minutes tick by. The angry hornet buzz of a distant motor bike penetrated the heavy wooden shutters and the closed window, deepening the heavy silence.

At last, he raised his head and looked at me. '*Sim*, yes, that is how it must be, *senhora*. I will tell you what I learnt from Roberto.'

Once he had made the decision to talk, Luís paced up and down my small kitchen, the words tumbling out of him. 'Roberto and I were very close. As close as twins.' He paused and swallowed hard. 'Until a few months ago. Then I began to see that we were not so close. He is gone for some days and does not say where he has been. When he comes back, he has many euros and drinks much. "Little brother", he says to me, "buy what you want." But he would not tell me where this money comes from. Then I see that he has bad friends, so I say to him I cannot take his money any more, as I think it is bad money. He gets very angry and says, "Money is money. With this money our mother can have much comfort. Do you not wish our mother to have this, little brother?" And what can I say? The Massaroco Hotel does not pay much.'

I pictured the sparsely furnished kitchen of the little house on the *levada* at Boa Morte, the sink with its single plate and cup on the draining board, and nodded.

'One night I ask him, "Those bad friends get the money from drugs, is it not so?" He has drunk much wine and he laughs and says, "Do not worry, little brother, the *polícia* will not catch us." So I know that is what he is doing. I tell him he must stop. I have heard that the *polícia* are watching the fishing boats. And he laughs and laughs and laughs and says, "They may watch the fishing boats as much as they like, but they will be looking in the wrong place." I grab his arm and say, "You will be caught, Roberto, and our mother will be shamed." He laughs again and says, "The *polícia* are so stupid. They look for the boats *on* the water, but they do not think of the little boats coming *under* the water from Porto Santo, little boats made of fibre-glass and wood."'

Submarines. Mini-submarines. All along we'd assumed that drugs were being moved in and out of Madeira by fishing or cargo boat and had concentrated our efforts accordingly. Mini-submarines hadn't entered our heads. I suppose someone should have thought of it, but no one had.

Luís sat down abruptly and buried his face in his hands with a muffled, 'I should have found a way to stop him.'

I put a hand on his shoulder. 'What could you have done?'

'If I go to the *polícia*, he not be dead.' The last word ended in a sob. I sat down beside him. As much to distract him from this despondent train of thought as in the hope it would help with my investigations, I asked, 'Do you know why he was killed?'

He looked at me. 'Ah, *senhora*, it is not only to me that Roberto talks of the submarines. When he has drunk much in the bar at Boa Morte, he again talks the big talk. I am afraid for him.'

'And you also became afraid for yourself? Did something happen to frighten you?'

He stared into space, seeing not my little kitchen, but the simple room beside the *levada* at Boa Morte. 'The day before Roberto was found in the harbour, when I get home from the bar, Roberto is already there. He is crying with fear. He say the men are going to kill him and me because I know too much. He say we must run off and hide. We arrange to meet in the church at Ribiero Brava and I stay to tell our mother what we are doing so that she will not go to the *polícia* when we disappear. I give him my credit card so he can get money.'

So that explained the initial misidentification of the body.

He stared into space. 'Then I go to Ribiero Brava and I wait a long time at the church, but Roberto does not come. At first I am angry, then I am worried. I wait and I pray. All night I pray. In the morning I decide I must go to the *polícia*. But then these men will kill us all, even my mother who knows nothing. Madeira can no longer be our home. I decide we go to England but no one must know this. At the Beerhouse I will tell you that I must leave Madeira quickly and ask you, who know about tourists, where in England is good place for waiters, a place where Portuguese people do not go, but I cannot ask you this where someone might hear.'

'I understand, Luís. But you did not come to the Beerhouse. Why was that?'

'After I leave the bar, I go back to the church but Roberto is not there. I wait until I must leave for our meeting, but there is accident on *Via Rápida* and I come late.' He buried his face in his hands again. 'And then I see ... I see Roberto's body being carried into ambulance, and I have much fear and I hide.'

'And your mother thought she could protect you from these evil men by saying Roberto's body was yours?'

He sighed and looked at me sadly. 'Yes, but it was a foolish hope. These men do not care which brother they kill. Still they are looking. They will only stop when both of us are—'

I stood up and went over to the phone. 'Listen to me, Luís. They will not find you – or your mother. As I said, I can arrange that both of you are taken to a safe place, anywhere of your choice. Will I make that phone call now?'

For the first time that night I saw him smile.

The heavy black hands of the clock in the vet's waiting room formed a perfect right-angle. At nine o'clock in the morning the room was as empty of patients as it had been just over twelve hours ago. Either the small domestic animals of Funchal were a particularly healthy breed, or Senhor Spinosa's fees were particularly steep – I suspected the latter. I hummed a little tune to myself. Things were looking up. There'd been no summoning phone call in the night, or what remained of it after Luís had been driven off, and better still, the receptionist had greeted me this morning with a bright smile and the news that I could take G home with me after the vet had made a final examination.

Yes, things were certainly looking up. Dead men tell no tales, they say, but through Luís, Roberto Gomes had spoken from the grave and another piece of the jigsaw had clicked into place. And as regards my coming trip to Porto Santo on Tuesday, I now had a definite lead to follow. On that small island, possible docking places for submarines, even mini ones, would be limited, very limited indeed.

I gave a cheery wave to a faint reflection of myself in the glass of a black-framed diploma on the opposite wall. What made this waiting room rather depressing was the array of sober black-framed certificates. Cheerful pictures didn't have a look-in as far as Senhor Spinosa was concerned. Perhaps he thought the sight of his qualifications would raise the spirits enough.

I heard the door to the street open. Reflected in the glass of the diploma, a woman came in struggling under the weight of a heavy pet-carrier. Senhor Spinosa had another client.

She placed her burden carefully on the floor and subsided onto a chair. 'Ooh, you *are* a weight, Blackie. I'll have to see about putting you on a diet. No more cheese biccies for you.'

I recognized the voice immediately. The woman with the cat-carrier was none other than Victoria Knight, the elderly widow I'd met on a previous case in Tenerife.

I swung round. 'Victoria! What are you doing here?'

Her plump homely face broke into a beaming smile. 'Fancy meeting you, Deborah. It's lovely seeing you again.'

I sat down beside her. 'You haven't given up that splendid house of yours, have you?'

'Oh no, dear.' She patted my hand. 'I'll never do that. I'm only over here for a few weeks' holiday, swapping houses with an old friend. She said the Flower Festival was a good time to come and, of course, I brought dear Blackie with me.'

I looked down at the pet-carrier. Blackie? She must mean Samarkand Black Prince. In Tenerife she'd offered to take care of the cat to save it from being sent to an animal sanctuary when its owner had been arrested and faced a long term of imprisonment.

The door to the corridor opened and we both looked up.

The veterinary nurse smiled at me. 'Senhor Spinosa says your cat is ready to go home. But first he has some words to say, Senhora Smith.'

I jumped up to follow her. 'We've a lot to catch up on, Victoria. See you on my way out.'

Gorgonzola was lying on the shiny metal examination table, eyes closed, a slump of ginger fur.

'Come on, G,' I said, gently tickling the back of her ears. 'Time to go home.'

She opened one eye and made a strangely human sound, halfway between a groan and a sob.

'Do not worry, *senhora*.' Spinosa sounded amused. 'She is only feeling sorry for herself. She has been frightened and she is hungry. We have offered her food, but she would not eat. That is quite often the case when cats come in for treatment, but when they get home, the appetite returns.'

I scooped her up. 'No dreaded cat-carrier for you, G. It's a taxi home for us.'

Spinosa smiled. 'This time your cat has been very lucky. Contact with lily pollen would be a very different matter. Ingestion is almost always fatal.' He held open the door. 'Ask the receptionist to phone for a taxi as you settle your account, Senhora Smith.' His white teeth smiled an expensive smile. 'And do not hesitate to contact me if there are any problems.'

'There'd better not be any problems, G,' I whispered into her fur. '*This* bill is going to make HMRC's eyes water.'

Victoria was still in the waiting room, empty pet-carrier at her feet. She was slowly stroking what appeared to be a thick, black, furry stole of the kind much favoured by Edwardian ladies. 'There, there,' she crooned, 'soon be better.'

'That just has to be Black Prince,' I said as I approached.

She gazed down fondly at the black Persian cat standing on her lap with its paws over her shoulder. 'Of course it's him, dear. I'd never leave Blackie behind. He's such a highly strung cat. So insecure.'

'Ah, yes,' I said, looking down at the limp ginger bundle in my arms.

Blackie, or Samarkand Black Prince to give him his pedigree name, had been an arrogant thug of a cat. In Tenerife, Gorgonzola had given him his come-uppance, transforming him into a timid shadow of his former self.

Miaooow. Black Prince's plaintive whine seemed to indicate that he had read my thoughts and was reliving that truly awful experience.

'So-oon be better, dear.' Victoria planted a kiss on his furry head. 'Blackie's got a small fishbone stuck in his mouth. I can't get it out by myself, so....' She turned her attention to Gorgonzola. 'But you didn't mention anything about having a cat when we were in Tenerife, Deborah. And a Persian too!' She unhooked Prince's paws from her shoulder and settled him on her lap. 'Look, Blackie, a little friend. What do you say to that?'

Prince's long-drawn-out *miaoooooooow* had a miraculously recuperative effect on Gorgonzola. She stirred, lifted her head, and stared with huge copper eyes in the direction of the mournful sound. I felt her stiffen. The hair on her body bristled and a loud vibrating purr, an exultant drum roll over a vanquished foe, rumbled from her throat.

The black fluffy mound on Victoria's lap imploded as Blackie attempted unsuccessfully to flatten himself into the folds of her skirt.

'Don't be a silly billy, Blackie. Deborah's cat is just being friendly.' She put her hands under him to gather him up, but he squirmed out of her grasp and vanished into the depths of the pet-carrier at her feet.

I tightened my grip on G and slammed the carrier door shut with my foot. 'Oh dear, she didn't mean to frighten him,' I lied. 'He really is nervous, isn't he? Perhaps you'd better let him stay where he is till you're called. If somebody comes in to see the vet, we don't want him running out onto the road.'

'I don't know what's come over him.' Puzzled, Victoria frowned down at the carrier.

I wasn't going to enlighten her. Blackie was recalling all too clearly his near-death experience at the paws of Gorgonzola who was now lying smugly in my arms, mission accomplished, point made. Time to beat a hasty retreat while the going was good.

'I'm filling-in here on a temporary basis with a travel agency,' I said. 'I'll probably be going back to England on the 25th, but we must get together before I leave. If you give me your phone number, I'll give you a ring.'

'That would be very nice, dear.' She fished out a scrap of paper from her bag and scribbled down a phone number. 'Come over and visit me and do bring your lovely cat.'

As I'd expected, the wad of euros in my wallet came nowhere near the sum needed to settle the hefty bill for Senhor Spinosa's professional services. While the receptionist processed my credit card, I stroked a contentedly purring Gorgonzola and thought what a small world it was. It would be good to see Victoria Knight again and catch up on how she was doing. But one thing for sure, I'd be going alone. G would not be accompanying me on that visit.

CHAPTER THIRTEEN

I'd hoped to keep well out of the way of David Grant, Exotic Cut Flower Exporter, and to that end I'd phoned the Massaroco Hotel and arranged a different venue for my office hour. Any clients wishing to consult me, would find me, not in the café bar, but on the terrace. A note to that effect had been put up on the Agençia de Viagens' noticeboard. But, best laid plans and all that....

David Grant could read too. And when I turned up on Monday, the first thing I heard as I strolled onto the terrace was the tinny rendition of *Land of Hope and Glory* from his mobile phone. Though his back was turned, I had clients to meet, so I didn't have the option of ducking back into cover and scuttling away. I couldn't avoid him for ever – I'd have to face him sometime. I just didn't feel quite ready to do so after the emotional battering I'd taken over the weekend.

I seated myself out of his immediate line of vision at a table under one of the green striped parasols and listened to him chatting away loudly on his mobile phone. I could only hope that the presence of clients might restrain him from making too much of a scene – or any scene at all. I opened my desk diary, laid out my pile of excursion leaflets and prayed for a client to come rushing up. If Dorothy Winterton was intending to come, she'd be here at ten o'clock sharp. But ten o'clock came and went. At five past, Grant's loud monologue stopped with a breezy *Ciao* and I could feel my luck running out. I bent my head and gave a letter from the Agençia my full attention.

A shadow fell across the page. A fist thumped down on the table, toppling the pile of leaflets. 'What the f— were you doing breaking into my shed, Smith?'

My hand holding the letter jerked, demolishing what remained of the pile of leaflets and sending a couple fluttering to the ground. I looked up into his face contorted with rage. Should I bluster it out or cringe in abject apology? A series of half-formed replies flashed through my mind, but in the event I just sat there.

He loomed over me and pushed his face close to mine. 'Nothing to say, eh? Out on bail, are you? Well, I've got you and that ruffian of a cat of yours on videotape and no slick lawyer's going to smart-talk you out of a prison sentence.'

'I'm very sorry, Mr Grant, if you're upset, but I was just curious, and after all, I didn't do any damage.' I summoned up a conciliatory smile.

They say that a gentle answer turneth away wrath, but not in this case. A speck of froth appeared at the corner of his mouth.

'Since your little escapade, madam, I've got myself a couple of Rottweilers and pit bulls. They roam free and if you come anywhere near my property again, they'll tear you to pieces.' There was no mistaking the menace in his voice. 'Cat or human, it's all the same to them. And, let me tell you, I won't be responding to any screams.' From the expression on his face he seemed to be enjoying the image of bloody, mangled flesh.

A voice cut in. 'Wow, Dave, what have you got in that orchid farm of yours – the crown jewels?' Neither of us had noticed the approach of Zara Porter-Browne.

The effect of her words was dramatic. It was as if she'd thrown a bucket of icy water over him.

He blinked, snarled, 'Bloody sights, I've—' The torrent of abuse spluttered to a halt. He took a deep breath, then his arm scythed across the table, sweeping desk diary, leaflets and letter onto the tiled floor. He surveyed his handiwork with some satisfaction, then without a backward glance, stomped off.

Zara tossed her green locks. 'Gawd, Deborah, what the shit did he mean by that?'

With some effort I laughed it off. 'He was probably referring to what would be left when his Rottweilers and pit bulls had finished with me.'

She helped me pick up my scattered papers, but like a pit bull herself, wasn't going to let the subject go. 'What *did* you do to bring that on, Debs?' She pulled up a chair, leant her elbows on the table and prepared to hang on my every word.

Damn. How was I going to get rid of her before another client came along? And how was I going to stop her recounting the whole incident with much embellishment to all and sundry?

I giggled. 'Took you in, did we? Genuine audience reaction! Great!

Dave's a leading light in the English Church Dramatic Society. They're putting on a play, a Victorian melodrama, and one of the cast has broken a leg, so I've been asked to stand in – only a minor part, luckily, because I'm no great shakes at acting. We were just taking the chance of a quick rehearsal.' I can be quite inventive in an emergency.

Her look of eager anticipation faded. 'Oh, bugger. And here was me thinking I'd come on a piece of the action at last. This dump is so shittishly *boring*.' She slumped in the chair like a wax candle melting under a hot sun.

'Sorry to disappoint, Zara.' This time my giggle was genuine. 'Now what can I do for you?'

'Sitting around here is driving me up the wall.' She pouted moodily. 'The place is full of old biddies and arty crafty types. At least when Chaz was around, I'd someone to talk to – or fight with,' she added as an afterthought. Signs of grief for the deceased Mason were conspicuous by their absence. 'C'mon, Debs, hit me with a tour that's not mind-numbingly bo-o-ring. None of those crappy garden visits, thank you.'

'What about the toboggan run from Monte?' I shoved one of the retrieved leaflets over to her.

'Been there, done it, got the straw hat.' She brightened, 'Yeah, that was all right. When that truck came straight at us on a bend, the old gent beside me nearly wet himself.' Her howl of mirth rang round the deserted terrace.

'Well, how about Wednesday's excursion to the São Vicente caves? They're old volcanic pipes. Not a flower in sight,' I said, hiding my amusement.

'Pipes?'

'They're tunnels left by lava flowing to the sea. It says here' – I waved the leaflet – '*Journey to the Centre of the Earth*. Of course, that's a bit of an exaggeration, but it's quite dramatic, in its way. ' I consulted the leaflet again. '*Walk the path opened by fiery magma four hundred thousand years ago.*'

Zara shrugged unenthusiastically. 'Anything's better than sitting around here, I suppose. OK, count me in.'

'I'm sure you'll enjoy it,' I said, jotting her name down in the desk diary. 'The *Agençia* agency told me this morning that there were only a few places left, so I'll send in your name right away.'

She slouched off in search of a drink and I went off in search of a phone in a David Grant-free zone.

'Senhora Smith here. The São Vicente caves on Wednesday, I've a booking in the name of—'

Before I had the chance to finish, Senhora Rosa Carvalho at the Agência snapped, 'Where on earth have you been, Deborah? I've been trying to get in touch, but the barman said there wasn't an office hour meeting in the café bar today.'

It hadn't occurred to me that the location of the office hour would be of any interest to the Agência. 'That's because I'm holding it on the terrace,' I said, with a bit of an edge to the words. 'I was told there might be competing noise from work being carried out in the café bar.'

In a more conciliatory tone she said, 'Well, I'm glad I've got hold of you at last. Ana's just had word that her father has died suddenly, so she has to fly home to Portugal. I know it's short notice, but I need someone to stand in for Wednesday, so I'm afraid I'll have to call on you to take the Wednesday excursion to the São Vicente caves.'

I put the phone down. Bugger, as Zara would have said. Well, look on the bright side – I wasn't being called in on Tuesday, so the Porto Santo investigative trip was still on. If I found confirmatory evidence of Luís's submarine story, Wednesday would have been the day to follow it up, but that couldn't be helped. Strings had been pulled to get me this job and I didn't feel I could wriggle out of a reasonable request just on the off-chance that I'd discover something in Porto Santo.

For the second time that day, I pinned up a notice.

Cancellation of office hour on Wednesday 19th. Please note: my day off is Tuesday this week. If you need help or advice on any of these days, hotel reception will contact Agência de Viagens on your behalf.

Celia's voice boomed from behind me, 'I say, that's a bit rich. Tuesday *and* Wednesday. *Two* days without help and advice.'

I closed my eyes and took a deep breath. Rarely had Celia come to an office hour seeking advice and help. She'd usually gone her own way, made her own plans for her painting excursions.

I swung round, hoping an apologetic smile would hide my irritation. 'I'm really sorry about that, but I've just learnt that I have to stand in for a colleague and escort the trip to the São Vicente caves, a whole-day excursion. So that's the reason there'll be no office hour that day.'

'Hmph.' A snort of disapproval. 'If there's no one available, that's just when something occurs that *needs* sorting out.' She flounced off in a swirl of blue and green smock.

Unlike Gorgonzola who likes to prowl the night, I hate getting up in the dark, but to catch the Porto Santo ferry I had no choice. Just after 7 a.m. I left her curled up warm and cosy on my duvet, and caught a taxi down to the harbour. Out to sea, a faint glimmer in the sky was heralding dawn, though on the dark mass of mountains round the bay the strings and clusters of streetlights still sparkled brightly.

Under the glare of powerful floodlights on the quayside it was already day. Iceberg-white, the side of the ferry towered above an organized chaos: cars and lorries rumbled into the hold; taxis arrived and departed; passengers searched in pockets, struggled with suitcases, hugged their last minute farewells. I pushed my way to where an official was electronically validating tickets, and while I waited, scanned the milling crowds for Dorothy and Celia. There was no sign of them. Hoping that they hadn't aborted whatever little scheme they had in mind, I made my way up the gangway and into the exclusive comfort of the leather armchairs, buffet and bar of the first class lounge. The semi-circle of plate glass windows showed a sky already lightening to a pale purple-grey. The houses on the encircling hills were now clearly visible, orange streetlights dulled to ochre. A short while later, the soft vibration of idling engines strengthened and the worn stones of the old fort guarding the harbour slid past.

What was the best way to handle the coming encounter with Dorothy Winterton and Celia Haxby? Just why had they concealed from me the fact that they were going to be on the ferry too? And if they *were* up to something, what measures would they take to make sure I left Porto Santo none the wiser? In hindsight I should have given this vital point a *lot* more consideration, but lulled by a hearty buffet breakfast and the gentle motion of the ship, I dozed off....

When I woke, the sea no longer stretched unbroken to the horizon. Ahead were the two distinctive conical mountains of Porto Santo, purplish brown against a grey sky. I knew it wasn't an island of tree-covered slopes and lush greenery, but as we approached, the almost complete lack of vegetation, the arid *emptiness* was startling. The capital, Vila Baleira, was a mere scatter of white houses hugging the ground in the valley between two low volcanic peaks. That thin line of colour must be the famous beach of golden sand, the island's main tourist attraction, but where were the customary lines of sun beds and umbrellas? I couldn't see any at all.

People had started to leave the lounge and I hurried after them down to the reception area. Still no sign of Dorothy and Celia among the fifty or so gathered there. I edged my way through the crowd, aiming to be amongst the first to disembark. I wasn't going to make the mistake of being stuck on the ship while they bowled off in a taxi to destination unknown. The exit door opened and I was carried along in the surge towards the gangway.

Just as I reached the doorway, from somewhere behind me Celia's voice said loudly and impatiently, 'No, Dorothy, it's *this* way to the car deck.'

A man elbowed me aside, ramming his suitcase painfully into my heel as I swung round craning to pinpoint the speaker. Before the press of bodies jostled me forward, I caught a glimpse of Dorothy's iron-grey perm reflected in the mirror ceiling tiles. All the way down the gangway I lectured myself on the crass stupidity of overlooking the obvious. *Of course*, I should have taken into account the possibility that they might take their car on the ferry. What better way of giving me the slip on Porto Santo? The best I could do now was to hope to commandeer a taxi and follow them.

I scanned the vehicles lined up on the quayside – a blue bus, an assortment of cars, mini-buses and vans and, the answer to my prayers, a sole taxi. What if somebody else got to it first? As soon as I stepped onto the quay I broke into a sprint, only to slow to a halt after a few metres. I was too late. The taxi was moving off in the direction of Vila Baleira. I stood there staring disconsolately after it. I'd have to catch the public bus to the little town and hope that Haxby and Winterton might stop off for a coffee there. Perhaps if I had a scout around, I'd spot that distinctive metallic-green car of theirs. If not, I'd hire a taxi to drive me round. On such a small island with its simple road network, the chances were that I'd come upon these ladies sooner or later, though what I'd do then…. Perhaps things *had* worked out for the best, for with roads so empty of cars and people, I now realized that to have trailed after their car in a taxi would merely have drawn their attention to the fact that they were being followed.

Poop poop. I spun round. I'd failed to notice the car coming up slowly behind me.

'Yoohoo, Deborah.' Celia waved a hand in greeting. 'Surprise, surprise! You didn't know we'd booked on the ferry too, did you?'

'Dorothy! Celia!' Genuine astonishment on my part, for far from sneaking off and trying to avoid me, here they were actively seeking me out.

Celia was beaming at me through the open car window. 'Going anywhere in particular? Can we give you a lift?'

That put me on the spot. I managed to come up with, 'Well, there's the Columbus House and museum, and ... er ... I thought I'd do a little island sight-seeing in one of those picturesque horse-carts.' I gestured in the direction of the one standing near the bus, a rhapsody in blue from wheel to roof, including the frilly curtains. 'Then if there's time, I'll see if I can try out the famous sand treatment for my shoulder – if they do that sort of thing at this time of year, that is.'

I was in for another surprise.

'Hop in.' Celia twisted round in her seat and eased open the rear door. 'Let's have a coffee together in town and you can tell us what's worth seeing.'

As we chatted in the five minutes it took to drive into Vila Baleira, my mind was busy with this unexpected turn of events. Could it be that in a desperate attempt to wrap up the case before the *comandante*'s deadline, I'd jumped to the wrong conclusion, quite misinterpreted Dorothy and Celia's innocent actions?

'Down here, Dorothy.' Celia was pointing to a parking area behind the handful of shops and bar-restaurants on the main road. 'There might be a nice little café near the sea.'

And indeed there was a café, right on the palm tree-lined promenade with a good view of the pier and the beach. As we sipped our coffee, the sun emerged from behind the clouds, transforming the sea to a startling turquoise-blue edged by sand so pale as to be almost white.

'Make a wonderful painting, don't you think, Celia?' Dorothy put down her cup and framed the view with her fingers. 'We could be in the Caribbean.'

'Those colours!' Celia produced a digital camera from her bag. 'I *must* capture those *colours*.' She pushed back her chair and wandered across the promenade to point the camera at the sweep of the bay.

'Celia's such a perfectionist when painting landscapes and still life, you know. She spends hours mixing those paints and getting things just right.'

I suppressed a smile. Dorothy was either being very loyal, or was a very poor judge of painting. The muddy greens and greys of the hilly landscape I'd seen in Celia's room were anything but natural. And as for 'getting things just right' – the only easily recognizable object in that picture with the pink teacup, apart from the teacup itself, was the slab of raw fish.

'Now to see what I've got. It's too bright out there.' Celia sank into her seat, held the camera on her lap in the shade of the table and peered at the screen. 'Hmm, not bad, but it's too empty. It needs a colourful figure in the foreground.'

Dorothy put down her cup. 'That purple outfit you're wearing, Celia, would make a good splash of colour. How about if I take your picture standing under that palm tree?' She held out her hand for the camera.

'No. I'm sorry, Dot, but your pictures are *always* blurry. Either that, or you cut off my head or my feet.'

'It's *Dorothy*, Celia. Not Dot. Just because last time the photos—'

'Why don't *I* take the photo?' I broke in.

'Would you?' Celia handed me the camera with alacrity and rose to her feet. 'I think if we go over there near the pier … oh, mustn't forget this. Need it for the picture.' She picked up her floppy hat from beside Dorothy's handbag on a vacant chair and jammed it on her head. 'Back in a sec, *Dorothy*.'

But by the time Celia had decided exactly where she was going to stand and had struck a suitable pose, it was a good deal longer than 'a sec' till we returned to the table.

'I knew this would happen, Celia.' Dorothy gave an exasperated sigh. 'Your coffees were stone cold. So I asked the waiter to take them away and took the liberty of ordering another pot – and some more of those delicious biscuits. Here you are, Deborah.'

'Now compare these two shots, Dorothy.' Celia took a quick swig of coffee, pushed aside her cup, and switched on the camera. 'Can you see why the composition is so much better in this one?'

I listened with half an ear to the discussion, drank my coffee and pondered my next move. I was convinced now that I had been wrong about Dorothy and Celia having an ulterior purpose in visiting Porto Santo. Suddenly aware that they had stopped talking, I looked up.

'Er, sorry.' I drained the cup and placed it back in the saucer. 'Did you ask me something?'

Dorothy smiled. 'We were wondering if you would care to accompany us to a delightful little bay just along the coast. You and I can sit in the shade while Celia exercises her brushes.'

'Yes, *do* come, Deborah. Dot gets a teeny bit bored with no one to talk to. You see, an artist must concentrate *totally* to capture the essence of a scene.'

Final proof that I had been on the wrong track. They definitely wouldn't want me along if they had something to hide.

'We-ll, I had thought—'

'Oh, you won't have to listen to me rambling on the whole time, Deborah. After getting up before dawn to catch the ferry, a little nap in the shade will definitely be on the cards.' She leaned forward, gazing at me intently. 'And I think you should have one too. You're looking a little tired, dear.'

I stifled a yawn. I *did* feel a bit drowsy. 'Well, thank you. If you're sure—'

'Quite sure.' Dorothy caught the waiter's eye, produced the car keys from her handbag and rose to her feet.

'Quite sure.' Celia echoed, picking up her camera.

The sand was soft against my cheek. I was lying on my side, the shoulder I'd injured at Monte buried in the warm therapeutic grains. I felt rested and relaxed … so relaxed that it was too much effort to open my eyes.

A man's voice penetrated the warm drowsiness that cocooned me. '*Desculpe, senhora*, it is not permitted to sleep on the beach.' A hand shook my arm.

I thought about this. How ridiculous. Any beach I'd seen was full of bodies stretched out and dozing in the sun. It was in my mind to say this, but I couldn't be bothered.

'*Desculpe, senhora*, it is not permitted to sleep on the beach when the sun goes down.' The voice was louder this time. 'I must ask you to leave.' The hand on my arm tightened.

Bloody Jobsworth. I couldn't have been asleep for more than a couple of hours, if that, so it wasn't anywhere *near* sunset.

'Please to open your eyes, *senhora*. It is time to go back to your hotel.'

Another voice broke in. 'Having trouble, Artur? Drunk too much wine, has she?'

What a nerve! My eyes flew open and I sat up, or tried to. I collapsed back onto the sand, fighting off a wave of nausea.

Two faces peered down at me. The older one frowned. 'The *senhora* was very foolish to drink and then to lie so long in the sun.'

I glared up at him. 'One and a half cupsh of coffee, *shenhor*.' I levered myself onto an elbow, and sank back again as the horizon performed a slow gyration.

'Told you, Artur. Drunk!'

'No, I'm shertainly not! But I think I *have* been too long in the sssun. I musht have fallen ashleep.' I realized I was slurring the words.

The younger man knelt beside me. 'What is the name of your hotel? I will call a taxi.'

'Massharoco,' I said. No, that wasn't right, was it? That is where I *work*. I live in a house with wisteria climbing round the balcony, the gingerbread house. I frowned. 'I'm ssorry I can't quite remember the name of the shtreet, but it'sh near the lido.'

'Lido?' Artur frowned back, as if frowning was infectious. 'There is no lido here. Could the *senhora* have come to Porto Santo on the ferry?'

'Yesh.' With the help of the young man I sat up slowly. 'I'd be awfully grateful if you could get me to the port. I'm feeling a bit dizzy and I'll be able to lie down on the boat.'

A snort of amusement erupted from Artur's colleague. 'Bit late for that, *senhora*. That's it away out there.'

I squinted against the light. I could just make out, halfway to the horizon, a white ship heading at full speed away from the island. I should be on it. What *was* I doing lying here on the beach? The events of the day were, for some reason, hazy, only half-remembered: I recalled boarding the ferry, standing on the quayside in Porto Santo, looking disconsolately after the one and only taxi disappearing in the direction of the town, getting into Dorothy Winterton's car, sitting with her and Celia at the café on the promenade, coming with them to this sandy cove....

But where *were* Dorothy and Celia? Surely they wouldn't have gone off to catch the ferry leaving me asleep on the beach? Celia must have finished her painting here and decided to drive on to another scenic spot. And I must have said I wanted to stay longer on the beach and I'd make my own way back to the ferry. But try as I might, I remembered nothing about it. Nothing at all.

How could I have been so *stupid* as to fall victim to the sun? I knew how strong it was at these latitudes, was always warning clients about the danger. I tried desperately to think of something to say to Artur and his sidekick that wouldn't involve that tricky letter 's'.

Artur was looking at his watch. 'It is possible for the *senhora* to get back to Funchal tonight.'

'Yesh? I mean, really?'

'There's a flight to Madeira in about an hour.'

'They won't take her, Artur. Under the influence of alcohol.'

'No, I'm not! I'm a bit under the weather, off-colour, ill!' I took a deep breath and enunciated the next words slowly and carefully, on guard against that treacherous, betraying 's'. If you can call a … er … car to take me to the airport, I will be very grateful.'

By the time the flight was called, helped by several glasses of water, a pot of black coffee and a sandwich, I was feeling a lot better. Groggy, but definitely on the mend. I stared out through the plate glass windows of the departure lounge at the star-studded sky and the darker mass of Porto Santo's low hills. If the short-staffed Agençia hadn't put me in charge of the next day's trip to the São Vicente Caves, being stuck on Porto Santo overnight would have been inconvenient but not really a matter of great concern.

All in all, I thought gloomily, I had nothing to show for the time and effort spent visiting Porto Santo. A whole precious day had gone to waste. I was no nearer wrapping up the case, and less than a week remained before the *comandante* had me frogmarched onto that London-bound plane.

CHAPTER FOURTEEN

'Bo–oring, bloody bo-oring.' Zara pouted like a sulky toddler. 'What do you mean by, "After we come out of the caves, we'll visit the cliffs of the north coast"? You kept that bloody quiet when you talked me into this trip. "Journey to the Centre of the Earth", you said, not "Journey to Dreary Old Scenery."'

'Sorry, Zara,' I sighed, 'but I know the caves won't be a disappointment and, if you really don't want to come with us to see those boring cliffs,' – I hid a smile – 'there's always the local bus that'll take you back to Funchal in an hour or so. But there's no need to decide now. You can let me know later.'

I left her pondering that one and went off to give out entrance tickets to the rest of the group, drawn from the Funchal hotels served by the Agençia. We joined the fifteen or so other people waiting for the guide to unlock the gate.

She clapped her hands for silence. 'We must keep in the group, all together in the group. No one must go into the places without the lights. With the lights no danger, where no lights, much danger.' She turned to me, peeling off an adhesive label and attaching it to my jacket. 'I give you new job. You, *senhora*, will come last of group, so you know that nobody is left.' She relocked the gate behind us.

The very mention of danger had altered Zara's mood. A look of anticipation had replaced her sulky pout, and I too had to admit that I felt a little thrill of excitement as we followed the guide into the depths of the dimly lit lava pipe. Drip … drip … drip of water, scuff of shoes on the concrete path, pools of yellow light intensifying the surrounding darkness, rough cinnamon-brown walls closing round us, mysterious, faintly menacing. At intervals secondary pipes branched off, like the bronchioles of a giant lung, an impression reinforced by the current of air in our faces and the faint hum of the ventilation generator.

The attack on me came totally unexpectedly. The chosen spot – an eerily beautiful subterranean lake. Under carefully placed spotlights the crystal clear water glowed a luminous emerald green. A moment before, Zara had thrust her camera into my hand.

'Do me a favour and take me with handsome here.' She flung an arm round the neck of a youth that I'm sure she had never set eyes on before and subsided onto a rock beside the lake, pulling him down with her. 'This'll make all the guys back home sit up! OK, Debs, shoot.' She pulled the startled youth's head down. 'C'mon, handsome. Light my fire.' She clamped her mouth to his with the enthusiasm of a lamprey attaching itself to its host. For Zara the wonders of the subterranean world obviously needed a little pepping up.

I was framing her in the viewfinder when without warning the lights went out, plunging the cavern into darkness, a thick velvety blackness that pressed on the eyes like a blindfold. Zara's distinctive high-pitched giggle cut through the startled exclamations and little screams.

The guide's torch clicked on. 'Lighting soon fixed. Only little problem. Two three minutes and—'

I heard a startled, 'Oh—' a clatter of metal on rock and the beam of the torch was abruptly extinguished.

'Keep *tranqüilo*, peoples. If you keep *tranqüilo*, there is no danger. No danger at all.'

I put an arm out as somebody blundered into me. 'Best to stand still till the lights—'

Rough hands seized my outstretched arm and twisted me round. At the same time other hands pinioned my other arm to my side.

Before I could let out more than a startled 'What—?' my feet were kicked from under me and I was lifted into the air in an operation so slick I didn't have the chance to struggle. My knees crunched painfully against the low wall that surrounded the lake. With the efficiency of a boat being launched down a slipway, I was shoved forward and down. I took a deep breath to scream just as my shoulders and face plunged into the icy lake.

Water rushed into my mouth. Choking … drowning....

Darkness enveloped me, the dark of the River Styx, river of the Underworld, river of Death.

I was lying on my back and somebody's lips were super-glued to mine. My eyes were closed, but somehow I knew it was Zara's mouth.

My eyes shot open. The cavern lights had come on again. Eyes stared into my own. Green eyes, green hair, definitely Zara. She gave a grunt of satisfaction and smiling, sat back on her heels.

I coughed and spluttered, only dimly aware of the ring of shocked faces staring down at me.

A voice, Zara's, saying, 'I don't often get the chance to practise the kiss, the kiss of life, I mean.'

The guide's face was close to mine. 'You have had the accident, *senhora*. Help is coming.'

No accident. There had been a carefully planned attempt on my life: the lights going out, hands seizing me, the rush of water into my mouth as I tried to scream.

'*Senhora*? How did accident happen, *senhora*?'

It had been no accident, but I didn't intend to enlighten her. I looked past the guide's head at the circle of concerned faces. Among them were my attackers.

I rubbed a hand across my eyes. 'All I remember is the lights going out ... somebody bumped into me ... must have fallen...' My eyes wandered round the ring of faces again.

Zara moved into my line of vision, eyes gleaming with excitement. 'Gosh, Debs! We all freaked out when the lights came on and we saw you with your head in the lake. You could have heard the screams all the way to Funchal! Somebody grabbed you by the hair and you were heaved out all limp and floppy.'

The guide draped her jacket over me. 'This young *senhora*, she runs forward and says she knows the way to make breathe the drowned person.'

I reached out and touched Zara's hand. 'Thanks.'

Faces smiled, hands applauded.

She blushed and muttered, 'Any time, Debs.'

The arrival of two men with a stretcher saved her from any further embarrassment. Wrapped in a blanket, I was carried through the tunnels. As the dark lava walls slid past my eyes, I pondered the narrowness of my escape. If those lights had come on a couple of minutes later ...

When the guide insisted that I wait at the first aid station until the doctor arrived, I didn't argue. The adrenaline rush of relief at being alive had died away, leaving me feeling decidedly weak and wobbly. The coach driver would have to decide whether to continue to the north coast without me, or cut the excursion short and return to

Funchal. All I wanted to do was lie down and sleep. I watched the coach driving out of the car-park, too tired to care whether or not the excursion had been curtailed.

To replace my wet shirt and jacket, the guide raided the souvenir shop and triumphantly produced a sweatshirt emblazoned with *The Caves of São Vicente. A Visit to Remember.*

'I'm really quite all right,' I lied to the doctor when he arrived. 'All I need is to get home and go to bed. Please just phone for a taxi.'

He pursed his lips. 'You are not fit to travel alone, *senhora*.' He opened the door to the outer office. 'I will get one of the guides to telephone for an ambulance. All your party has gone and, without someone to accompany you, I cannot give permission for you to go home by taxi.'

Resigned to losing the argument, I slumped back.

The guide, busy at her desk filling in the accident report, looked up. 'One of the *senhora*'s party is still here. She is waiting for a bus, but I think she has long, long time to wait.' She pointed through the open door.

On the other side of the car-park a green-haired figure was leaning somewhat disconsolately against the bus stop. Zara was destined to come to the rescue again.

As the taxi sped back along the *Via Rápida*, I said, 'I'm afraid all that must have spoiled the excursion for you, Zara.'

'Oh no, Debs!' She leant forward, eyes shining. 'That was a wow of a trip. And not boring at all! The last time I got such a buzz was in a nightclub when I caught a guy spiking my drink. I tell you, Debs, he didn't know what hit him!' She hooted with laughter. 'It was the toe of my Manolo Blahnik!' She hooted with laughter again.

Spiked drink. I sank back against the seat closing my eyes, not in weakness, but in shock, as a memory of yesterday in Porto Santo returned: Dorothy and Celia staring at me across the café table … as if looking for something. And now I knew what that had been: a sign that the drug they had administered was taking effect.

After Zara had helped me into bed, I slept a sleep too deep for nightmares and might have slept longer, if an insistent paw hadn't tap-tapped, tap-tapped, tap-tapped my shoulder till I opened my eyes. The newly risen sun was slanting through the half-open shutters, lighting up the room with a pinkish glow. I turned over slowly to see a furry face looking enquiringly into mine.

'You're asking me how I'm feeling, G?' I thought it over and decided the answer was, 'Fragile but in pretty good shape, all things considered.' And definitely, most definitely, hungry.

G was an expert mind reader, particularly where food was concerned. She leapt lightly from the bed and stalked to the door, looking back, tip of tail twitching with impatience. 'What are you waiting for? I'm starving' was unmistakable.

'You can't possibly be as hungry as I am. What about that large bowl of food Zara put out for you yesterday afternoon?' I sat up and saw the alarm clock: 8 a.m. With a shock I realized that eighteen hours had passed. 'I take that back, G,' I said, swinging my legs out of bed. '*Both* of us are starving. Breakfast in ten minutes.'

But it was more than ten minutes before G and I tucked into our respective breakfasts, for pinned to the kitchen table with the point of my favourite vegetable knife were several sheets torn from the notepad I kept by the telephone.

Hi there, Debs! Didn't want to worry you seeing that you were so bushed, so I didn't say anything on the way back in the taxi. That was no accident in the caves, I just know it!!!!!!! First that mugging near the toboggan place, then that hit and run with the car when Chas bought it, now THIS!!!!!! You should be WARNED that I think one of your clients is out to get you!!!!! But don't you worry. You can count on me to suss out who it is. No point in trying to talk me out of it. I'm going to start with that old bat Winterton. She gives me the creeps. Z

Don't worry! I hurriedly pulled out a kitchen chair and collapsed onto it. That was all I needed. Zara blundering about. If Winterton or Haxby were indeed behind those attacks on me … I put my head in my hands and groaned. Too late now to stop her. And she'd had nearly a day to wreak havoc. I reached for the telephone and tried her room at the hotel, but if she was there, she wasn't answering. I left a message with the receptionist for her to call me, stressing that it was urgent. For the moment there was nothing more I could do.

A heavy paw trod on my bare foot and remained there, reminding me that there were other priorities – at least, as far as G was concerned.

'OK, G,' I sighed. 'We'll both feel better when we've eaten.'

After a leisurely breakfast I did indeed feel much restored, but not enough to call in at Police HQ to report the incident at the caves. Tomorrow would be time enough. My attackers were long gone and would probably never be traced. It might be worthwhile, though, to have a search made of the subterranean lake and the nearby rocks. To be able to deal with me so quickly and efficiently in that pitch dark cave would have necessitated the use of night-vision goggles. They'd have whipped them off and thrown them away before the lights came on, but after that there'd have been no opportunity to retrieve the goggles without being noticed.

My office hour at the Massaroco Hotel was looming and I didn't really feel up to going there either. Fortunately I'd had the foresight to ask Zara to put a message on the Agência noticeboard: *Due to unforeseen circumstances Thursday office hour is cancelled.*

She'd doubled up with mirth. 'Just wait till those old bags, Haxby and Winterton, see this! They were moaning enough about today's cancellation, though they bloody well weren't going to come to your office hour anyway. Said they were going off to the Nun's Valley again. I don't know what they see in the place. Once was enough for me.'

A day of leisure stretched ahead. I sat in the garden with Gorgonzola on my lap and, trying to keep my mind off what Zara might be up to, pondered the evidence against Winterton and Haxby. They'd spiked my coffee on Porto Santo, I was sure of it. I'd had all the telltale symptoms: confusion, slurred speech, dizziness, loss of memory. Those visits of theirs to the Nun's Valley might have significance. Or again, might not.

The warmth of the sun on my face and the rhythmic *purr purr* of a contented cat were highly conducive to dozing off ... It was the ringing of the telephone in the kitchen that woke me. As I rose to my feet, G leapt indignantly off my lap and went off to sulk in the shade of the nearest bush.

I picked up the receiver. '*Olá?*'

There was a long pause. Then a flustered voice said tentatively, 'Oh, er, have I got the right number? I was wanting to speak to Deborah Smith.'

'Yes, speaking,' I said.

'It's me, Victoria Knight, dear. I was wondering when you might be able to come over. I'm so looking forward to having one of our little chats again.'

'Love to.' It might be the only chance to see her before I was deported back to London. 'As it happens, I've got the day off. How about today?'

'Come as soon as you can, dear. I can't wait to ask your advice about something.'

The Quinta Jacaranda was an impressive nineteenth-century stuccoed building set in extensive grounds surrounded by a high stone wall smothered by creepers and assorted ferns.

I'd just reached the top of the wide stone steps to the front door when it was flung open. Today Victoria was wearing an unstylish but comfortable green caftan, from behind the folds of which peered an apprehensive Blackie, ready to flee at the first glimpse of the dreaded Ginger Monster.

'Lovely to see you.' She gave me a motherly embrace. 'You're looking tired, dear.' She scooped up the cat. 'Blackie's come to meet his new friend. But where is—? Not still under the weather, is she?'

I embroidered the truth a little. 'Oh no, fully recovered. She didn't come when I called. You know how it is with cats. Minds of their own.'

She kissed the top of Blackie's head. 'They have, haven't they?' She ushered me into a glass-enclosed veranda, its tiled floor scattered with wicker chairs and glass-topped low tables. Through open double doors I could see dark wood floors and a red-carpeted staircase with brass stair rods.

Over coffee I caught up with all her news over the past year. '… and before I left for this little holiday in Madeira, I decided I would replace every painting in my new house with something I'd chosen myself. That's what I need advice about.' She delved into the pile of magazines under the table and produced the lavishly illustrated catalogue of a well-known London art gallery. 'I've put a bookmark at the ones that took my fancy. Have a look and tell me what you think, while I get us a bit of lunch.' She handed me the catalogue and in a swirl of green disappeared in the direction of the kitchen. Blackie stared at me with alarmed eyes and scuttled after her, obviously fearful that this hench-woman of the dreaded Gorgonzola would carry him off to an awful fate.

I studied the pictures Victoria had marked. The first three were land-scapes, and I'd definitely put all of them on *my* walls – if I could have afforded them. While dishes clinked in the kitchen, I flicked idly through the rest of the catalogue towards the last bookmark. After the

Landscapes section came *Portraits*, followed by *Abstracts*. The colours of some of the abstracts were quite pleasing; others were muddy, drab, and just plain dull, or a ghastly splodge and smear of clashing colours. The sort of thing, in fact, that Celia Haxby churned out. People were obviously prepared to pay through the nose for that sort of thing.

It was in the last section, *Still Life*, that I made the breakthrough – in the shape of *Still life with Kipper* by John Byrne. A week ago when Gorgonzola and I had snooped in Celia Haxby's room at the Massaroco, a picture of that selfsame giant pink teacup looming over a slab of fish had been leaning against her wall. I stared at the page. A painting offered for sale by a prestigious art gallery would not be stored against the wall of room 316 in the Massaroco Hotel.

If the pink teacup painting was a copy of a famous painting, perhaps the muddy landscape, the English-type landscape of muddy green and grey hills, was a copy too? At the time it had struck me as being so out of place, so foreign to any place Haxby could have seen on one of her Madeiran excursions. There was nothing illegal in copying a work of art, of course, but passing off the copy as a valuable *original* most certainly would be.

I opened the catalogue at the *Landscape* section again, on the lookout for green and muddy landscapes. A few fell into that category, particularly one by Sir William Gillies selling at more than £25,000. Had Celia Haxby copied it with express intention of passing it off as a genuine Gillies? A forgery scam would certainly explain all those pictures in room 316. From the beginning, I'd had a feeling that there was something suspect about Haxby and her paintings. Could I manage to get into her room again, photograph them and get an art expert's opinion?

'Did you find anything else of interest, Deborah?'

I looked up as Victoria placed a laden tray on the coffee table. I certainly had.

CHAPTER FIFTEEN

The following morning I still had heard nothing from Zara. I'd make a point of seeking her out, but first I had that scheduled meeting with the *comandante*.

In the public entrance hall of Police Headquarters I caught sight of Raimundo beckoning me from behind the desk.

'*Bom dia, senhora*. I, Raimundo Ribeiro, have the interesting information for you.' With the air of a conjuror producing a rabbit out of a hat, he whipped a video tape from a drawer.

'Tourist video, is it?' I asked unenthusiastically, my mind on the forthcoming interview. How would she receive my account of what happened at the São Vicente Caves? Would she accept that it had been a serious attempt on my life, or dismiss it contemptuously as yet another example of that incompetent Sshmit's clumsiness? So I replied, 'Thanks, Raimundo, but I've seen them all.'

The moustache bristled, the dark eyes gleamed. 'But this one, I promise, you have not seen.' A tobacco-stained finger tapped the side of his nose.

I reeled back in mock shock-horror. 'You wouldn't be offering me, an unmarried lady, a sex film, would you?'

He slapped his hand on the desk and roared with laughter. 'You make fine joke, *senhora*. This I must tell everyone.' He turned and yelled to his colleagues, 'The *senhora* make fine joke. She says ...'

And I had to stand there in acute embarrassment as my words were gathered up by the fine acoustics of the domed entrance hall and broadcast to police and public alike. Loud guffaws, amused smiles, scandalized looks – all of this I could have done without. I could only stand there smiling weakly, pretending I was enjoying the joke.

At last he recovered enough to splutter out, 'No, no, *senhora*. This is CCTV tape.' He lifted the desk flap and motioned me to follow him into the inner office. 'It is tape from the Massaroco Hotel. Every week

I have the job to look, to see if any suspicious peoples creep around. This I do this morning, and I see....' He paused dramatically. 'I see ... *this*.' He slid the tape into a video machine.

The camera's field of view was a secluded area of the Massaroco's garden, near the outer wall. The date was yesterday, the time 7.45 a.m. In the early morning light a man was standing half-obscured by the drooping branches of a bottlebrush tree. He turned his head and looked at something off to the right, then moved forward as another figure came into view.

Raimundo pressed a button and the picture paused and zoomed in, magnifying the man's face. 'We have here bad character. His name is Silvestre Gonçalves and he is arrested many times for the drug dealing.' He pressed another button and the tape resumed.

At first little could be seen of the other figure. Back to the camera, he or she was wearing one of the Massaroco's distinctive mono-grammed towelling bathrobes with the hood pulled up. Then the camera pulled back for a wide shot, and from the legs and sandals I could tell that the figure was a woman.

From under his jacket the man produced four small packages and handed them to the woman who slipped them into the pockets of the robe. After a few moments of what seemed to be amicable conversation, the woman turned away and walked back in the direction of the hotel. For a few fleeting seconds her face came into shot, then she moved out of camera range.

Raimundo stopped the tape. 'Well, *senhora*, we know the man, but who is the woman? Perhaps you are able to tell us?'

I hitched myself forward to peer at the screen. 'I'll give it a try. Can you rewind to where she comes into shot, then zoom in, and advance it frame by frame?'

Frame followed frame, but the shadow cast by the bathrobe's hood and the flatness of the early morning light blurred the face, even in close-up.

After the third run-through I gave up and sat back with a sigh. 'I'm sorry. It's no use – she could be anybody.'

With a sigh of disappointment, Raimundo switched off the machine and ejected the tape.

He looked so downcast that I hastened to add, 'But that was good work, Raimundo. She is obviously a guest at the hotel. That gives me and the cat something to work on.'

I dearly wanted it to be Dorothy Winterton, but the bulky robe had concealed all physical characteristics apart from the legs and feet. Though there'd been a glimmer of refracted light, hinting at spectacles, this would count for nothing as far as proof of identity was concerned.

It was as I was walking along the corridor towards the *comandante*'s office that I remembered I'd seen packages like those in the garden of the Massaroco Hotel two weeks ago when Dorothy Winterton had rummaged in her handbag with its unusual security lock. That would be something to report to the *comandante*, something to mollify her, for I was going to be in for a hard time of it when I confessed that I had fallen victim to yet another attack. I knocked on the door and went in.

'... and so,' I finished, 'I was saved only because the lights came on and Senhora Porter-Browne gave me the kiss of life.' I waited with some apprehension for the *comandante*'s reaction.

Much to my surprise, she showed those perfect teeth in a congratulatory smile. 'At last, Officer Sshmit, you must be doing *something* right.' In the warm breeze from the open window the strelitzias in their tall blue vase nodded their agreement.

'I am?' I said puzzled. I'd expected her to treat the news of Wednesday's incident with, at best, resigned impatience.

She raised her eyes heavenward and sighed. 'Why do I always have to explain things to you, Sshmit? I asked you to observe the suspects and uncover their secrets, peel away the layers of the onion. This latest attempt on your life can only mean that you are nearing the heart of the onion.' She gave a short nod of satisfaction.

The peeling of an onion is very often accompanied by tears, and so far the tears had mainly been mine. I tried to look pleased that I'd been the victim of a murderous attack.

'Fourteen days ago you came to me with a list, Sshmit.' An impatient blood-red fingernail tapped the desk. 'Who is now at the top of that list?'

I'd been expecting that question. As I sat in the garden yesterday afternoon with Gorgonzola, I'd had plenty of time to think about my list of suspects: Charles Mason was dead and whatever he might have done in the past could not have been responsible for this latest attempt on my life; Zara Porter-Browne, if she'd wanted to kill me, would not have saved me in the caves. She'd just have stood by and let me drown; as for David Grant, whatever he was up to with his plants, it had nothing to do with drugs. However, I might as well ask London to send information on what the criminally minded would find profitable about plants.

'I've narrowed it down to two people,' I said. 'The widow, Dorothy Winterton, and the artist, Celia Haxby.' I told her about *Still life with Kipper* and my thoughts about how Haxby could be passing off forgeries as genuine.

She frowned. 'There is one thing that is troubling me. If this Haxby has something to hide, is up to the no good, why would she invite you into her room where all these pictures are to be seen?'

I didn't meet her eye. 'Well, er ...'

The *comandante* reached forward and picked thoughtfully at one of the strelitzias, shredding with a sharp fingernail first one silken orange petal, then another, till tattered strips of orange fluttered in the draught from the ceiling fan.

'Perhaps the door was open when you passed along the corridor?'

As if I hadn't heard the question, I continued, 'Of course, Haxby would have to have a "front", an outwardly respectable gallery to sell the copies, but that wouldn't be too difficult to set up.'

The *comandante* attacked the remaining orange petals of the strelitzia with vigour. 'This may be as you say, Sshmit, but what connection has this Haxby person with the murder of Gomes?'

At least she was listening. With more confidence I continued, 'I think there is a connection: Celia Haxby is always in the company of Dorothy Winterton who I have reason to think may be engaged in drug dealing. They seem to have very little in common but—'

Her fingers beat an impatient tattoo on the desk. 'You say that this Haxby has nothing in common with Winterton, so what keeps them together?'

Surely her astute mind would have worked that out, but maybe this was just another little test? 'If Haxby is making money from selling fake masterpieces and has set up a gallery to offer them to the public,' I said, 'and if Winterton *is* engaged in drug dealing, they'd be ideal business partners because such a gallery would be an easy way to launder money. On Tuesday they took the ferry to Porto Santo together. They knew I, too, was on the ferry, and gave me the slip—'

'Slip?' The *comandante*'s brow creased in a frown of incomprehension.

'I couldn't follow them, as I was held up by what I suspect was a pre-arranged incident.' I hurried on before she could ask what that incident was. I didn't want her to find out that, like a naïve greenhorn, I'd fallen for one of the oldest tricks in the book – the spiked drink. 'But I am sure that they were up to something they didn't want me to know about.' Suspecting that she was about to probe further into that pre-arranged incident, I produced my rabbit out of the hat. 'What I did find out was that they transfer the drugs between Madeira and Porto Santo using a homemade mini-submarine made of plywood and fitted with a snorkel.'

'*Homemade?*' she snorted. '*Snorkel?* Is this your English humour, Sshmit?' She gave a short mirthless laugh.

'No, not at all, *Comandante.*' I said coldly. I'd been so sure she'd see this as a breakthrough in the investigation. 'Luís told me that his brother let it slip when he was drunk, and so, on my visit to Porto Santo—'

'*Drunk.* Enough, Sshmit!' She swept the little heap of shredded petals into the bin and flipped open the lid of the laptop on her desk. 'I remind you that you now have only four days before I say *adeus* for ever.'

I drove back along the Estrada Monumental seething at the *comandante*'s cavalier dismissal of my carefully thought-out conclusions. *She* might be treating it as mere conjecture and surmise; *I* was convinced my conclusions were right and that it all fitted in. But how was I going to get the proof with only four more days remaining before I was igno-miniously shipped off and returned to sender?

Forced to a halt opposite the dome of the casino by the usual tail-back of traffic, I stared moodily at a fenced-off patch of waste ground where tangles of red and yellow nasturtiums and the tall purple spires of massaroco created nature's own artwork among the tall grasses.

I had only four more days. I made a sudden decision. I'd take digital photos of all the Haxby paintings, send them to London and get an expert opinion. I glanced in the mirror, made an illegal U-turn and shot back to the gingerbread house to collect my camera. At the Massaroco Hotel, Haxby and Winterton would be taking their lunch on the terrace. It had become quite a set routine. How could I make sure that they stayed on the terrace? If I was caught red-handed in Haxby's room, it would be an ignominious send-off on the *next* plane, ending all chances of a successful outcome to the investigation.

The hideous *clang clank clang clank* took some time to penetrate my thoughts. In the mirror, a flashing blue light signalled a police car on a mission. I smiled. It could only be Raimundo making the most of some traffic violation. Mine, as it turned out. As I slowed to let him pass, he made the internationally understood sign to pull in.

'*Senhora*!' A wave of tobacco and garlic engulfed me as he bent to lean his elbow on the window. '*Senhora*, you know it is illegal to make the turn on the Estrada Monumental. This is most serious offence.' The stern expression was accompanied by the slow conspiratorial lowering of one eyelid.

Encouraged, I smiled sweetly. 'Sorry, Senhor Officer. But it is permitted to make such a turn if there is an emergency, is it not?'

The bushy moustache twitched. 'Of course. And do you need police assistance for this so serious emergency?'

'No.' Then as an idea formed, '... Er, yes indeed,' I said. I needed an uninterrupted session with those paintings – and the solution to the problem had just presented itself.

From my position of semi-concealment behind a large pot plant, a particularly fine specimen of an ornamental fig, I had a good view of the Massaroco reception desk and a splendidly severe-looking Raimundo Ribeiro standing beside it.

A petulant, 'Now what's all this about?' heralded the arrival of Winterton and Haxby. They moved into my line of vision, Dorothy leading the way and a disgruntled-looking Celia trailing behind.

Raimundo whipped out his notebook and with a theatrical gesture flipped it open. I could see that he was relishing his role.

'Senhora Winterton?'

'Yes.' There was no hint of apprehension in her voice or expression.

Had I been grasping at straws, my case against her, mere wishful thinking?

He consulted his notebook. 'You are the driver of rental car?'

I didn't wait to hear more. I turned and walked quickly to the service stairs. A couple of minutes later, I was closing the door of room 316 behind me. Celia's portable folding easel was standing ready for action beside the stacks of paintings. She'd been busy. There were now four pictures in each of the three stacks. I didn't have time to photograph them individually, so I moved the easel to one side, propped the first four of the newly added paintings against the wall, and took a snap of the group.

One of them was a landscape – but a very strange one: a melon-shaped moon and brown and purple clouds floated above greenish humps of hills, and what appeared to be a white oilrig was poised to take off from an orange mound.

The couple of still lifes were in the rather naïve style she seemed to favour for this type of picture: two colourful jugs and a brown fish on a table; a cream vase with a green plate on a folded beige tablecloth, each object heavily outlined in black. I almost didn't bother with three of the other paintings. One canvas looked as if it had been used to clean off a very wide brush: it was just a rectangle of red shading off to black.

Some misfortune had befallen the other two works: in one, ugly white horizontal streaks splattered a scene of a white Indian canoe reflected in a green lake; the other had suffered serious water damage. What might have been trees in a yellow field with a background of purple hills or storm clouds had been reduced to black, brown and green watery splodges perhaps by one of the sudden torrential rain-storms that could occur at this time of year. Why would she keep something so obviously ruined? I never ignore unexpected departures from the normal. It was this that decided me to include these three in my photo gallery.

I worked quickly, putting the photographed pictures back in position, careful to keep them in the order I'd found them. In a few minutes I'd finished. I stood for a moment, inspecting the room to make sure I'd left everything exactly as I'd found it. Satisfied, I put the digital camera back in my pocket and prepared to beat a circumspect retreat to my car.

I nearly missed it: a piece of card sticking out of the drawer that formed part of the easel. Had it been there when I moved the easel to photograph the paintings? I was sure it hadn't. I'd have noted it. To leave something out of place is the professional's way of checking whether someone has been poking around. I gave the card a quick glance as I slipped it back through the sliding frame.

Looking for original pieces by renowned contemporary artists?
Find them in St. Ives, Cornwall, at Avant-Garde Art.
All pictures carry a certificate of authentication.

I took a photo of it and shoved the card back out of sight. I'd email the pictures and check up on that gallery as soon as I got back to the office. I'd told the *comandante* that I thought Haxby's paintings were copies of valuable works of art. If London confirmed this, that *should* persuade her to take seriously my suspicions about Dorothy Winterton.

My next port of call was Zara's room on the next floor.

I rapped loudly. 'Ees room service!'

No reply. I put my ear to the door. No telltale movements inside. A quick tour of her usual haunts – café bar, terrace, swimming pool – also drew a blank. From the café bar I phoned reception. Yes, the *senhora* had been given my message. Yes, the *senhora* had been seen early this morning. Who could forget the so-green hair? No, unfortunately, the present whereabouts of the *senhora* were not known.

Was Zara deliberately avoiding me? More worryingly, was she at this very moment engaged in hot pursuit of her quarry? She hadn't responded to my earlier message, so I could visualize her merely crumpling up and binning another on the same lines. I thought for a moment and scribbled down, *Hi, Zara, Hold everything. I've a suspect under investigation. Must see you soonest. Debs.* I went back to her room and pushed the note under her door. What I would say to her, if she contacted me, I hadn't the faintest idea.

When I left the Massaroco, Ribeiro's old wreck had gone. I risked putting my foot down on the way back along the Estrada Monumental. The sands of time were running out.

Screened by a clump of almond-scented oleander bushes, Zara Porter-Browne watched DJ's car drive out of the car-park. With a satisfied smile she closed the paperback she'd been reading and stowed it in the little bag slung over her shoulder. Now was her chance, her first chance ever, to stand in the Nike trainers of investigators Kinsey Millhone and Stephanie Plum. Not that they were *real* people, of course, only the creations of ace crime novelists Grafton and Evanovich, but they were her kind of women, taking no crap from the likes of old witch Winterton and that bastard Mason.

This was the opportunity she'd been waiting for to search Winterton's room. The old bat and her equally obnoxious sidekick Haxby, slaves to routine, would be on the terrace feeding their faces. She'd spent yesterday afternoon working out how to get into Winterton's room. A cinch for Millhone and Plum – they'd just pick the lock. Well, she had no picklock, wouldn't know what one looked like, but she'd had a brill idea. The chambermaids always cleaned the bathroom before fixing the rest of the room and, while they were making the beds and sweeping the balcony, someone could slip into the bathroom unseen. Yes, sneak in, hide behind the shower curtain, that's what Kinsey and Stephanie would do. She'd tried it out yesterday, getting unseen into her own room while the maids were in, and the scheme had worked a dream.

She had it all worked out: if the maids caught her in the bathroom – no sweat. She'd flourish a notebook and be toting a pile of those boring excursion leaflets, just like Kinsey and Stephanie made use of an official-looking clipboard. She'd say she was from the Agençia making an inspection of the accommodation, looking for mouldy silicone in the shower.

The only flaw in this grand master plan was that all too recognizable green hair of hers. But she'd fixed that too. She'd spent this morning in the hairdresser's salon. Gone that trendy green, in its place – for a short time only – her normal mid-brown, swept up into a stylish French roll to impart a businesslike air.

Preparations complete, she'd avoided all the places anyone – especially Debs – might look for her, and now that Debs had taken herself off, the coast was clear.

CHAPTER SIXTEEN

When Zara had made no effort to contact me by ten o'clock on Friday evening I wasn't really surprised. The little madam had jammed her Sherlock Holmes hat firmly on her head and any blundering detective work of hers could have dangerous repercussions for us both. With Gorgonzola on my knee, I sat in the warm darkness of my veranda debating whether to go off, late though it was, to the Massaroco and find out exactly what she'd been up to.

'Damage limitation, that's what's needed, eh, G?' That had always been top priority for Gerry Burnside, Director of Operations on my previous assignment in Tenerife. I'd cooked up a storyline I hoped would convince her that she was completely on the wrong track: that the police had informed me they had a suspect under surveillance and didn't want him alerted by *anyone* snooping around asking questions. But first I had to get hold of Zara.

'Would this be the best time to catch someone who's been avoiding me, or should I wait till tomorrow?' As I eased forward on the chair, G's sharp claws dug through the thin cotton of my trousers, indicating a firm intention to stay where she was. 'You're right, G. Better leave it till tomorrow. Tonight she might very well be living it up at some club or other.' At crack of dawn I'd definitely catch her in her bed.

But I didn't. First light found me at the Massaroco, but there was no response to my persistent knocking on her door. No drowsy, 'Whadyawant? Buzz off!' No shuffling footsteps crossed the tiled floor. Of course! I should have remembered that Zara was one of those night birds that don't return to the nest till well after dawn. That time I'd returned from the market and seen her draped elegantly over the rail of the Beatles Boat, the sun had been up for over a couple of hours. I stood back and pondered my next move.

She wasn't going to give me the slip this time. A frequent check of her room every half-hour should make sure of that. I wandered out to the terrace overlooking the gardens. Early as it was, the gardeners were already at work turning on sprinklers and brushing paths. On the far side of the extensive lawn I caught glimpses of a ponytailed jogger on one of the paths winding through the subtropical bushes. Nice to have the leisure, and the cash, to keep fit in a five-star setting.

I consulted my watch. There'd be time to stroll round the gardens before checking Zara's room again. I wandered round towards the back of the hotel where a particularly fine specimen of wisteria dipped mauve-blue petals into the dark waters of a small pond. A peaceful spot, no traffic hum, only the sharp *clink clink clink* of an unseen bird calling from deep within the branches of a tree.

I was sitting on a nearby bench watching the reflections change as cat's-paws of breeze ruffled the surface of the water, when I heard the *slap slap* of running feet approaching along the path behind. The feet slowed, labouring lungs gasped and wheezed. The seriously unfit jogger tottered past and with heaving sides collapsed over the small section of ornate railing that guarded the outflow of water from the pond. There was something familiar about the way that figure draped itself over the rail – ponytail, baseball cap, vest and running shorts, Nike trainers. Replace with curtain of long *green* hair, silk mini-tunic and strappy sandals – Zara. At last I'd find out what she'd been up to.

I gripped her shoulder and turned her to face me. 'Didn't you get my note, Zara? Why didn't you get in touch?' I made no effort to hide my exasperation.

'Oh, hi, Debs.' Gasp. 'You won't *believe* how busy I've been.' Gasp.

'Busy?' I said. Perhaps I'd got it all wrong. Perhaps her enthusiasm for detective work had flitted out of her butterfly head as quickly as it had come. 'You mean at the hairdresser? What's happened to the green hair?'

She straightened up, her breathing more under control. 'Yes, it's a disguise. All part of being a PI, a private investigator, you know.'

'Disguise?' It was as bad as I'd feared. Worse, as it turned out.

Zara did a little jig of excitement. 'I thought of *everything*: if the maids saw me coming into the old cow's room, I'd say that the Agência had sent me.'

I walked to the bench and sat down heavily. 'You'd better tell me all about it.'

She followed me over. The words tumbled out of her. '… so there I was standing behind the shower curtain. When I heard the maids leave, I nipped out and rummaged through her stuff.' Her face clouded. 'Didn't find anything, though.'

Sweat filmed my forehead. 'But … but … if Mrs Winterton notices her things have been disturbed she'll know that someone has searched her room.'

Zara laughed. 'Don't *worry*, Debs. I put everything back more or less where I found it.'

More or less where she'd found it. Oh, my God! I stared at her.

'I know what you're thinking. You're wondering how I managed to be so good at all this private eye work, aren't you?' She tapped the side of her nose knowingly. 'I'll give you a clue – Plum and Millhone.'

If there had been a wall nearby, I'd have beaten my head against it. 'So that explains this early morning jog?'

She clapped her hands delightedly. 'You've got it. When Kinsey's trying to figure out her next move, a three-mile jog gets the little grey cells working.'

Little grey cells! The catchphrase of Hercule Poirot. Now she was morphing into him!

'And what have you come up with?' I dreaded the answer.

She jumped to her feet. 'I'm off to search her sidekick Haxby's room, of course. *Ciao.*' Zara Plum-Millhone and her Nikes trotted off.

Victorian ladies would have been left with an attack of the vapours, but twenty-first-century ladies are made of sterner stuff. I headed for the bar and a very strong black coffee.

I was always surprised how the heat built up in the tiny office space allotted to me by the *comandante* even when there was little sun. I went through the routine of flicking the ceiling fan to high and throwing the window wide open. Zara's amateurish search of Winterton's room – and presumably Haxby's – was a time bomb ticking away. But with less than seventy-two hours left to come up with results or be slung out of Madeira, I had more pressing things on my mind.

I settled down to write an email to London with attached photographs of Haxby's paintings. I red-flagged the message as urgent and clicked on the Send button.

That done, I decided I might as well try to nail David Grant too: the high security on the orchid farm, his over-reaction to me seeing those plants behind the locked doors of his laboratory. Smuggling rare orchids into Britain – could that be Grant's little dodge? If so, HM Revenue & Customs would most certainly be interested. I was certain that it all added up. Another query email winged its way, this time to DEFRA, the Department for Environment, Food and Rural Affairs.

I put copies of the sent emails in the filing cabinet and turned my attention to the contents of the in-tray. It usually contained, if anything, sharp notes from the *comandante* and so was never my first port of call, on the principle that if I hadn't read them I couldn't act on them. And indeed, there was a message waiting for me in my in-tray.

I picked up the first sheet of paper. There were only three words, printed in bold capitals. **TWO DAYS, SMITH**; tomorrow the message would be, **ONE DAY, SMITH**; and on Monday, **SMITH, TOMORROW ADEUS**. I crumpled the paper into a ball and lobbed it out of the window in direct defiance of the *comandante*'s anti-litter campaign.

I picked up the remaining sheet of paper in the in-tray. As I scanned it, my pulse quickened. Raimundo had come to my aid again. Clipped to the paper was a police mug shot of Silvestre Gonçalves, the man I'd seen on the videotape in the Massaroco Hotel gardens. The most memorable thing about him were his ears, close to the head but very long and slightly cupped. His hairline had receded to leave a U-shaped bald patch with an island of sparse hair on the centre top of his fore-head. A light stubble covered cheeks and chin.

I skimmed the attached official report that Raimundo had dug out of the files for me. *Unemployed … small time crook and known associate of drug dealers … three previous convictions for carrying and small-scale dealing … seen in the company of Roberto Gomes on several occasions.* I let out my breath in a sigh of disappointment. No new lead here after all.

Then I saw the lines scrawled at the foot of the page.

My second cousin, Maria, she lives in the Curral and cleans the church there. She tells me that she has seen him many times in the cemitério in the early morning. He does not have family buried there, so she tells me about his visits as she knows information like this is useful to a policeman.

The Curral das Freiras, the Nun's Valley, was a spectacular crater-like hollow surrounded by towering peaks, forty-five minutes' drive from Funchal and only accessible by mountain path till sixty years ago. I'd visited it by bus a couple of times. The information Maria had passed on to Raimundo wasn't much to go on, but it was all I had. I pulled out a map from the drawer. The village of Curral das Freiras lay deep in the mountains north-west of Funchal and directly north of Câmara de Lobos. A deep ravine slashed through from the village towards the sea; a dotted line marked a rough footpath ending at the main road above Câmara. I picked up the map and went in search of Raimundo.

I found him crouching down behind his car securing the exhaust with a piece of wire. He spread out the map on the bonnet of the car.

'Ah, *senhora*, many old paths lead into the valley, and there is indeed a path as you say, along the Ribeira dos Socorridos but it is very, very dangerous, so dangerous that walkers are warned about it. There have been many fatal accidents. In old times the path over the mountain pass was the most important route into the Curral, but it is three hours' walk and you have to have the feet of a mountain goat. You are not thinking of taking that path?'

I could tell by his voice that it wouldn't be a good idea. 'No, no,' I hastened to reassure him. 'But it would be possible, for someone who is familiar with the mountains?'

He nodded. 'Of course. But there is a shorter way. An easy path starts here.' He stabbed a finger down on the map. 'Behind the *miradouro* at Eira do Serrado it goes down the cliff through the chestnut trees. In less than an hour you are down at the Curral walking through the streets of the village.'

He slipped behind the wheel and started the engine. *Clang clank clang clank clang clank.* I grabbed the map just before it slid off the bonnet and bent down to the open window.

'That information from Maria might be worth following up,' I howled above the din. 'I think I'll take the cat for a sniff around the Curral cemetery.'

And no time like the present. I could go all the way to the Curral by bus. The buses were usually full, so I'd have the advantage of arriving as one face in the crowd. The snag was Gorgonzola. No way would G lie low in a rucksack for the hour's bus journey. Her antics would make me a talking point and the focus of attention. Going all the way there by car would involve driving round hairpin bends with a drop of a thousand metres on one side, which I didn't fancy a bit. Besides, down in the village there was nowhere to tuck away the car, nowhere that I wouldn't be seen stuffing a reluctant G into my rucksack. I decided to take the car to the *miradouro*, park there, and go the rest of the way on foot by that path down though the chestnut trees.

Up, up I drove, past the stands of eucalyptus trees, a wooden army of ramrod-straight camouflage-mottled trunks. Up, up past the mimosas smudged with the sulphur yellow of tiny pompom flowers. Ten minutes later I was looking down on the tops of these same trees, level with the low clouds that drifted wraithlike through the branches of pines and laurel. The air was colder now. I closed the car window and concentrated on the narrow, winding road ahead.

A blue notice, *Eira do Serrado*, marked the entrance to a cobbled lane snaking off to the right. I drove carefully up it and parked outside the building that served as tourist centre and hotel. Leaving Gorgonzola catnapping on the warmth of the just-vacated driver's seat, I sat down in the weak sunshine outside the café and ordered a milky *galão* and a large piece of chestnut cake to fortify me for the walk down into the village. I sipped and ate, watching chiffon scarves of mist trail round the jagged peaks and fluffy kapok-ball clouds chase each other across the bare slopes, casting patches of blue shadow on the other side of the valley. From the village far below, sharp in the clear air, drifted up the excited barking of a dog and the chime of church bells.

Back at the car, I yanked the door open. 'Come on, then, you pampered cat. Walkies!'

With G stepping daintily ahead of me at the end of her lead, I set off along the narrow path winding steeply downwards through the chestnut trees. Last year's leaves rustled crisply underfoot and through the grey haze of bare branches I could just make out, far below, a scatter of red roofs.

Halfway down, the head-high tree heathers edging the path thinned, revealing the road, a narrow grey tarmac strip corkscrewing down from Eira do Serrado to the Curral, the white blocks of its safety barrier a frail protection against a 300-metre drop. Several hundred metres above on the cliff edge the treetops were tossing in the wind, but down here, sheltered by the shoulders of the mountain, all was still.

Tukk tukk tukk. A bird's sharp clear call rang out like a hammer chipping away at stone, its source impossible to pinpoint in the sounding bowl of the mountains.

The lead in my hand tightened. G was in stalking mode, homing in on a tiny blue-grey lizard basking in the sun, its splayed fingers suckered to the rock. Just as her muscles bunched to pounce, a lizard eye swivelled and, with a flicker of movement her prey was gone.

'Mind on job, G,' I said a trifle unfairly as *her* job was not going to begin till we got to the cemetery.

I would set G loose there to sniff. If drugs were being brought in over the mountains or along that dangerous *levada* track from Câmara de Lobos, what better place to leave packets than amongst graves? Who'd think of rummaging in a mound of funeral wreaths or upending a vase of flowers? If any drugs were stashed away, G would find them.

And if she didn't? If I reported back to the *comandante* empty-handed, three days from now I'd be boarding a plane at Funchal Airport. David Grant, Exotic Cut Flower Exporter, would no doubt hear of my deportation and be there to give me a triumphant two-fingered salute from the public viewing terrace.

'I'm relying on you, G, to save the day,' I said.

At the first signs of cultivation I stopped, shrugged off the rucksack and opened it invitingly. 'OK, G, time to rest your paws, time to go undercover.'

I didn't have to ask twice. With a plaintive *miaoow* she leapt in, and before I'd time to unhook the lead, sank into the depths of the rucksack with a longsuffering sigh. I wasn't taken in. It was just her little ploy to make me feel sorry for her, ensure a bigger helping of food in her bowl this evening.

With G safely out of sight, I descended a steep flight of steps and headed off in the direction of the church. Leaning on the cemetery wall, I looked down at a line of cypress trees standing sentinel over a grit path lined with low box hedges. Somehow I'd expected the cemetery to be overgrown and neglected, affording hiding places a-plenty for illicit packages. To my surprise, it was well tended: a mass of flowers and an ornate white or black metal cross marked each low mound.

I descended the short flight of steps, pushed open the gate and let G out of the bag under cover of the cone-shape bulge of the first cypress tree, running my finger round her collar to remind her of her sniffing duties.

'Search!' I pointed in the direction of the nearest grave.

I watched as she stepped carefully round the collection of glass and silver vases filled with white carnations and lilies. While she continued to work her way methodically along the double row of crosses, I trailed after her along the path, reflecting, as one does in such surroundings, on those who have died – a young man smiling shyly out from an oval plaque; an old woman, her once-red cardigan bleached pink by the sun; a man standing stiffly proud in his Sunday suit, carnation in button-hole. The distant shouts of children and the sharp *clink clink* of a hammer seemed to underline the unbridgeable gulf that separates us, the living, from the dead.

'Poignant, eh, G,' I said, when I caught up with her in a slightly neglected area at the far end of the cemetery. Here, half-a-dozen metal crosses were propped haphazardly against the wall of the church, the photographs of the dead water-marked and faded, the flowers plastic and leached of colour.

G had abandoned her search and was sitting on the lid of a sarcoph-agus constructed of flat slabs standing on end. Eyes closed, she was swaying gently, her face lifted to the warm sun.

'How about earning your keep and finishing the job?' I said sharply. Disappointment at her failure to find anything had made me edgy.

Her eyes opened. Affronted by the unfairness of the reprimand, she stared at me for a moment, then narrowed her eyes and sheathed and unsheathed her claws. Guiltily I reached out to pat her head, but she sprang out of reach. Stiff-legged she walked slowly to the edge of the slab and, with an expressive wiggle of her bottom, leapt down into the narrow gap between the sarcophagus and the wall of the church. From experience I knew that she'd play hard to get till she judged that I'd realized the error of my ways.

Despondently I sank down on the lid of the sarcophagus and leant back, eyes closed, face turned to the sun. It seemed that those visits by Gonçalves to the cemetery had an innocent explanation, after all. I'd been so sure I was on the verge of a breakthrough, had anticipated snapping the cuffs, so to speak, on Winterton and her sidekick, Haxby. Morosely I contemplated the now inevitable ignominious send-off and the equally ignominious reception in London.

The hornet-like buzz of a motor scooter on the road above, almost drowned by the loud rustle of leaves turned over by G's questing paw, infiltrated these gloomy thoughts.

'Sorry, G,' I sighed. 'How could you *possibly* find something that wasn't there? It was mean of me to take out my frustrations on you. I'll make it up to you tonight with—'

The rustling stopped. Two paws followed by a gingery face appeared above the stone lid, only to vanish abruptly.

I looked over at the mountainside and the towering buttresses of rock. Somewhere up there was the path that I'd descended so hopefully such a short time ago. I'd planned to return the same way, but since there was no drug drop-off in the Nun's Valley, it didn't matter now if I attracted attention by carrying a cat in a rucksack.

I levered myself off the sarcophagus and set the rucksack down on the ground. 'C'mon, G. Let's go for the bus.'

From the narrow gap, no sound, no movement.

'C'mon, G. The bus. We'll miss the bus.'

The rustling among the dried leaves recommenced with a new vigour. She was still miffed and I had only myself to blame.

'No need to be like that, G. I've said I'm sorry, haven't I?'

The rustling stopped. Silence. At the far end of the cemetery, the gate *sque-a-ked* open and *cla-nged* shut. At that moment, *purr purr purr*, the sound I'd given up hope of hearing, rose softly up from behind the sarcophagus.

G was signalling a find.

'Atta girl, G.' I flung myself across the stone lid and peered into the gap.

A pair of copper eyes stared back at me. She was sitting in front of a triangular hole between two of the upright slabs – a hole that before G's excavations would have been well-hidden by a thick pile of dead leaves. I reached down and groped in the cavity. My fingers touched sacking, touched – and pushed the object further into the hollow interior of the tomb.

'I should have trained you to fetch, G,' I grunted, straining to reach in just that little bit more. The edge of the stone bit painfully into my armpit as I inserted my hand and wrist into the hole as far as I could, curving my fingers in an effort to get a grip on the object. Again my fingers made contact with it, only to push it further in. Another nudge and it would be out of reach.

'If only I had claws like yours, G,' I muttered.

I withdrew my hand from the cavity and rested for a moment. Perhaps I *could* make use of G to hook the packet out? I picked up a couple of dead leaves, held them inside the cavity, and closed my hand. *Scrunch*.

G stiffened and her ears pricked up. She lowered her head and stared intently into the aperture. *Scrunch, rustle*. I whipped away my hand. She quivered. A clawed paw streaked into the aperture. *Thunk*. It hooked onto the sacking. She withdrew her paw. And with it, the packet.

'Well done, G. You're a star.' I tickled her behind the ears and patted her head.

Her long loud *purrr* signified acceptance of praise due.

Gripping the packet, I wriggled backwards and levered myself upright, then sat there brushing the dirt off my knees. The sacking-wrapped package of drugs weighed about half a kilo. But anyone could have put it there. I needed to link this packet to Gonçalves. We already had the CCTV evidence of a connection between him and a woman at the Massaroco, so....

As I sat there in the warm sunshine, the key to the operation in my hands if only I knew how to turn it, the rustling resumed in the depths of the narrow gap behind me. G was making further probings of that enticing cavity, on her mind something very different from the problem that I was grappling with.

Two quick footsteps *crunch crunched* on the grit path. A rough hand snatched at the package in my hands.

'I'll take that.' Gonçalves was looming over me, his face contorted with rage.

The package was torn from my grasp. I lunged forward and made a grab, knocking it from his hand. It sailed through the air and thumped down beside the stack of metal crosses. I got there first, but only just. His full weight landed on top of me. As I gasped for air, he plucked the package from my unresisting hand and scrambled to his feet. A kick aimed at my head gave me the chance to clutch his boot and give a quick upward heave. Off balance, he staggered back and fell with a crash onto the stack of crosses.

I scrabbled forward and snatched at the package. For a few seconds we tussled for possession. Brute strength won. His fist slammed into the side of my head and I found myself flat on my back staring dazedly up at the sky. I heard the scrape of metal on metal, saw him towering over me with a heavy metal cross raised above his head. Another second and it would come smashing down on me.

But it didn't. There was a gingery blur of movement. Metal clattered on stone. With a scream he tottered back, arms semaphoring wildly as he tried to protect his face from a scratching, clawing cat.

A door banged open, a woman's scandalized voice shrieked, '*Mãe de Deus! Deus me livre*! Heaven forbid that there is such a happening on holy ground!' I sat up, groggily aware of running footsteps and the shrill voice screaming, 'Silvestre Gonçalves, God sees all the evil you do. You cannot run away from God.'

A small body rubbed itself against my side and I looked down to see G staring anxiously up at me. I gathered her into my arms and sat there pressing my throbbing face into her soft fur.

'The *senhora* is hurt? That no-good Gonçalves has robbed you? I call police.' The woman plucked a mobile phone out of her apron pocket and stabbed at a button.

'No, please, I—'

Ignoring my protests, she put the phone to her ear, '*Esta*? Raimundo? Yes, it's Maria. I was right. That scoundrel Silvestre Gonçalves is up to no good and I have seen it with my own eyes. He has just attacked a tourist, Mãe de Deus, in the cemetery. *Sacrilégio*!' The hand holding the phone touched forehead and breast in a rapid sign of the cross. 'No, I didn't *actually* see the attack, but—' A look of exasperation crossed her face. '*How* do I know? I was in the church trimming the candles when I heard—' She listened for a moment. 'Where is he now?' The *sque-a-k* and *cla-ng* of the cemetery gate gave the answer. 'He has just run—'

I got unsteadily to my feet. 'Excuse me, *senhora*. You are speaking to your second cousin, Senhor Raimundo Ribeiro?'

Her excited outpouring stopped abruptly, her lips still forming the word she was about to utter. After a moment she said slowly, '*Sim*, Raimundo Paulo Ribeiro. You know him, *senhora*? How is this?'

'I am also police, English police.' Not quite the truth, but near enough. 'Senhor Ribeiro and I are working together. May I speak to him?'

Dark eyes full of speculation, she held out the phone. On the road above, a two-stroke engine *stut stut stutted* into life, followed a moment later by the high-pitched rasp of an over-revved engine as a scooter sped away.

'Raimundo? Deborah Smith. Yes, I found what I was looking for, but Gonçalves has it now. No, no, I'm not hurt.' Which was true, if I ignored my bruised and swollen cheek. 'No arrest, please. If we can catch him handing it over.... Yes, yes, I know, but Comandante Figueira doesn't *have* to be informed. Who's going to tell her? Gonçalves isn't, is he? Leave it to me to put in a report.' Both of us understood that a report was never going to appear in the *comandante*'s in-tray. 'Now this is what I suggest we do....'

CHAPTER SEVENTEEN

Needless to say, by the time Maria had administered first aid in the shape of a pack of frozen peas and a cup of tea, the four o'clock bus had come and long gone. That a pet cat would accompany an Englishwoman on police business, she seemed to put down to the eccentricity for which the English are well known.

On my way to the bus stop I purchased a traditional Madeiran woollen hat with trailing earflaps, ideal for concealing my swollen face, and Gorgonzola, sensitive to shocks to the system, slept off the recent traumatic event in the dark security of the rucksack, so neither of us excited any comment on the bus journey back up the mountain.

I was in buoyant mood by the time I got home. Despite the attack on my person, I felt the journey to the cemetery in the Curral had been worthwhile. The loss of the package, far from being a set-back, could be the chance to bring the Madeiran operation to a successful conclusion. This time when Gonçalves handed over the package to that mystery woman in the grounds of the Massaroco Hotel, we'd be monitoring the CCTV and be ready to swoop. I was convinced that the woman would turn out to be Dorothy Winterton.

'Thanks to you, we've got it cracked, G,' I said, and poured myself a generous measure of *poncha*.

Modestly she raised her head from the chunks of prime espada fish and purred agreement.

I should have remembered that too hard a congratulatory pat on the back can make you fall flat on your face. As I found out when I walked briskly into Police HQ on Sunday morning. The first intimation that not all was well was Raimundo's doleful expression.

'Alas, *senhora*, when I went an hour ago to Massaroco garden to check why the CCTV camera does not give picture, I find it is gone.'

'Gone?' I repeated.

'*Sim*, it is gone. There is no camera, only the cables are left.'

I stared at him, momentarily at a loss for words, reluctant to acknowledge that along with the camera had gone the chance of wrapping up the case before I was due to leave the island. Worse still, the theft of the camera pointed to the fact that someone suspected the police were taking an active interest in what was recorded on that particular tape.

Raimundo swivelled his eyes in the direction of the *comandante*'s office. 'Today,' he hissed, 'she has the face like the storm.'

This was not good news. The last time she had come in at the weekend had been to deal with the furore over my break-in at David Grant's laboratory. It would be politic to keep out of her way by beating a hasty retreat from the building – but first there were those files to tidy up in readiness for my departure on Tuesday. Swivelling my head like a meerkat on watch for danger, I scuttled off to my office.

My heart sank. From the doorway I could see that another *Explain, Smith!!* memo had landed on my desk. Gingerly I approached. It bore the ominous heading **YESTERDAY'S INCIDENT IN THE CURRAL CEMETERY**. As I scanned the page, it became clear that the story had snowballed, gathering accretions, each more sensational than the last. Evidently Raimundo's second cousin Maria was an incorrigible spreader of gossip. Within hours, therefore, it had come to the *comandante*'s ears that a tourist and a strange-looking cat had been involved in an unseemly brawl in the cemetery at the Curral. These reports, the *comandante* had meticulously set down. I'd just reached the foot of the page where she had scrawled spikily *Don't even try to explain, Smith!!* when there was a tentative knock at the door and Raimundo sidled in.

Avoiding my eyes he mumbled, 'The *comandante* say to give you this.' He handed me an envelope and hovered as if waiting for a reply.

The envelope contained two air tickets to London – the first in the name of Deborah Smith, the second for the transportation of one cat (Persian).

He shuffled his feet uncomfortably. 'It is my fault, *senhora*. I should have told Maria that everything was top secret and she must not tell anyone *anything*.' In an attempt to cheer me up, he added, 'However, the *comandante* did not suggest the handcuffs when I take you and the cat to the airport on Tuesday.'

I stared thoughtfully at the one-way tickets. An idea was forming in my mind.

DJ Smith was out. But definitely not down.

The view from the 757's window was limited, but not so limited as to prevent me from making out the triumphant sneer on the face of David Grant, Exotic Cut Flower Exporter. Elbows on the low rail of the terminal's observation terrace fifty metres away, he was savouring the public deportation of DJ Smith, client liaison for Agência de Viagens Madeira. The *comandante* had stage-managed it with maximum publicity – a police car with blue flashing light had drawn up in front of the terminal building; a policeman in uniform (Raimundo) gripping me tightly by the arm had escorted me through the airport to the very foot of the aircraft steps. David Grant was to be left in no doubt that the full weight of the law had descended on my hapless head.

The engines whined into life and the 757 began its pushback. As the observation terrace slid slowly past, David Grant straightened, smirked, and raised his fingers in an unmistakable two-finger gesture. A few metres behind him, Raimundo raised an arm, and gave a conspiratorial thumbs-up. I smiled and waved back vigorously, taking not a little satisfaction from the fact that the Exotic Cut Flower Exporter would think this action was directed at him.

The engine noise rose to a roar; the 757 strained against its brakes. We surged along the runway, the green hillside dotted with red-roofed houses skimming past the wings; a steep climbing turn over the sea and my last view of Madeira was a cloud-shrouded glimpse of the knobbly sea-horse-shaped São Lourenço peninsula.

I was not in the least downcast. I was leaving, but I had already set in motion plans to return: yesterday morning I'd phoned Mrs Knight to tell her I would have to leave for a few days on an emergency visit to England. As I'd hoped, she had immediately offered to look after Gorgonzola. 'Delighted,' she'd said. Blackie wouldn't be at all delighted, but he hadn't been consulted.

I'd phoned again this morning for a last minute bulletin. The news was good – there'd been no pining for me and no attacks on the rightful resident, Blackie. G, it seemed, was purring happily on Victoria's lap while a no doubt disconsolate black Persian cat was making do with a pillow on the sofa.

'Blackie's still a bit shy,' she'd confided, 'but I'm sure they'll soon be the best of friends. Now, don't you worry, dear, everything will be fine.'

And everything was. When I had checked-in the empty cat-carrier as part of my normal luggage, Raimundo had turned a blind eye to the fact that the designated occupant was conspicuous by her absence. Indeed, a slightly raised eyebrow was the only sign that he had noticed. When we reached the aircraft steps, he'd said, 'Now I can report to the *comandante* that both you and the cat *box* were on the plane.' Lurking behind that moustache, the trace of a smile. 'Till we meet again, *senhora.*'

My abrupt departure from the Massaroco had been efficiently handled. The *comandante* had made arrangements with the Agença, and by now my replacement would have held her first office hour, informing Winterton and Haxby and the others that I'd been summoned home due to serious family illness. That suited me very well. Believing that I'd gone for good, Winterton and Haxby would relax. If they felt secure, they would perhaps become a little careless....

And with my departure, the timebomb of Zara Porter-Browne's bungling attempts to be a PI had been defused. I settled back in my seat. As soon as I got back to London, I'd chase up the answers to these emails I'd sent on Saturday in an effort to gain something incriminating on Haxby – and Grant. Gut instinct told me I was onto something with them both, and that's why I'd left Gorgonzola behind. I knew I'd be back.

Jim Orr, senior investigating officer for HM Revenue & Customs, wasn't too pleased at my sudden ejection from Madeira and consequent appearance in the London office. No smile, no warm greeting, just a brusque, 'Take a seat.'

He got straight down to business. 'Comandante Figueira, it seems, is rather upset, Deborah. Single-handedly you have somehow managed to sour three hundred years of cordial relations between England and Portugal – an offence, I believe, on a par with the episode when Captain Cook fired on Funchal's fortifications.' Selecting a sheet of paper from a file open on his desk, he fixed me with a stern look. 'While seconded to her department, you contrived to ... break and enter the premises of a respectable businessman ... conceal and fail to inform her of the existence of a suitcase of Class A drugs ... engage in an unseemly brawl in a village cemetery. It may be,' – he regarded me steadily for a few seconds – 'it may be, that you have a perfectly reasonable explanation for this conduct?' I hitched forward on my chair, but before I could reply, he continued, 'Suppose you run it past me for credibility.'

I relaxed. This was a pet saying of his, always employed in jocular fashion, a sort of in-joke. It was a signal that this dressing-down was more bark than bite – confirmed by the almost imperceptible twitch at the corner of his mouth.

I flipped open the pocket file I'd brought with me. 'As a matter of fact, I have *three* good explanations.' I held up the replies I'd received to the emails I'd sent from Madeira. 'And here's the proof that I'm close to bringing home the goods.'

'If not your cat, eh?' This time he permitted himself the faintest of smiles.

How did he find *that* out? For a moment it threw me – exactly as he'd intended. Jim Orr prided himself on not letting anyone slip something past him.

'Don't keep me in suspense, Deborah.'

'Er, er, yes … well….' Hoping to dodge further questioning on the whereabouts of Gorgonzola, I held up the reply from DEFRA. 'You see, I broke into the premises of that outwardly respectable businessman thinking I was going to find a heroin or crack cocaine laboratory. When I opened the door and saw all those lights, I ditched that theory in favour of a cannabis factory. But on closer inspection, the seedlings bore no resemblance to cannabis plants.'

'Get to the point, Deborah.' He held out his hand for the DEFRA email.

I passed it over. 'You see, I knew that with all that security, Grant was obviously up to *something*. So I sent an email to DEFRA. According to them, there's a considerable amount of money to be made from the illegal propagation and sale of rare orchids.' I sat back and waited for his reaction.

'Hmm. I think you might be on to something there.' He rubbed his chin thoughtfully and muttered something that sounded like 'sites'.

'Sites?' I repeated. What on earth did he mean?

'C-I-T-E-S,' he spelled out. 'The Convention on International Trade in Endangered Species. Also known as the Washington Convention, it restricts or bans the trade or movement of rare plants from the wild. You can't just stroll into the jungle and pick orchids from trees, you know. And if you try to pull a fast one and smuggle them in, you don't get off with just a slapped wrist and a caution. Nowadays it's up to seven years in the clink and an unlimited fine.'

'But Grant's plants aren't—'

'Yes, yes, they're laboratory grown. But the regulations apply to artificially propagated plants as well as those from the wild. We've a specialist Customs' Cites team at Heathrow to catch people who smuggle in prohibited plants – and animals – for personal gain. *Anyone* carrying a pet carrier, occupied or *not*, Deborah, is the focus of attention.' He leaned back, his expression that of a poker player holding the winning card.

So that's how he'd known about Gorgonzola. I'd been under discreet surveillance at the airport. 'Er, yes,' I said, again hurriedly changing the subject. 'But I just can't believe it would be worth risking imprisonment for a *flower*.'

'Believe me, Deborah, when it comes to acquiring a rare item, the sky's the limit as far as some collectors are concerned. They're prepared to pay any price for something others don't have. Passions can run pretty high.'

Something was stirring at the back of my mind. I closed my eyes in concentration trying to recall that time on the terrace at the Massaroco when Grant was threatening me with Rottweilers and pit bulls … Zara had made some remark to Grant. That was it, something on the lines of, 'There must be something pretty damn valuable in that orchid farm of yours.' And Grant's reaction had been to sweep my papers off the table onto the ground, shouting … *shouting*, 'Bloody sights!' At the time, that's what I'd *thought* he'd said. He'd actually let slip what he was up to.

'We've got him!' I punched the air in exhilaration.

Jim Orr was looking at me with raised eyebrows. 'Just had a eureka moment, Deborah? Care to share it with me?'

I did. 'So,' I finished, 'that's the case against D. Grant, Exotic Cut Flower Exporter, sewn up.'

'Celebration a little premature, I'm afraid, Deborah.' Jim Orr tapped the email. 'A raid on the laboratory will certainly wrap up the Madeira end and put the gentleman in question behind bars, but what I'm interested in is the bigger picture – *how* he is smuggling the plants out, and *where* they are going. Any ideas on that?'

'How about if he conceals them in one of his above-board shipments to a nursery or wholesaler?'

'Poss-ib-ly.' He frowned. 'But there'd have to be someone in the know at the receiving end to spirit away the prize. And in a box of orchids, all very similar, just how is our special orchid to be singled out without drawing attention to it?'

Three weeks ago while I'd been waiting for G's plane to land, I'd watched home-bound passengers putting their cardboard boxes of plants on the dedicated trolley waiting to be wheeled into the specially heated hold on the plane. 'It would be quite easy,' I said, confident that I was on the right track. 'Nobody would remark on a box slipped onto the plant trolley in Departures, or during loading. And there are, of course, those who will, for payment, take a box to England, or France, or Germany, pretending it is theirs.' People like Celia Haxby and Dorothy Winterton.

Orr nodded thoughtfully. 'OK, we'll not make an issue of that breaking and entering of yours. But we still have the little matters of your concealment of that suitcase of class A drugs and the – er –unseemly brawl in the cemetery, do we not?'

I filled him in with the details and waited while he mulled them over. In the silence a plane droned overhead carrying holidaymakers to some far-flung destination. Some thousands of miles away in Madeira, no doubt Gorgonzola was snoozing in the shade while Victoria prepared a light lunch; Raimundo would be tinkering with his car or, if he had angered the *comandante*, wrestling with a recalcitrant computer; David Grant, Exotic Cut Flower Exporter, would be calculating his profits from illegal propagation and celebrating my expulsion from Madeira and his life. And Winterton and Haxby – what would *they* doing?

'A penny for your thoughts, Deborah. No, let me guess … you're planning to go back and close the case. Am I right?'

Damn. Nothing, but nothing, slipped by him.

'We-ell …' I hastily changed the subject. 'I thought I might drive down to Cornwall to look at some paintings.'

'Hmm … no doubt you're about to enlighten me as to the reason for this expense account trip?'

'I'm going in search of a gallery called Avant-Garde Art so that I can …' I paused, but infuriatingly, he didn't say a word, just waited for me to finish. Another plane rumbled overhead. I caved in first. '… so that I can turn the key in the lock of Celia Haxby's prison cell.'

His hand had been hovering over the expense account forms. Now he picked up a pen and started fiddling with the spring top. *Click Click*

Click. Click Click Click. Click Click Click. A subtle way of reminding me that the time allotted for my interview was running out. Putting pressure on me.

'Those paintings I found in Haxby's hotel room,' I said hurriedly. 'I emailed the photos to our art fraud department. And the expert said that they appeared to be—'

'Works by famous artists.' Jim was disappointingly lukewarm, a decidedly wet blanket. 'There's nothing illegal about making copies – until or unless Haxby adds a counterfeit signature and attempts to sell them as genuine.'

'But that's *exactly* what she intends. I'm absolutely sure of it. That picture of a giant pink teacup looming over a slab of fish is a copy of *Still life with Kipper* by John Byrne, worth a couple of thousand pounds.'

'Hardly earth-shattering.' *Click Click Click.*

'Well how about a cool twenty-five thousand for a landscape of muddy green and grey hills by Sir William Gillies?'

The *click click* stopped. I'd caught his attention.

'And,' I rushed on, 'recently someone shelled out one and a half million for the original *Abstraktes Bild* by Gerhard Richter.' The canvas I'd thought Haxby had used for cleaning her brush!

That afternoon, expense account forms tucked away in my bag, I drove down to Cornwall, making good time down the motorway. Being a fan of Daphne Du Maurier, a stop at Jamaica Inn was essential – I'd just passed a 'Tiredness Kills' notice, after all. Though I was only halfway to St Ives, I believe in slipping into an undercover role early so that when the moment arrives it comes as second nature. To that end, I'd discarded my workaday trousers and trainers in favour of a modish jacket and calf-length dress bought in a charity shop in the Portobello Road after my early morning interview with Jim Orr. So it wasn't DJ Smith of HM Revenue & Customs, but the Honourable Deborah Smythe of the landed aristocracy, who pushed open the door of the eitheenth-century coaching inn and with the other tourists soaked in the ambience of dark wooden beams and leaded windows.

While I worked my way through a pot of tea and wolfed down a Cornish pasty, I reviewed my strategy for approaching the art gallery when I reached St. Ives. In the boot of the car lurked an abstract work by the paw of Gorgonzola, feline artist. Life is stressful and we all need a way of unwinding – for some it may be alcohol, a cigarette, or drugs. For G, it was something rather out of the ordinary – for cats, that is. If presented with dishes of acrylic paint, she'd dip in a paw and daub a surface with the various colours, creating interestingly abstract designs that were, to my mind, decidedly superior to those in Celia Haxby's hotel room. Three weeks ago, when I'd collected G from Funchal airport and brought her back to the gingerbread house, I'd pinned up sheets of paper to give her the opportunity to unwind in her special way. She'd produced two *oeuvres*, one a sombre arrangement of black streaks unrelieved by any colour, and two days later, another – a firework outburst of joyful colours.

With an approach to Avant-Garde Art in mind, I'd had the latter expensively framed before I left Madeira. My plan was to ask for a valuation at the gallery, with the explanation that G's painting was a legacy from a recently deceased relative. Then I'd show an interest in buying one or two of the works on display. By means of a camera hidden in the frame of the plain-glass spectacles I'd be wearing, and a voice-activated recorder disguised as a silk rosebud pinned to a lapel of my jacket, I hoped to provide enough evidence for the HMRC's art expert to reach a conclusion.

St Ives, Mecca for artists and tourists alike, was living up to its picture-postcard image of golden beaches, sparkling blue sea and colourful boats bobbing in the little harbour. Since the holiday season was not yet in full swing, I found a parking place with only a little difficulty, then with G's bubble-wrapped picture under my arm, wandered through the narrow streets that climbed up from the harbour. As in many other picturesque Cornish villages, art galleries, tearooms and souvenir shops outnumbered those premises devoted to selling the necessities of everyday living and I spent a very pleasurable hour window-shopping. All as part of my cover, you understand.

Though I assumed that Haxby was safely beavering away in Madeira at the production of yet another batch of *oeuvres*, I kept to my Standard Operating Procedure. I never take anything for granted. My approach to Avant-Garde Art for a valuation had to appear fortu-itous, without arousing suspicion that I'd deliberately sought the gallery out. So I dawdled in front of various gallery windows and went into a couple to try out the legacy story and ask for a valuation: one of them mentioned a sum less than the price of the expensive frame;

the other offered a surprisingly large amount that I resolved to conceal from Gorgonzola on the grounds that she would expect to be accorded celebrity status. After that piece of heady news, with the aid of the map provided by Tourist Information I was all set to tackle Avant-Garde Art.

The shop itself, like many of those in St Ives, was a converted fisherman's cottage, and consequently by modern standards the display window was tiny, mostly taken up by a child-sized easel. Propped against it was a weirdly abstract painting. I walked past, then returned and studied it for a couple of minutes. I was genuinely intrigued. Could a tangle of black lines and a few red squiggles on a cream background be termed Art? Behind it in the brightly lit interior, I could see several other abstracts, equally bizarre. I hitched G's *oeuvre* more securely under my arm, and went in.

At the sound of the buzzer a young man materialized through an open door at the back of the shop. Dark hair gelled to sleek perfection, dark suit tailored to a perfect fit, cuffs and teeth a startling white, to my professional eye he oozed conman from every pore.

'Can I be of assistance to madam?' The cut-glass accent conveyed that here was a man – and a business – that had all the integrity of the Bank of England.

Two could play at that game. I summoned up a haughty expression worthy of the Honourable Deborah Smythe. 'Indeed you can.' I didn't add 'my man', but it hovered wraith-like in the air between us. 'I have here an abstract picture for which I require a valuation.' I let my eyes rove round the room. 'Your establishment seems eminently suitable for that.'

His eyes roved over me, assessing. I clearly passed some sort of test, for he said, 'Of course, madam. May I?' He took the bubble-wrapped parcel from me and placed it reverently on a low table.

While he opened up the layers of plastic, I gave him the spiel. 'It's a legacy from my aunt, Lady Felicia. Can't say I've taken to it, and if it's not of much value, I've no room for it in my collection of abstract art.'

He held up G's masterpiece at arm's length, calculating its money-making potential. 'Quite an interesting piece, but unsigned.' He pursed his lips. 'That takes down *any* value, I'm afraid.'

'Oh dear,' I tutted. 'In that case, I'll just have to donate it to the village auction in aid of the church roof fund. If you could just wrap it up again....'

'I'm sorry to disappoint, madam. A signature, now, that would have made *all* the difference. Unfortunately, all our clients require a signed work.'

Shit. That was something I hadn't bargained for. That carefully thought out strategy of mine had fallen at the first hurdle.

'No chance of it being an unsigned Hodgson, I suppose? Haw, haw, haw,' I brayed.

His hand reaching out for the parcel tape stopped in mid-action at the thought of the lucrative possibilities of a famous artist's signature on that unsigned work.

'No chance at all, madam. But ... as madam is selling it in aid of the church ... and to save the considerable inconvenience of carrying the picture all the way back home, perhaps madam would consider accepting twenty-five pounds in aid of the church fund?'

'Well ... I don't know ... oh, all right. I can't bear the thought of Auntie's picture not selling at the auction and ending up in a *charity* shop.' My wrinkled nose and curled lip said it all.

'So if madam will give me a moment ... as you will appreciate, our business is normally transacted not with cash, but by way of banker's draft or credit card.' He dematerialized through the door at the back of the shop.

I took the opportunity to snap several of the paintings on the wall with the tiny camera hidden in the frame of my glasses, then wandered over to study the picture in the window. I leant over the painting to bring it in range and took a photo of it. At the discreet cough behind me, I turned to see him advancing, cash in hand.

'Now, this here is rather an interesting work.' I indicated the abstract of tangled black lines and red squiggles.

He slipped the money into my hand. 'Emilio Vedova.' Each syllable was deferentially caressed.

'Vedova? The Italian Jackson Pollock?' This was the wildest of wild guesses, a stab in the dark.

'Vedova – a *pioneer* of abstract revolutionary art, sadly no longer with us.' He cast his eyes to heaven as if seeking a nod of agreement from the illustrious departed. 'This powerful painting is one of the works from his *Protest Cycle No. 4*.'

'It's certainly powerful,' I agreed. 'But perhaps a little too large for my collection. Now that one there—' I darted over to a garish painting illuminated by two spotlights on the back wall. 'Yes, this is more what

I'm looking for.' I peered at the signature, taking a snapshot with the concealed camera as I did so. 'A Patrick Heron. *Jan 14:1983.*'

An odd title for an odd painting. On a background one third basically blue, two-thirds a washed-out red, a large lime green oval liberally smudged with red floated in a ferment of bright green bubbles. I studied the work with the rapt contemplation of an admirer. Was it an abstract of sunrise viewed from outer space – the sun taking a bite out of the darkness of planet earth? Or … I tilted my head on one side. If the picture was rotated one turn, perhaps, just perhaps, it represented the head and shoulders of someone in a blue top.

Genuine or counterfeit? I said slowly, 'Well, that's certainly *strange….*' Frowning, I tailed off. I waited for his reaction. It might give me a clue.

The immaculately manicured hands rubbed together in sudden unease. 'Madam has a question?'

'That title. The date is the title, is it?'

He stepped forward, disguising his relief with extravagant gestures.

'This particular artist, madam, favours titles of this type. We have *Greens and Grey (Red Line): June 1983.* Or *Violet Disc in Lime Yellow: June-December 1982.* Then—'

I prepared another ambush, stemming the flow with a sharp, 'It comes with a certificate of authenticity?'

'Naturally, madam. Supplied by an expert from—' He named an establishment of impeccable reputation.

That seemed to be that, then. Oh dear, everything had seemed to fit so well. I'd been so very confident that the signature on the certificates supplied by Avant-Garde Art would be a name unknown in the art world.

I nodded as if reassured and, to buy time in case my disappointment showed, pretended interest in a nearby picture. I was staring at the image of a weird blurred face. I blinked and looked again. It was as if the artist, in a moment of pique, had taken a rag and smeared it across the wet paint.

Behind me the salesman murmured, 'Perhaps not to everyone's taste, but we do have a most enthusiastic core of collectors.'

Well, I certainly wasn't one of them. I turned away. I couldn't resist bolstering his hopes by casting a lingering look at the blue and red abstract with the lime green oval. 'I must say I prefer this one, Heron's *Jan. 14:1983.*' Then cruelly dashed those hopes by adding, 'But it's not a decision I can rush. If you'll give me your card, I'll be in touch.'

Enveloped in a black cloud of disappointment, my carefully constructed theories blown sky high, despondently I made my way back through the picturesque streets of St Ives. On the drive to London I gave the delights of Jamaica Inn a miss. That was an item on my expense account that, alas, couldn't now be justified.

CHAPTER EIGHTEEN

I handed over the voice-recording and digital photos from the hidden camera to the tech guys for further investigation, not holding out any hope. So next day, when I received a summons from Jim Orr, I was convinced that it was to tell me that he was taking me off the case.

You could have knocked me down with the proverbial feather when he waved me to a chair and said, 'Send in an expense chit for that little excursion to St Ives yesterday, Deborah. I think there's every chance you'll soon be turning that key in the lock of Celia Haxby's cell door.'

There was a momentary pause while I mentally shifted gears. I stared at him. Had I heard right?

'Yes, Deborah,' he was saying, 'a pat on the back for taking those close-ups of the paintings in St Ives. I'm confident you're onto something. Our art fraud boys examined the artist's brushwork in the photos you took yesterday. Brushwork is as individual as a signature, and extremely difficult to forge well enough to fool an expert – unless you've the skill of that celebrated forger, Van Meegeren, of course.'

'So they *are* copies then?' With difficulty I suppressed the urge to do a little victory dance.

'Yep.' He slid my close-up photos of Vedova's *Protest Cycle No. 4* and Heron's *Jan. 14:1983* across the desk. 'As you see, they've indicated the discrepancies with the real McCoy.'

I studied the annotated red circles with interest.

'They've also made discreet enquiries about the expert who authenticates Avant-Garde's pictures. And—' He tugged thoughtfully at his lower lip.

After a few moments I prompted, 'And?'

'And he's conveniently dead'.

So, it was in an entirely different mood that, two days later, I sat in the 757 looking down on the spine of the dragon-shaped São Lourenço peninsula as the plane made its steeply angled approach to Madeira's runway. Celia Haxby, though she didn't know it, was painting her last pictures as a free woman. We'd arranged for Passport Control to alert Customs when she arrived at Gatwick Airport. Undercover agents would hopefully be able to link her and her paintings with the art gallery in St Ives. And once we'd done that, the photo evidence from her hotel room at the Massaroco should be enough to slam the cell door shut on the Flamboyant Artist for a very long time. That floppy yellow sun hat and Picasso artist's smock would certainly brighten up one of HM's prisons. There was only one niggling little loose end to be tied up – why had she gone to the expense of travelling all the way to Madeira when she could be tucked away in England daubing merrily at her canvases?

I thought about it as we touched down. The roar of reverse thrust engines filled the cabin, and the hillside of red-roofed white houses rolled past the window, slowed and came to a stop. Was it as simple as Haxby hankering after a holiday in an exotic location, thus combining business with pleasure? Or did the answer lie in a link with that upper-class English lady abroad, Dorothy Winterton?

I undid my seat belt and collected my holdall from the overhead locker. I'd established that Haxby was most probably selling fake masterpieces. In spite of failing to get video evidence of Winterton's connection with the well-known drug dealer Gonçalves, and in spite of the *comandante* rejecting my theory out of hand, I was more convinced than ever that Winterton and Haxby were partners in the business of laundering money.

I thought about this as the bus transferred us from aircraft to terminal. After all, Avant-Garde Art was an ideal channel to convert drug money into what would appear, on the surface, to be legitimate profit. A few of the paintings in the gallery had displayed the red spot denoting a sale, and in due course those paintings would disappear off the wall, the sum ostensibly paid appearing in the income column of the gallery's accounts. Yes, it all fitted.

Though I didn't think it would occur to the *comandante* that the summarily deported Sshmit might return to Madeira, I was just a little bit on edge as I shuffled in the queue towards Passport Control. I needn't have worried. The bored policeman gave me only a cursory glance before thumbing lazily through my passport and pushing it back under the glass screen. Unchallenged, I re-entered Madeira.

Yesterday I'd telephoned Victoria Knight to let her know that I'd be arriving on today's flight. 'I'll come straight to you from the airport, so I should be at the villa around midday,' I'd finished.

'Oooh, that is a lovely surprise, dear. Now before you even ask, Gorgonzola's just fine, hasn't really missed you—' She'd paused and hastily rephrased. 'Oh, what I mean is that she hasn't pined, isn't off her food, or anything like that.'

'She and Blackie are er … getting on all right, then?'

'Oh yes, dear. They're nearly always together. She's taken quite a fancy to him. Any chance she gets she tries to mother him.'

Smother him was more like it. G had a long memory, and didn't quickly forgive attacks on her person. Blackie might no longer be the arrogant, spoiled thug that had attacked her on that previous assignment in Tenerife, but she'd be taking no chances. Pre-emptive strike strategy, I think the military call it. It was just as well I was coming back to Madeira.

Gorgonzola was gratifyingly pleased to see me, but not nearly so pleased when I produced the cat-carrier and whisked her into it. She realized that a cease-fire had been unilaterally imposed from on high, that Blackie was no longer a legitimate target, and that war game fun stopped now. Watched by an ecstatically mewing Blackie, I stowed the cat-carrier with its thwarted incumbent on the floor of the rental car.

Victoria gave me a farewell hug. 'Come back soon, dear. Blackie's already missing his little friend.'

Turning a deaf ear to G's grumbles, I drove along the Estrada Monumental passing the gingerbread house, now awaiting a new tenant. Its faded green shutters were firmly closed, the racemes of purple wisteria clinging to the pale stucco walls were beginning to wither at the tips. Old houses have a soul that needs to be cherished. It was as if in my absence its life-force had drained away.

Before my enforced departure from Madeira I'd found an agreeable substitute for the gingerbread house. In preparation for my return I'd rented a tiny studio apartment in an old house that drowsed on a hand-kerchief-sized scrap of land bypassed by the modern world. From the main street all that was visible above a high wall and a rippling green sea of banana fronds were terracotta roof tiles faded by more than a century's exposure to sun and rain.

The entrance to this hideaway was via a cobbled lane too narrow for modern vehicles. I parked on the street and opened the rear door of the car.

'Time for you to go undercover, G.' I zipped the cat-carrier into a capacious holdall brought expressly for the purpose and started off up the lane.

After a few metres I stopped. The holdall was emitting disconcertingly loud yowls. So much for the planned undercover arrival at my new abode. I slid the zip open a few centimetres and hissed, '*Shut up*, G. This is *work*. You're being unprofessional.' She wasn't wearing her working collar, but it had the desired result – silence. A reproachful silence. Followed by an anguished mew, faint but unmistakable, craftily designed to wound. Suitably chastened, I made my way up the lane, the scuff of my shoes loud on the cobbles.

The rented studio was plainly furnished and scrupulously clean. As a bonus, louvre doors led directly onto a shady patio-courtyard complete with lime-green metal table and a couple of chairs, French café-style.

With a bright, 'Very nice, eh, Gorgonzola?' I unzipped the holdall, lifted out the cat-carrier, unfastened the catch and flung open the door. 'What do you think of your new home?'

I waited a moment for a response, but there wasn't one. I knelt and peered in. 'C'mon, G, forgive and forget,' I pleaded.

This time I got a response. It sounded most decidedly like a fart.

That did it. 'I've been up since three to catch that early morning flight, G. I'm *tired*. T-i-r-e-d. I'm going to take a short power nap. We've work to do tonight. I hope you'll be in a better mood when I wake up.'

I took off my shoes and flung myself on the bed. I was tired. My eyes closed…. A moment later, or so it seemed, a large paw tap tap tapped my arm. I didn't open my eyes. Hot breath fanned my face … taptaptap.

'Watch my lips, G. T-i-r-e-d. T-i-r-e-d, do you hear?' I muttered drowsily.

Just when I thought she'd given up and I was drifting once more into slumber … taptaptaptaptaptap.

'Let – me – have – that – power nap, G,' I said through clenched teeth.

And eventually she did. But not before I had staggered over to the nearby supermarket in search of a conciliatory offering that would satisfy her gourmet tastes.

*

On the flight back to Madeira I'd made the decision to stake out the somewhat seedy block of flats in Funchal where Gonçalves holed up. I parked my car a short distance away. The CCTV footage of Gonçalves being the best lead I had – indeed the only firm one – I was prepared to lie in wait for him all night, every night.

Within an hour I glimpsed a movement in the dark recess of the doorway. A moment later a man emerged. At first I wasn't sure if it was Gonçalves, but as he passed under a streetlight, that U-shaped bald patch on the top of his head told me my vigil was at an end. He advanced on a motor scooter parked by the communal rubbish bin and kicked it off its stand. The glowing tip of a cigarette arced into the gutter and without a backward glance he sped off towards the centre of town.

At a discreet distance I followed. I wasn't altogether surprised when he took the road towards Camâra de Lobos, the coast end of that old mountain path, the route whereby I suspected drugs were being trans-ported into the Nun's Valley. And Haxby, with Winterton in tow, had made no secret of her visits to Camâra, ostensibly to plant her easel in the very spot where Winston Churchill had set up his. But had there been *any* views of the fishing village among the paintings in Haxby's room? I mentally reviewed the stacked works…. No, not one – circum-stantial evidence to back up my theory that her visits there had been for an entirely different reason.

Pondering this new train of thought, I almost missed the brightening of his brake lights as Gonçalves slowed, bumped over a low kerb and turned into a narrow alleyway between two buildings. Anxiously I scanned the road for a parking place. Fifty metres ahead a car moved off and I swooped into the vacated space. After a quick glance in the mirror to check for oncoming traffic, I flung open the door – then eased it shut. Gonçalves had reappeared and was walking briskly along the pavement towards me. Any sudden movement would have attracted his attention, so I just sat there, hoping that he'd be so intent upon his own affairs that he'd pay no particular attention to a woman, head bent, rummaging in her handbag.

Once he was a safe distance ahead, I picked up the rucksack. At 11 p.m. there were enough people wandering around in Câmara de Lobos to make me inconspicuous as, keeping to the shadows, I followed on foot Silvestre Gonçalves' wiry figure. The up-turned crescent moon sailed out from behind a bank of cloud, silvering the far side of the street and plunging the near side into still deeper shadow. The *thump thump thump* of heavy metal music spilt from the open doorway of a bar. Off to my left, under the shelter of a clump of palm trees a line of blue and green fishing boats slumbered on the cobbles of the harbour like ground-roosting exotic birds. A few metres from the shore, the jagged ribs of an old hulk lay half-submerged in the dark waters as if picked clean by the razor-sharp teeth of a shoal of the espada fish it once hunted.

The rucksack on my back twitched as its occupant detected the alluring aroma of fish wafting up from the array of nets strung on racks and spread on the quayside. G was registering temptation, but temptation heroically resisted – a subtle way of underlining that when she was *officially* at work, she was the total professional. This afternoon's unfortunate episode of the holdall had been forgiven, but not forgotten.

He was heading away from the harbour in the direction of the huddle of narrow lanes round the fish market. Now that there were fewer people about, I dropped further back. He rounded a corner, and I lost sight of him. I quickened my step, but the dimly lit street stretched emptily ahead: the façade of the fish market stared blankly back at me; a shutter hanging loose on one of the houses opposite rattled mockingly in the freshening breeze.

I walked slowly down the street on the lookout for something, anything, that might indicate where he'd gone to ground. At the end of the street I set the rucksack down and unzipped it. G's tousled head emerged and immediately swivelled to target the fish market.

'*This* side, G.' I pointed to the row of houses. 'Let's see what you can nose out.'

I really didn't have much hope, but with Gorgonzola scouting ahead, I walked back up the street. Halfway along, a movement flickered in the shadows – only a skinny white cat scavenging in an overflowing municipal rubbish bin. It eyed Gorgonzola appraisingly, saw in her scruffy coat an unwelcome rival for the treasures of the bin, and took mean and vicious action. With a blood-freezing *tchaaaargh*, claws slashing like scimitars, it hurled itself at G.

My brain was still clunkily taking in the situation as G's alley-cat genes launched her into a counter-attack. Her opponent had made the fundamental error of going for the throat. While its claws were entangled in the thickest area of G's patchy fur, G sank her teeth into the back of its scrawny neck, and with a toss of her head, hurled her attacker into the road.

With a contemptuous *yeeerh*, G fluffed herself up and advanced, ears flattened, stiff-legged towards her dazed assailant who leapt to its feet with an ear-splitting *hooowooool* and shot off to a safe distance from where it screamed raucous defiance and abuse.

Somewhere above me a window was flung open. 'Shurrup, I say, *shurrup!*' A hand holding a jug of water appeared and I just had time to flatten myself behind the malodorous bulk of the rubbish bin, when a sheet of water splatted to the ground right on target.

A particularly piercing *yaoooooooooooooo* cut off abruptly. The scrawny cat, flattened fur exposing skeletal thinness, blinked water out of its eyes. *Hissss* – Gorgonzola ever the opportunist, sprang forward to administer the *coup de grâce*. *Splatt*. With an expertise honed by years of practice, the hand at the window delivered a second jugful. Gorgonzola's aggressive hiss deflated like a punctured air-cushion. Drenched and slimmed to half her size, abandoning her plans for GBH, she dived for cover under the bin.

The Portuguese equivalent of 'Gottcha, you bastards!' drifted down from above. The window slammed shut. G's bedraggled head poked tentatively out of her refuge and I'd just crouched down to scoop her up for a consolatory cuddle, when the faint squeak of un-oiled hinges made me look up. Across the road, a small door inset into one of the fish market roll-down shutters was slowly opening.

A finger of light spilt across the tarmac towards the bin, seeking me out. I was sure I'd found Gonçalves, but I certainly didn't want him to find me. Any movement by the bin would catch his eye. I had a few precious seconds while his night vision was adjusting. I lowered my head, tucked my chin into my shoulder, and prayed that my leg muscles would be able to hold their uncomfortable position.

'Quiet, G,' I breathed.

A tremor ran through her, whether of victory thwarted or of shock delayed, it was hard to tell, but training won and she lay motionless beneath my hands.

I stared at my knees. I heard the click of the door closing. Silence. Perhaps he'd sensed movement by the bin and was even now creeping towards me, knife in hand.... My straining ears picked up a faint sound, the quiet pad of rubber soles. The hairs on the back of my neck prickled, instinct screamed at me to jump up and defend myself. But had I *really* heard something? Was it merely my overheated imagination? Gonçalves might just be standing there checking the area or lighting a cigarette. Leaping up from behind the bin would precipitate the very thing I feared: he'd rush at me, knife in hand. I took a deep breath and stayed down.

Mustn't–look–up, mustn't–look–up. I tried not to picture my bowed shoulders, neck exposed like the bull's for the fatal thrust of the matador's sword. Mustn't–look–up. Twenty of those little incantations and he'd have walked away up the street, and I'd be safe. Mustn't–look–up ... fourteen. Mustn't–look–up ... fifteen. Mustn't—

My calf muscles signalled surrender. At the same moment, my stomach rebelled against the putrid stink of decomposing fish and decaying vegetable matter erupting from the bin. I lurched to my feet, trying not to retch. If Gonçalves was there, all he'd have to do was hold out his blade and I'd fall on it.

But he wasn't there. The street was deserted. Even the scrawny cat had slunk off to investigate less perilous treasures. I reeled away from the foul smell and leant against a house wall, massaging the circulation back into my aching leg muscles. A barely audible, plaintive *miaow* issued from beneath the bin. Gorgonzola was pointedly rubbing in the embarrassing fact that while the captain had cravenly abandoned the stinking ship, G had dutifully remained at *her* post.

I limped over and gathered her up. She lifted a woebegone face and stared at me wide-eyed, milking the situation for all she was worth.

'Dear, oh dear, let's see what we can do,' I fussed.

I set her down and did my best to dry her off by rubbing her with my jacket. Then bundling her up in it, I tucked her under my arm and walked across the road to investigate. I hadn't seen the person who had emerged from the fish market and consequently couldn't be *sure* it was Gonçalves. Perhaps I was wasting my time investigating, but it was worth a try.

I studied the door. The lock was of the simple Yale-type, all that was necessary for a fish market out of working hours. I could have opened it with a paperclip, with my picklocks it was simplicity itself. I fished in my pocket with my free hand and within five seconds was inside the building.

Moonlight filtering through roof lights opaque with salt and dust struggled to reach the floor where I stood listening. Gradually my eyes accustomed themselves to a gloom that smelled strongly of fish and salt water. The bundle under my arm nosed that heady bouquet and made a miraculous recovery, quivering with the excitement of a child let loose in a sweet factory. I set G down, keeping one finger in her collar as a reminder that this paradise for cats was a *working* environment for a HMRC drug detector.

The narrow beam of my pencil torch revealed continuous rows of stone tables stretching off into the darkness. If drugs *were* here, they'd be carefully concealed. I wasn't going to find a row of packages neatly laid out for my inspection on one of these slabs.

'Find!' I waved Gorgonzola forward. She had been trained to sniff out narcotics. Her low crooning call would tell me if she found anything.

Tail erect, she walked out of the beam of light. A wraith-like shape, she began a run along the rows of stone tables. I could trace her progress by the soft thud when she leapt down, followed some moments later by the scutter of claws as she leapt up to start on the next row.

I switched off the torch and waited. I couldn't afford to draw a blank here. I had no other leads. To date, the only evidence against Winterton was that CCTV tape of a woman meeting with Gonçalves, something that a smart lawyer would easily demolish. Time was running out to build a watertight case against her. In a few days she and Haxby would be returning to England, their holiday in Madeira at an end.

With the minutes passing and still no signal from Gorgonzola, my hopes faded. Expectation gave way to resignation. By now, G must have almost completed her search. There was nothing for it but to stake-out Gonçalves' house again. But this time he might not emerge for hours – or at all. And when he did, the chances were that he would just head for the nearest bar.

Where *was* G? I suddenly realized that I could no longer hear the faint scratches and thumps that marked her position. Could she, oh treacherous thought, have stumbled on a succulent fishy morsel and even now be tucking into it?

My fingers closed on the ultrasonic whistle in my pocket. One blast would bring her back. I hesitated. What if I called her back just when she was within a sniff of success? No, I'd give her one more minute, just in case.

I gave her two minutes, then pulled out the whistle.

Purrrrrr. I jumped as if I'd been jabbed with an electric cattle prod. The triumphant crooning call came from somewhere off to the left. *Purrrrrrr.* I switched on the torch and made my way towards the seaward entrance of the market. *Purrrrrrr.* G's eyes flashed yellow-green as the beam caught her. She was crouched on a pile of old nets, proprietorial paw firmly planted on a battered red ball-float of the kind used to mark lobster pots.

'*Well done*, G. How *could* I have doubted you!' I gathered her up and planted a rather guilty kiss on her nose. 'Now, clever girl,' I unbuckled her working collar, 'the place is yours!'

She squirmed out of my arms and streaked off to home-in on a temptation previously resisted. I put on a pair of thin latex gloves, pulled aside the tangle of torn nets, and picked up the red ball. Judging by its weight, more than a kilo, Gorgonzola had hit the jackpot.

I laid it on the nearest stone table and played the torch over its battered surface. A raised seam ran round the circumference like an old-fashioned ball valve in a cistern – at a guess, that's probably what it had once been. So it should unscrew…. But it didn't. My hands were too small to give me leverage. Carefully I replaced it under its screen of nets.

The drug courier would need to pick it up before the fish market opened on Monday and, I glanced at my watch, it was already Sunday morning. I'd have to alert the *comandante* quickly. But how was I going to avoid recriminations over my return to Madeira, and the accompanying hostility and unpleasantness that would waste valuable time?

'Enough, Sshmit,' she'd hiss, thumping her fist on the desk. 'As of the 25th of April, you have had no official presence here.' The orange heads of the strelitzias would nod unanimous agreement. And that would be that.

'Time to go home, G.' I called, and she appeared, chewing at a cherished fish tail, like a desperate smoker taking the last frantic puff before boarding a bus. 'You've earned it, G,' I said and loaded her and the fish tail into the rucksack.

I played the flashlight over the pile of nets, and satisfied that everything was as it had been, let myself out. The door clicked softly shut behind me. Perhaps on the drive back to Funchal I'd think what to do.

*

191

When I unzipped the rucksack in the banana grove of the studio apartment, G stepped leisurely out and sat on the cobbles, meticulously cleaning her face and whiskers of the last traces of fish supper.

'Full moon, and one o'clock in the morning, best time for cats on the prowl,' I said heartily. 'Only don't bring me any little presents.'

Gorgonzola's eyes narrowed at thoughts of dessert. The last I saw of her was the waving tip of her tail as she disappeared among the shadowy fronds.

I slung the rucksack onto my shoulder and headed off up the road to the little bar at the corner that stayed open till the last customer left. I chose a quiet spot at the back of the small courtyard and ordered a *poncha* to assist in the thinking process. Half an hour later, I still hadn't worked out what to do about the drugs in the fish market. An anonymous tip-off about drugs in the fish market wouldn't be acted on before Monday morning. So to get action I'd have to identify myself. And then the *comandante* would view it as a challenge to her authority that I'd been brazen enough to return against her express orders. It would be like a red rag to a bull. I sipped disconsolately at a second *poncha*—

Suddenly I had something else to worry about. Someone was watching me, I was sure of it. In my line of work you don't last long if that basic survival instinct is not highly developed. The trick is to surreptitiously identify who is taking that special interest. If the surveillance comes from behind, you're in trouble, but my chair was against the wall of the small courtyard so that was to my advantage.

I took another sip, put the glass down, and gazed vaguely ahead, chewing my lip as if deep in thought. That way, I'd avoid eye contact. Only two of the tables directly in front of me were now occupied. At one, three young men were slouched over an array of empty glasses and bottles; at the other, an old man in a battered black hat was gazing morosely into his drink, not taking the slightest interest in me. But somebody was. I could sense it. That unsettling feeling of being watched was, if anything, stronger.

With my elbow I nudged at a beer mat till it fell to the ground. I reached down to scrabble for it and as I slowly straightened up, studied the tables to my right. Nobody was looking in my direction.

Hrmm. The cough came from beside my left shoulder. As a shadow fell across the table, I was conscious of the stale smell given off by a chain-smoker's clothes. I swung round. My eyes focused on a pale-blue shirt with a thin red stripe, and flicked up to an all too familiar face and bushy moustache.

'Yes, *senhor*?' I said, my face betraying no sign of recognition. Would he follow my lead and permit me to remain under cover, under wraps?

An interminable pause, then he said slowly, '*Disculpe, senhora.* Excuse, please. I think you are someone I know.'

'Many people mistake me for my sister.' My smile was open and innocent.

'Ah.' He pulled out a chair and sat down. 'I am a friend of your sister. Perhaps you can tell me what she is doing now?' He put up a hand to stroke his moustache and hide his amusement.

I leant towards him, lowering my voice, though no one appeared to be taking any interest in us or in our conversation. 'She has a problem, *senhor*, a big problem. You see....'

Later, fully awake, I lay in bed gazing at the strips of moonlight slipping silently through the louvre bars onto the tiled floor. Dead to the world, Gorgonzola snored softly near my feet, twitching as she chased an elusive dessert through the shadowy banana jungle. *Would* Raimundo act on my tip-off? All the while that I'd been telling him about my visit to Câmara de Lobos, he'd puffed thoughtfully at one of those awful cigarettes and said nothing.

'... and so,' I'd finished, 'I'm certain that the courier will come some time today, before the market opens on Monday.'

He'd stood up. 'Tell your sister to take care,' he'd said and walked away without a backward glance.

I shifted restlessly under the thin cotton sheet, causing G to stir in protest. Could I count on him? Perhaps he'd feel it his duty to tell the *comandante* about my return.... Brain too active for sleep, I lay there watching the infinitesimal slide of the moonlight bars across the tiles.

CHAPTER NINETEEN

Twenty-four hours later, in the early hours of Monday morning, I was again watching the play of moonlight on shutters, but this time I was crouched in a derelict two-storey building just down the street from Gonçalves' flat. I'd gained entry to the building, as had others before me, by prising aside some loose boarding at a downstairs window. Trying not to breathe in the nose-wrinkling odour of stale urine and wet rot, I'd picked my way to the stairs through the assorted detritus such places attract – beer cans, bottles, syringes, discarded clothing. Now from my position at a window on the upper floor I had an angled view of the entrance to the block of flats opposite. As before, his scooter was parked by the rubbish bin.

Some time after midnight I'd watched Gonçalves weave his unsteady way home from the nearby bar. On Saturday night I'd seen him come out of the flats within an hour of my taking up surveillance, but this time I was having no luck. Unfortunately for me, he seemed to be sleeping the sleep of the unjust instead of puttering off on some nefarious business, giving me the opportunity to search his flat and maybe find something to implicate Dorothy Winterton. But as the minutes passed, it seemed increasingly unlikely that I'd be given this opportunity.

I eased myself into a more comfortable position, envying Gorgonzola, probably now stretched out on my bed after her nocturnal stalk through the banana plantation. Before I'd left I'd opened a tin, but she'd made it clear with a disparaging sniff at the bowl, that snack-on-the-hoof activated the taste buds more than snack-on-the-plate.

In the street outside nothing moved, not even a stray cat in the shadows. In Gonçalves' block of flats the windows were dark except for one where a faint glow behind thin curtains showed that someone apart from myself was still awake. Though to tell the truth, I wasn't fully awake: last night's lack of sleep was taking its toll. I'd lain in bed worrying most of the night and it hadn't solved a thing. I still didn't know what action Raimundo had taken over the drug stash at Câmara de Lobos. Or if a trap been set for the drug courier. Or if the *comandante* now knew of my presence in Madeira. I had a sudden depressing thought: Raimundo might have decided it would be more prudent to forget all about our meeting. What if...?

I woke to a flurry of rain against the window and the steady *drip* ... *drip* ... *drip* of water through a gaping hole in the lath and plaster ceiling. No helpful moonlight now to aid my surveillance of the dark street, just the yellow glow from the metal lamps fixed at fifty-yard intervals to the buildings. Between the faint pools of light everything was in deep shadow. One of the lamps illuminated the rubbish bin and the scooter still in position beside it. I heaved a sigh of relief. I hadn't missed him while I was asleep unless ... unless he'd gone off on foot. There was no way of telling. Oh well, I'd just have to—

I leant forward. A man was zigzagging unsteadily from one pool of light to another, a sailing ship battered by squalls, tacking to harbour. His woollen Madeiran hat was pulled low, practical earflaps down as protection against the driving rain, internal warmth supplied by the contents of a bottle that glinted as he lifted it to his lips. Idly I watched him weave his way to the doorway of the flats, bounce off the jamb on his first attempt to negotiate the entrance and stand there, swaying gently as he negotiated his key into the lock. He lurched inside and I settled back to my boring vigil....

For the second time I lost the battle against sleep.... It was the sound of an engine stuttering into life and the receding high-pitched buzz of a two-stroke speeding away that jolted me awake. Rubbing my eyes and yawning, I knelt and peered through the grimy glass. There was an empty space beside the rubbish bin where Gonçalves' scooter had been parked. Now was my chance. I got stiffly to my feet and made my way down the stairs and out into the street.

In the doorway of Gonçalves' block of flats out came my latex gloves, a second-nature precautionary measure against those incriminating fingerprints. All I had to do now was find the right apartment. A metal grid hanging by one screw on the jamb had, in more prosperous days, held the names of the householders, but now any names in the spaces were defaced and illegible. I wasn't too worried. Gonçalves' name would be on his door to avoid the disaster of an illicit consignment being delivered to a neighbour. With the picklock I had less trouble gaining entrance to the flats than the man in the Madeiran hat, and moments later I was walking towards the stairs. My pencil torch shone on peeling walls of an indeterminate colour and a stained and littered passageway. The wet footprints of the drunk in the Madeiran hat petered out as I climbed. I didn't stumble over his prostrate body, so he'd obviously made it to wherever he was going.

It was on the second floor that the narrow beam picked out Gonçalves' name scrawled on a torn piece of card taped to a door surprisingly strong and in good repair compared with the others I'd passed. This door with its intricate mechanism designed to safeguard the secrets of a professional took me considerably longer. But at last, *click*. The picklock worked its magic and the final lever yielded.

I pushed open the heavy door – and immediately wished I hadn't. I don't know what I'd expected to see, but it certainly wasn't Gonçalves' dead body pinned to the kitchen table by a traditional Madeiran half metre-long meat skewer. He was staring up into the harsh light of the bare overhead bulb, eyes and mouth wide in a ghastly re-enactment of Munch's *Scream*.

I swallowed hard, took a deep breath, and stepped forward. The blow to his throat had been delivered with such force that the point of the triangular steel rod had embedded itself deep in the table. Blood had spurted from the wound onto the floor. How long had he been dead? Tentatively I touched the back of the hand dangling limply on my side of the table. Still warm.

I dragged my eyes away. Dominating the room in stark contrast to the cheap kitchen chairs, grimy bed coverings, blackened pot and frying pan on the tiny stove, was the latest in home cinemas, sound muted to a whisper. On the screen a distraught blonde cringed in terror as two men slashed viciously at each other with knives. In front of the screen a comfortably upholstered black leather and chrome chair lay on its back, the only sign that Gonçalves had put up any kind of a fight. He must have known his assailant. Wary of visitors, he wouldn't have opened the door to an unknown. And by dozing off twice during my two-hour vigil, I'd missed not only the murderer's arrival, but his departure. I realized now that was what had wakened me – the revving engine as the murderer made his getaway on Gonçalves' scooter.

The slam of car doors in the street outside brought home how incriminating it would be if I was found here, standing on bloodstained floorboards beside the body of a man who'd just been brutally murdered. That *would* take a lot of explaining away. I turned and made for the door.

BAM BAM BAM. The thick panels trembled under a violent pounding.

'Police! We know you're in there, Gonçalves. Open up!'

BAM BAM BAM.

Rooted to the spot, struck dumb, heart in mouth – clichés, I know, but an all too apt description of the physical state of DJ Smith, HM Revenue & Customs.

BAM BAM BAM.

'Open up, you bastard, or we'll shoot off these fancy door locks.'

I took a deep breath, and with a hand that shook, took hold of the key and turned it.

'Sso-o, Sshmit.' The *comandante* spread her long fingers on the polished desktop and studied her nails, for this occasion painted execution-black. 'Let us go over your story once again. Do not leave anything out.'

Standard police procedure. When suspects retell their story many times, if they have something to hide, the chances are they will trip themselves up. Interrogators are on the lookout for any inconsistencies, any vital detail that might differ, something on which they can pounce.

With a sigh, I launched yet again into my account, '... and in the two hours I was watching the flat, *nobody* went in, except, of course, the drunken neighbour who—'

With a sudden flash of insight, I realized I'd *seen* the murderer. The man in the Madeiran hat. That drunk was fumbling not with keys, but with picklocks at the entrance to the flats; those footprints, still wet, on the stair were those of the murderer. But there was only my word for it that he even existed.

The *comandante* took a closer interest in her nails. 'This drunk, Sshmit, you are thinking of telling me that this man is the murderer? This is very convenient for you that such a person comes along to pull you off the hook, is it not?'

I had to admit that his appearance on the scene *did* seem rather too opportune, too neat a means of shifting the blame off myself.

'*If* this person exists,' – her tone conveyed that this was most unlikely – 'you will, of course, be able to give me a description of him.'

'Well, no, I can't, *Comandante*. You see, it was dark, it was raining and—'

She slapped the flat of her hand hard on the desk, startling me. In their vase, as one, the phalanx of strelitzias swung sharp beaks in my direction, marksmen lining me up in their sights.

'Enough, Sshmit! Is this the only street in Funchal that does not have lights?'

'Street lights do not penetrate the sideflaps of a woollen Madeiran hat,' I said wearily. Why didn't they just get it over with and charge me? I'd had little sleep in the past twenty-four hours and I was past caring.

Comandante Figueira's perfect teeth smiled the smile of a cat that has just finished playing with a mouse. 'At last, Sshmit, you have given me the helpful answer.' From the top drawer of her desk she produced a clear plastic evidence bag beaded with moisture. It contained a Madeiran woollen cap.

'That, my dear Sshmit, was found under the leather chair lying in front of the television. How did it get there?' She tilted her head back and gazed thoughtfully at the ceiling. 'Gonçalves leaps up when he sees the intruder. The assailant forces Gonçalves towards the table. They struggle. The hat falls … the chair falls…. Then comes the blow that kills.' She switched her gaze to me, and her eyes narrowed. '*You*, of course, could have been wearing the hat, as a disguise. It could have been *your* hand that delivered the fatal blow.' She paused. The silence lengthened.

Indeed, I could very well be guilty. And looking at it dispassionately, I had little chance of proving otherwise. The evidence against me was pretty damning: I'd been found in the room with a man who had just been killed, the door locked from the inside. I'd been wearing gloves….

'Yes, we have considered this. And' – she let me squirm for a few moments longer – 'we have evidence that the murderer is someone other than yourself. We found in the blood the mark of a shoe. We compare it with your shoe, and it is not the same.'

So that's the reason they'd taken away my boots. I stared at her. The *bastards*. 'You mean,' I snapped, 'you subjected me to this pantomime of an interrogation when you *knew* I was innocent?'

A flash of white teeth. 'Innocent? Not entirely innocent, I think. Your hand was not the hand that drove the *espetata* skewer through the neck of the unfortunate Senhor Gonçalves, that is true. But *why*, Sshmit, was someone given the order to kill him? We must ask ourselves that, must we not?'

It sounded as if she already knew the answer. And after a moment, so did I. Raimundo *had* passed on my tip-off to Comandante Figueira, and the raid on the fish market had signed Gonçalves' death warrant. Gangland killings had a language of their own: he had been killed in a way that would be a warning to other informers.

'I see that you understand me, Sshmit.' She nodded in satisfaction. 'That fleabag Gonçalves, who is no longer troubling us, was just the small fish. The next question is ... now that we have the evidence against her, how do we close the trap on the big fish Winterton?'

'Evidence? Winterton?' I said, stunned.

The Comandante seemed to be taking more than a little satisfaction from my astonishment. 'Officer Ribiero, who like you, causes me much trouble, yes much trouble....' She paused for a long moment, gaze unfocused as she mentally reviewed Raimundo's past misdemeanours. '... has for once done something right. Yesterday, he has the clever thought. He looks again at the CCTV tape taken ten days ago showing the woman with Gonçalves in the Massaroco gardens, and he notes the meeting was in the early morning. He thinks to himself, Ribiero, someone stole the camera on Sunday morning because there has been another meeting between the woman and Gonçalves. Then he looks at the Sunday morning tape on camera two which is covering another area of the grounds, and he sees another person who is out so early. Someone who is running for the exercise.'

'Jogging,' I said. *Could* it be Zara in Kinsey Millhone mode?

The *comandante* was riffling through a file of papers. 'Officer Ribiero thinks this person may have seen a meeting with Gonçalves and this mystery woman in the bathrobe, so he goes to the hotel and finds out who is running in the morning for the exercise, questions her and brings her here to make the statement.' She selected one of the papers and studied it briefly. 'And this person, it seems, is the same Senhora Porter-Browne who in the Caves of São Vicente prevented you from drowning.' She ran her eye down the page. 'I read you the impor-tant bit. She states, "Every morning I run round the hotel gardens. On Sunday morning I was finishing my run when I spotted old bag Winterton skulking in the bushes with a man. Got to give it to her, didn't think she had it in her. The grumpy old bat is never up that early. Kinsey Millhone would have gone on running as if she saw nothing, and doubled back through the bushes, so that is what I did".'

She looked up, frowned. 'I understand, Sshmit, that these words "bag" and "bat" indicate that the *senhora* does not have a great respect for the suspect Winterton, but perhaps you can explain who is this person Kinsey Millhone to whom she refers?'

'Senhora Porter-Browne,' I said with a smile, 'reads many crime novels, and Millhone is one of the detectives she much admires.'

'Aah, like Sherlock Holmes,' she nodded and continued reading. '"Those big flowery bushes made good cover, so I got quite close. Might have known her taste in men was the pits. This guy had weird pointy ears, and a big baldy patch. Gave me the creeps. I heard her say something about Monday and she handed him a stash of notes. Well, someone like her would have to pay for sex, wouldn't they?" '

The *comandante* gazed thoughtfully at me. 'The *senhora* identified Gonçalves from the photo in our files. At last, Sshmit, we have the evidence of a business arrangement between Winterton and the most unlamented Gonçalves. So, as I said, the next question is ... now that we have the evidence against her, how do we close the trap on the big fish, Winterton?'

It sounded as if she already knew the answer to that one. And something told me that, whatever I was about to hear, I wasn't going to like it.

She pinned me to my seat with her piercing stare. 'My dear Sshmit, I tell you what you must do. You must frighten this Haxby and Winterton. Yes, you must arrange that they will take actions that will lead to their arrest. How this is done, I leave to you.' The two neat rows of perfectly matched teeth smiled their crocodile smile.

My first thought when I left the *comandante* was to go off in search of Raimundo. I drew a blank. He was nowhere to be found – not behind the public counter stabbing fitfully at the keyboard, nor tinkering with his car in the police yard. My enquiries were met with a shrug, expressive of 'Ribiero? Who knows?' I scribbled a congratulatory note and left it propped up against the computer.

Easel set up on the tiny terrace overlooking the terracotta rooftops on the far side of the harbour, floppy yellow sun hat pulled low over her eyes, blue and green artist smock flapping in the light breeze, Celia Haxby was giving her undivided attention to painting the scene before her. Unnoticed, I crept up and peered over her shoulder. Pinned to the easel was a small postcard depicting one of Winston Churchill's oil paintings of Câmara de Lobos.

'Thought I'd find you here, Celia.'

She looked up, in her expression surprise – and something else. 'You're back!'

'Mmm.' I made a show of studying the painting. 'Copying Sir Winston, eh? Pretty good, Celia. If *his* signature was on it, it would sell for thousands.'

'Oh!' The loaded brush shot across the paper trailing green in its wake. She was rattled, just as I'd intended.

'Dear, dear, dear! Will you be able to … er, fix it?' I whipped out a tissue and dabbed frantically. The resultant green smudges were much more disfiguring than the original thin streak.

'Bloody hell!' She snatched the canvas off the easel and flung it on the ground. 'Don't you know better than to sneak up on an artist when a work's in progress?'

'What a shame! I'm so sorry,' I said with feigned concern. After a moment's silence in memory of the spoiled masterpiece, I said cheerfully, 'I was looking for you to give you the good news. Starting from tomorrow, my office hour in the Massaroco will be back to normal.'

This was not greeted with any detectable enthusiasm.

'Humph.' She turned away and snatched up brushes and paint tubes. 'It's no use me continuing with this. Too late in the day now to capture these colours. Light's going.'

'Well,' I said sunnily, 'must be off. Better luck tomorrow, eh? Might pop along to see how you're getting on.'

She surged to her feet, thunderous scowl signalling, 'I bloody well hope not.'

I sauntered back to my car, well-satisfied with that little performance. So far, the *comandante*'s master-plan was going well. Next on my list was Dorothy Winterton. But that part of the plan would be put into operation after I'd given Celia time to contact her with the unwelcome news of my return.

So with time on my hands, when I arrived at the Massaroco I went in search of Zara. When she wasn't in any of her usual haunts – sitting on a high stool in the café bar, swimming in the pool, or lying stretched out on a sunbed, I asked reception to call her room, but there was no reply.

I was standing at the desk gazing around, when a young woman came through the swing doors to the foyer, a bulky carrier bag in each hand. It took a couple of seconds for me register that it was Zara: short brown hair, clothes casual but not outrageously trendy, nothing about her that would immediately catch the eye.

She caught sight of me and hurried across. 'Didn't expect to see you so soon, Debs!'

'Just got back.' I studied her for a moment. 'What's with the new image, then?'

She giggled. 'That's the point – merge with the crowd. Kinsey and Stephanie couldn't carry out their investigations if they drew attention to themselves.' She put down the carrier bags, flexing her fingers to restore the circulation. 'These are a ton weight. I've legged it all the way from the English Book Shop and frankly, I'm bushed.'

'Looks as if you've brought the shop with you.' I stooped to peer into the bags. 'Are these *all* Grafton and Evanovich books?'

'Yep. I'm going to make an in-depth study of Kinsey and Stephanie's methods and then....' She slipped her hand into her shirt pocket and pulled out a white business card. 'I've had these printed out. What do you think?'

I stared at the card, trying desperately to think of something tactful to say.

ZARA PORTER-BROWNE INVESTIGATIONS
Worried? Suspicious? Why not put your mind at rest?
Discreet, resourceful. No case too small.
Undercover Work a Speciality

I pride myself on coming up with the right words in the trickiest of situations, but this time I was at a loss for words. I could only stutter, 'Well, it's ... it's ...'

She didn't give me time to finish. 'But you'll never guess what's happened!' Her eyes gleamed with excitement. 'Just wait till I tell you— Oh, no!' She clapped a hand to her mouth. 'I've been sworn to secrecy, mustn't say a thing.' She put her mouth close to my ear and hissed, 'Winterton's in trouble with the police! *Sex!*'

'But—' I gasped.

'They said no one staying at the hotel was to know, so telling *you* doesn't count, does it?' She grabbed hold of my arm. 'Come up to my room and I'll dish you the dirt.'

*

I found Dorothy on the terrace, sitting at one of the tables beside a magnificent flowering plant in a tub. From its huge white trumpets the sweet scent of honey drifted towards me in the warm twilight. I wandered casually towards her.

'Hello, Dorothy, I hoped I'd find you here.'

She placed a finger in her book to mark the place and peered at me over the top of her spectacles.

'So you're back, Deborah. Well, this *is* a surprise.'

I had the strong impression that it was no surprise at all. I smiled a guileless smile. 'I've just popped by to put up my office hour notice. I'll be here on the terrace tomorrow to make up for the days I've missed, so if there's something you want me to arrange before you go home next week....'

With a murmured, 'I can't think of anything at the moment', she picked up her book, plainly signalling that the conversation was at an end.

'Well, if anything comes up and you've missed me, my mobile number's on the noticeboard.'

As I wandered down the steps of the terrace onto the lawn, she called after me, 'I'll let Celia know you're back.'

Good try, Dorothy, but I was convinced that a panic phone call from Celia had already alerted her to my unwelcome return.

Screened by a bed of purple massaroco, I fished in my shirt pocket for the ultrasonic whistle and summoned G from the bushes where I'd left her. *Rustle rustle.* She slipped out from under an overhanging branch to twine herself round my legs. Large copper eyes looked up at me enquiringly.

I put my hand on her working collar and pointed up at the terrace. 'Search, G.'

Purring softly she walked daintily up the steps, tail erect and twitching in anticipation of a challenge.

On several occasions I'd seen Winterton petting the hotel cat, so I knew she wasn't one of those people with a cat phobia. If, as I suspected, Winterton knew about the sniffer cat that had detected drugs in the Gomes suitcase, the sudden appearance of G should in itself ruffle her composure. And that was the whole purpose of my visit here tonight. I waited.

Silence. Then from the terrace above came a sharp, '*Shoo!* Get away!' The scrape of a chair being pushed back was followed by a small scream and an angry, 'Go away, damn you!'

Fatally attractive words to a cat, as cat phobes all too often find out. Cats seem to take a perverse delight in pressing themselves upon someone who dislikes their presence. Such fussing and flapping would only add to G's entertainment.

'Stop it! Stop that *now*, I say!'

I smiled in satisfaction.

I heard the metallic clatter of a chair toppling over, then sounds of hurried departure. A blast of the sonic whistle brought G leaping down from the terrace. I gathered her up into my arms.

'Mission accomplished, G.' I murmured. 'You haven't detected any drugs, but I've got the result I wanted.' All I could do now was wait.

It was after nine o'clock before G and I were strolling through the little banana plantation to my studio apartment. After all this activity both of us were starving, so as soon as G was wolfing down her bowl of tuna, I headed for the little bar on the corner and ordered a pepperoni pizza and bottle of Coral lager to celebrate getting off a murder charge after being discovered in a locked room with a newly dead corpse. I sat at a table mulling over the other successes of the day … those engineered encounters with Haxby and Winterton had gone well. I plunged my knife into the soft crust of the pizza.

I reacted instinctively to the soft footfall behind me. I threw myself sideways onto the floor, sending the chair toppling. Raimundo was looking down at me.

He helped me up. 'It is not the requirement to throw yourself at my feet, *senhora*, even though I am Policeman of the Week.'

To the barman craning from behind the counter I waved and called an embarrassed, '*Disculpe, senhor*. When I leant down to pick up the napkin, I fell off the chair. Bring another plate for my friend and another Coral lager.'

'Well, Policeman of the Week,' I said, as I slid half the pizza onto his plate, 'Comandante Figueira told me she is very happy.'

'Ah.' A heavy sigh. 'But I, Raimundo Paulo Ribiero, am not happy.'

'*No?*'

'No, *senhora*. She says to me "Ribiero, you have done well. I think you make good detective. So next week I move you from traffic department." And she smiled that smile. But I want to stay free, go where I like.' His shoulders drooped. 'What can I do, *senhora*?'

'Comandante Figuera says this because she is pleased with you.' I chewed thoughtfully on my pizza. 'What you must do is make her not pleased.'

Smiling, we clinked glasses to the Big Foul-Up.

Later, I sat in my little patio-courtyard at the lime-green table with Gorgonzola on my lap, listening to the sounds of the night.

'I did try, G, to wriggle out of us being the bait in the *comandante*'s little scheme. I said to her "But how can I go anywhere near the Massaroco, *Comandante*? David Grant will there. He'll call the police as soon as he sets eyes on me." That should have done the trick, shouldn't it?'

But it hadn't. This had been met with an airy wave of the hand and 'Don't worry about the Exotic Cut Flower Exporter, my dear Sshmit. The agents from CITES raided his orchid farm this morning. The *senhor* is even now being interrogated about the prohibited plants they found in his laboratory.'

I stroked G's back. 'I have to admit, G, that the *comandante*'s master plan has gone smoothly enough so far. Between us we've certainly rattled Winterton and Haxby, but what's worrying me is what they're going to do now.' I watched her claws gently sheathe and unsheathe. 'Comandante Figueira's quite unscrupulous, you know. She's staked us out like the tethered goat for the tiger hunter, hasn't she?'

I tickled Gorgonzola behind the ears. My fingers slowed as I contemplated the likely fate of the goat.

I picked Gorgonzola up and held her tight. 'We'll have to be *very* careful, G, *very* careful indeed.'

was halfway through breakfast the next morning when the call came to my mobile.

'Senhora Smith? I am Elizabete Teixeira, assistant to *veterinário Senhor* Artur Spinosa.'

'Yes?' I was puzzled. It had been more than two weeks since I'd collected G from the vet. She seemed to have completely recovered from the attempted poisoning. Why would he be contacting me now?

'You will remember, *senhora*, that when the cat was here we made the test of the blood. The results have just come, and … er … I do not wish to cause the anxiety, *senhora*, but there is a worry with the blood count.'

I looked down at G who was vigorously rasping her tongue over her coat in her post-breakfast wash and brush up. She sensed my eyes on her and paused for a moment before resuming. Could there really be something wrong with her, something *seriously* wrong?

Heart racing, I said, 'I'm sorry. I don't quite understand. You tell me that Senhor Sousa thinks that Gorgonzola is *ill?*'

'Senhor Sousa says you must bring the cat to him as a matter of urgency. He can see you in half an hour.'

'But what is wrong? Can I speak to the *senhor?*'

'A moment, *senhora.*'

Crackle crackle. Infuriatingly, the line started to break up. Senhor Spinosa's voice was very faint. '… blood count …' *crackle crackle* '… dangerously low for …' *crackle crackle* … I could make out only the occasional word. Then the line went dead.

Breakfast forgotten, I rushed over to where G was settling herself in a patch of sun. I scooped her up. Her eyes were bright and clear with no sign of the extra eyelid, that indicator of ill health in a cat. But if Senhor Spinosa was worried….

I put G down, and with shaking hands retrieved the cat-carrier from under the bed. Abandoning the usual prolonged niceties needed to persuade her into the hated box, I made a grab and stuffed her in before she had time to utter more than an astonished squeak.

'Sorry, G. Emergency.'

Ignoring G's outraged mini-yowls, I rushed out to the car, placed the carrier on the floor, and sat behind the wheel for a few minutes trying to calm myself. The carrier was quivering and juddering as she threw herself against its sides. Taking comfort from the fact that she wasn't behaving as one at death's door, I turned the key in the ignition and eased my way out into the stream of traffic on the Estrada Monumental.

There are not many traffic lights in Funchal, but every single one was at red. The wait at each seemed interminable. Progress was slowed further by narrow side streets obstructed with parked vehicles. Nevertheless, nerves shredded, within the half hour stipulated by Senhor Spinosa I was just a street away from the vet.

'Fingers crossed for a space near the surgery, G,' I muttered. 'Hold on in there. We'll soon have you in Senhor Artur's expert care.'

I glanced down at the cat-carrier. Her furious face stared at me through the grid. She didn't look as if she wanted care, expert or otherwise. What she wanted was OUT. O-U-T accompanied by abject apologies and succulent snacks in recompense for that rough and unceremonious bundling into the box.

My two previous visits had been by taxi so I hadn't then had the worry of seeking out a parking place. As I turned the final corner, I could see that the street was lined with vehicles on both sides. I cruised slowly up the street. At the end I turned and drove slowly back.

I'd just decided to double park and risk being towed away, when I spotted a movement in the line of cars as a small van began to nose its way out. I held back till it had completed its manoeuvre, then with a sigh of relief, swung into the vacated space. It only took a moment to go round the car, open the passenger door and pick up the cat-carrier.

I started across the pavement towards the surgery door. Closing my ears to G's piteous yowls and sobs, artfully designed to rend the heart and embarrass me in front of any passer-by, I quickened my step.

Thump. I felt a violent blow between my shoulder blades. The cat-carrier was snatched from my hand and I was sent sprawling on the pavement. In a way, the thugs did me a favour. With both hands empty, I could break my fall and prevent my face smashing into the concrete.

Winded and shocked, I groggily turned my head. A boot swung to target me full in the face. I rolled on my side and made a frantic grab. It was enough to deflect the full force of the attack. Off balance, my assailant staggered. At a shout of 'Leave it!' from the white van standing in the middle of the road, engine revving and rear door open, he abandoned the attack and flung himself into the already moving vehicle. With a roar and a scream of tyres it shot off down the street.

Shakily I got to my knees and stared after it. The cat-carrier had gone. And with it Gorgonzola.

From down the hill, a blare of horns marked the getaway route.

A woman's voice enquired, 'The *senhora* is hurt?'

I looked up to see a ring of concerned faces gazing down at me. Amid a babble of excited voices, someone helped me to my feet. Blood was trickling from a cut on my cheek, my right knee was throbbing where it had made contact with the pavement and both hands were grazed and bleeding.

'I'm all right,' I lied. 'I must speak with the *veterinário*.'

Somebody must have summoned him from his surgery, for by the time I gathered myself together enough to limp the short distance across the pavement, Senhor Spinosa and his assistant were hurrying towards me.

'My dear Senhora Smith, what has happened? What are you doing here? Is your cat ill?'

The surprise in his voice made it all clear. The phone call had been a ruse to lure me to the ambush. Whoever was behind it had made sure I'd be in the right place at the right time.

And I'd fallen into the trap.

For a moment I could only stare at him, close to tears. I swallowed hard.

'You didn't telephone me to bring in Gorgonzola for the results of a blood test, did you?' I knew the answer before he shook his head. 'Would you be good enough to call the police, *senhor*? G-Gorgonzola's been … stolen.' The quiver in my voice was embarrassingly obvious.

'What we must ask ourselves, my dear Sshmit, is why this thing was done.'

Justinia Figueira leant back in her chair and studied the ceiling as if seeking the answer from the large black spider crouched in the centre of the web anchored between the light flex and the cheap plastic shade.

Its thought transfer rate must have been markedly sluggish, for minutes passed and she continued to stare fixedly at the ceiling. Her eyelids slowly closed. A soft *p ... p ...* escaped from her slightly parted lips, the sound of someone sinking into slumber.

Action! I wanted, I *needed*, action! Every second counted. I couldn't bear to think about what could be happening to Gorgonzola. I was convinced that Winterton had master-minded the snatch, and while the *comandante* took a leisurely post-lunch nap, the gang might be—

And I was doing *nothing* about it. *Nobody* was doing *anything* about it. I found myself standing in front of the desk gripping the vase of strelitzias with the intention of hurling to the floor these aloof symbols of Justinia Figuiera's indifference.

Her eyes snapped open, and closed again. My flushed face, white knuckles, and rapid breathing had not seemed to register. What *would* it take to get some action, *any* action, from this woman of stone? I took a deep breath and raised the vase high above my head, ready to hurl it to the ground with a bloodcurdling scream.

Her eyes remained closed. Her lips moved.

'Calm yourself, my dear Sshmit. The cat is in no immediate danger. It is obvious that they have taken the scruffy creature to use for the bargaining. We must wait. Yes, what we must do is wait.' She settled herself into a more comfortable position in the high leather back chair.

With hands that trembled I set the vase down, spilling drops of water onto the polished desktop. I collapsed onto the hard chair reserved for interviewees, took a deep breath and thought about what she had said.

In Dorothy Winterton's eyes the main threat came from myself – so why had *I* not been the main target outside the vet's? There'd already been several attempts to eliminate me, so why had they held back on this occasion? With the seizure of the shipment of drugs at Câmara de Lobos, it was clear that the police net was closing in. Just how close, must have been plain to Winterton when I'd set Gorgonzola to sniff out her handbag on the terrace of the Massaroco. I tried to put myself in her shoes.... Top priority for her now must be how to make her escape from Madeira. With the authorities on the alert, the obvious air or sea routes were closed – unless.... Yes, the *comandante*'s words made sense. Gorgonzola was being used as a bargaining tool.

I gazed up at the ceiling. The spider was testing the strength of its web, plucking at the filaments with the sureness and practised delicacy of a concert harpist. Satisfied, trap set, it stretched out motionless once more. I put my mobile on the desk and, like the *comandante*, settled down to wait.

The call came an hour later, by which time, they hoped, my fears for G's safety would have made me desperate. And that wasn't far from the truth, I have to admit. I snatched up my phone.

The *comandante* shot upright in her chair. 'A moment, Sshmit.' She leant forward, deftly extricated the mobile from my hand and studied the display. 'This number shows that the call comes from a public phone box. It is unlikely to be genuine, one of your Agência clients. We will not answer it. We play the waiting game, and this time it is *they* who must wait.' Keeping a firm grip on the mobile, she settled back in her chair and closed her eyes.

Short of committing an assault on her person, there was nothing I could do. I count myself an old hand at the waiting game, something of an expert in fact. In my line of work I've often had to sit hour after hour in a vehicle, or less comfortably, lie flat on my stomach under a bush, waiting patiently until someone made a move. I have some well-tried ways of passing the time – but none of them worked for me now. I sat on that hard chair and the leaden minutes dragged on. Above me the spider hung motionless in the centre of its web. It too was waiting.

At midday the *comandante* stirred. 'I do not think it will be long now, Sshmit. We must hope that this time they speak on their mobile phone. In exchange for the animal, they will ask for something. You will say that it is necessary to have the time to do this, so they must call again in an hour. Then we strike.'

I nodded. Phone network technology can use a mobile's signal to locate its position very accurately. Meanwhile it was back to waiting. I tried in vain to find a comfortable position on the hard chair.

A fat bluebottle made a noisy entrance through the open window. Idly I followed its progress round the room. Several circuits of the ceiling later, it blundered into the carefully laid ambush of the spider's trap. The web master stirred, then having identified a prey, darted across to clasp its victim in a deadly embrace. But the outcome was no neatly trussed victim, only a gaping hole and a web in tatters – a timely reminder to me not to take anything for granted. The *comandante*'s carefully constructed plans might very well fall apart. And the consequences for G ... I didn't want to think about it.

I tried to shut out my dark thoughts by staring at the shadowy shapes of flower stems in the blue vase on the desk. At that moment the call came to the mobile. The *comandante* sat up, studied the incoming call number and nodded in satisfaction.

'It is from mobile, not from public call box. Of course, we can only track her while her phone is switched on. We need to know where she is when the call is ended. So, Sshmit, you must say you will phone her when you have done what she asks.' She scribbled the incoming number on her pad and handed me the phone.

I took the call. 'Yes?' The tremor in my voice was not an act.

'I presume I am speaking to Deborah Smith?' It was unmistakably the voice of Dorothy Winterton, but hard and authoritative, totally unlike the familiar timid delivery of the elderly widow, avid partaker of the Massaroco's afternoon teas.

'Yes. I-I believe that you have my cat—' I caught the *comandante*'s eye. She nodded her approval. The break in my voice was calculated to convey that I would do anything to get G back – including helping Winterton escape arrest. I pushed away the uncomfortable thought that perhaps this was the truth.

'Listen carefully, Smith, if you want to see the brute again. *Alive*, that is....' The long pause that followed was designed to play on my nerves, as of course, it did.

When I glanced over at the *comandante*, she was talking quietly on her own line, setting up the trace. Whatever I said would have to ensure that Dorothy Winterton kept her phone switched on in expectation of a return call confirming that the authorities were meeting her demands. Could I manage it without rousing her suspicions?

My audible gulp broke the silence. 'Wha-what do I have to do? I take it there's going to be a trade-off?'

Winterton appeared to ignore the question. '*Such* a well-fed cat,' she mused, her voice silky. 'Accustomed to two good meals a day, I'm sure.' Another pause, then, 'I don't have to spell it out, do I? You're an intelligent woman.'

Across the desk, the *comandante* opened and closed fingers and thumb in a 'keep her talking' signal.

I waited as long as I dared before replying. 'I-I don't know what you mean.'

'Well then, let me ask you a question, my dear. Did your cat have a good breakfast this morning? With perhaps a nice little drink of milk or water, eh?'

'Ye-es,' I stammered. 'But, but—' I sensed what was coming.

'I believe I read somewhere that a cat can survive without food for an amazingly long time – now, how many days was it? I really can't remember off hand, but let's say thirty. Without water, of course, that will be *quite* another matter. Survival time will be *considerably* reduced.' Her voice hardened. 'Shall we find out, Ms Smith?'

I ran my tongue over dry lips. I thought of G, a desiccated bundle of bones, too weak to raise her head.... Hour after hour she'd lie there, trusting that I'd come—

'No, no,' I burst out. 'I'll do anything, *anything*.' And I meant it.

The *comandante* looked up sharply.

Dorothy Winterton's quiet laugh was unnerving. 'I see that you understand me. So kind of you to supply the cat-carrier, by the way. It will fit most snugly into the place I have in mind. And there'll be no chance, no chance at all, of the beast clawing its way out.'

'Just tell me, tell me what you want me to do, and I'll—'

The *comandante* gave a satisfied thumbs-up sign as she replaced her receiver on its rest. The mobile had been traced.

Dorothy Winterton's tone was briskly businesslike. 'What I intend, my dear, is to be on the flight that leaves for South America tonight. A ticket, one-way, of course, to be left for me at the desk. *When* I reach my destination, and only then, will I tell you where the cat's hidden.'

I played for time. 'You're asking a lot.'

'A word of warning, Ms Deborah Smith, or whatever your real name is. You do realize, don't you, that the authorities will set more store on arresting me than rescuing that scruffy animal? Do I make myself perfectly clear? No amount of police questioning will make me reveal the location of the cat. If you inform the police, you can say goodbye to Ginger.'

I drew in a deep breath. 'I've no choice, have I? I'll phone you when I've set it up. But if I leave a ticket at the airport, and you catch the flight, how do I know you'll make that phone call?'

There was no reply.

'Hello? Are you still there?'

Silence. *Call ended* came up on the display.

The *comandante* raised a perfectly shaped eyebrow. 'So, Sshmit, let me guess. Provided that we do not arrest her at the airport, she will tell you where she has hidden the cat, yes?'

I nodded, not trusting myself to speak.

'Câmara de Lobos ...' she said slowly. 'At the moment that is where the signal it is coming from. But if Winterton switches off the phone we can no longer locate her.' Thoughtfully she tap-tapped a glossy fingernail on her notepad. 'Or ... perhaps this very clever woman knows that the phone signals her location, gives it to another person to mislead us and vanishes into the air – like that!' She flicked a hand in an airy gesture signifying a dematerializing Dorothy Winterton. 'We cannot allow this woman to slip through the fingers. No, this we cannot do.' Her eyes refused to meet mine.

I knew why. Dorothy Winterton's words were echoing in my head. *'You do realize, don't you, that the authorities will set more store on arresting me than rescuing that scruffy animal?'*

Justinia Figueira stared at a point above my head. 'What we must consider most carefully is tactics, my dear Sshmit. There is only one place where we can be one hundred per cent sure that we will find this Winterton, and that is at the airport. Yes, she will walk up to collect her ticket. And then we close the net.' On the notepad one black nail beat a slow funerary march for G.

There was one chance, one slim chance left to save G and it depended on me getting hold of Raimundo. I'd caught a glimpse of him in the office as I'd rushed into Police HQ after she'd been snatched. Please, *please*, let him still be on duty. I ran along the corridor, my heart pounding. As I neared the entrance hall with its public benches, I made myself slow to a brisk walk. I mustn't draw attention to myself, mustn't let the fact that I'd sought him out get back to the *comandante*.

There behind the desk was that unmistakably moustached figure. I let my breath out in a long sigh of relief. He didn't acknowledge my presence. Eyes down, finger hovering in search of the correct key, he was engaged in his usual battle with the computer. I leant over the desk to bring my head close to his.

'Raimundo, I must speak to you,' I whispered.

'Moment, *senhora*.' A nicotine-stained finger stabbed down on a key.

'G-Gorgonzola's been–been—'

A sob choked off the rest the sentence. To my dismay a tear trickled down the side of my nose and dropped onto the back of his hand.

His finger froze on the key sending jjjjjjjjjjjjjjjjjjjjjjjjjjjjjjjjjjjjjjjjjjjjjjjjjjj zipping across the screen. For a moment he stared mesmerized at the display as the line marched on. jjjjjjjjjjjjjjjjjjjjjjjjjjjjjjjjjjjjjjjjjjjjjjjjjjjjjjjjjjjjjjjjjjjjj.

213

'*Merda!*' He snatched his hand away, and looked up at me. My brimming eyes and flushed face brought him to his feet. 'Something bad has happened, *senhora?*'

I managed to stutter out, 'I need your help. The *comandante* intends to – intends to—' I couldn't go on.

Fortunately he made no attempt to put a comforting arm round my shoulders – sympathy would have rendered me a blubbering wreck – but motioned me round the desk and led the way to the inner office, giving me the chance to pull myself together.

'Tell me, *senhora*,' he said.

And I did. As I poured out my story, it was impossible to tell from his expression what his reaction was going to be. I finished. Without saying a word he went over and closed the door to the outer office.

A tiny spark of hope flared as he said, 'What do you want me to do, *senhora?*'

'Five minutes ago the mobile phone trace showed that Winterton was in Câmara de Lobos. She's an old woman, Raimundo, out of touch with modern technology, and might not realize that her location has been tracked by her mobile phone. So if she remains where she is until it is time for her to go to the airport.... And if I drive over there right now and—'

'But, *senhora*, she may be gone. Already she may have—'

'That's what I'm afraid of, and that's why I need your help. You're my only chance of getting back Gorgonzola.' I brushed away a tear.

For what seemed an age he took a deep interest in the scuffed tiles on the floor, tracing the grout lines with the toe of his boot. At last he looked up. 'The signal is still being traced?'

I took a deep breath to steady my voice. 'Yes, and what I need to know is if the signal moves away from Câmara de Lobos.'

'I understand, *senhora*. But if Comandante Figueira discovers—' He slashed a finger across his throat.

He was right. I was asking too much. Why should he put his career on the line for the sake of a cat?

The spark of hope flickered and died. I shouldn't have asked. I turned away. 'It's all right, Raimundo. Don't worry about it.'

I wasn't going to give up while there was still a chance. It would take me about twenty minutes to reach Câmara de Lobos. Dorothy Winterton *might* still be hiding out in one of the picturesque little houses of the sleepy fishing village.

I had my hand on the door when he said softly, '*Un momento, senhora*. The Ogre, she does not know everything. When I contact you, nothing has to be spoken.' A smile lurked under the moustache as he pulled his mobile out of his pocket. 'No one hears if I *text* you the position of the Winterton. And if Figueira does find out....' He shrugged.

I was lucky. The traffic on the outskirts of Funchal was lighter than usual – that, and putting my foot down at every opportunity, brought me to Câmara de Lobos in only fifteen minutes. I found a parking place on the road that swept up the hill towards Cabo Girão and sat staring through the windscreen at the picturesque cluster of red roofs huddled on the small headland overlooking the harbour, the scene captured in oils all those years ago by the Great Man himself. The fact that I'd heard nothing from Raimundo indicated that Winterton was still holed up somewhere, perhaps among these very houses. But now that I was actually within striking distance, I realized with sinking heart that I hadn't actually worked out *how* I was going to rescue Gorgonzola.

'She'll kill you, G,' I whispered. 'If she catches sight of me, she'll guess that somehow she's been traced. Something that could only have been done by the police. Enough to sign your death warrant. She'll know the net is closing in.'

And it was. Nothing would prevent Comandante Figueira making that arrest at the airport. G would die. Panic and despair gripped me. I'd been deluding myself, been crazy ever to think that I could save her.

In keeping with the black pit of depression into which I'd plunged, a pitter patter on the windscreen heralded a flurry of rain, soaking the ground, intensifying the colours of the blue and orange boats drawn up on the shelving beach. I looked over to Cabo Girão to see that low clouds had swept down from the interior mountain range and were now draping the soaring cliffs in a thin grey veil. A shroud for G. No! There *had* to be something I could do. What? What? *What?* I punched the rim of the steering wheel in frustration.

One thing was certain: if I did nothing, Winterton would be arrested at the airport, and G *would* die. But if I tackled Winterton *now*, there might be the slimmest of slim chances. Decision made, I flung open the car door and swung a foot out onto the pavement.

Perleep perleep perleep peep peep. I snatched up my mobile from the front passenger seat and stared at the text message. Winterton was on the move.

Shaking, I slid back behind the wheel. From where I was parked, I'd be able to spot that metallic-green car if she came past the harbour. But what if *she* saw *me*? What if she'd changed cars? What if she wasn't holed up amongst those red-roofed houses, after all? What if she slipped by unnoticed?

Nerves. I took several deep breaths. It didn't matter if I didn't see her passing by. Raimundo's text messages would tell me where she was. The really important thing was to stay hidden, not alert her in any way. I slithered down below the level of the windows and lay on my side across the passenger seat.

In this rather uncomfortable position the minutes ticked slowly on, marked by the swish of passing cars and the roar of an engine as a laden truck laboured to climb the hill.

I stared at the mobile willing it to ring again. 'C'mon, Raimundo, c'mon, *c'mon.* Tell me where she's going.'

I knew he wouldn't text me till the signal gave a strong indication of a new position, but the long delay began to alarm me. Had he lost his nerve? Had a furious *comandante* discovered that I'd gone against her orders and put a stop to the text messages?

At last, *perleep perleep perleep peep peep.* The message, *Cabo Girão.*

I had to wait an agonizing couple of minutes while yet another laden truck, followed by what seemed an interminable stream of cars, crawled past. At last I was on my way – at the tail end of the line and moving slowly, oh so slowly. The road was narrow and winding, offering no chance to overtake even one car. As we crept uphill, I fumed and fretted at every approaching side road, willing the truck's indicator to blink.

I had time to ponder why Winterton had gone to Cabo Girão. It certainly wasn't to enjoy the famous view from the *miradouro*. And what was she up to *now*? Was she at this very moment hiding the cat-carrier among the scrub on the headland? My grip on the wheel relaxed. If so, all I'd have to do was lurk till she'd driven off. Searching among the bushes might be like looking for the proverbial needle in a haystack, but G would respond to me calling her name and blasts on the ultrasonic cat whistle. To rescue G wasn't going to be so difficult after all. I managed a smile.

Time is relative, speeding up or slowing down depending on whether one dreads or looks forward to the coming event. Though it seemed to take an age to reach the turn-off to Cabo Girão, when I glanced at my watch I was surprised to find that barely twenty minutes had passed.

'Not long now, G,' I whispered as I drove along the stretch of tarmac road leading to the car-park.

The rain had cleared the headland, though inland, grey clouds were resting heavily on the shoulders of the mountains, leaving the air humid and cool. Tourists were conspicuously absent, the car-park almost deserted.

There'd been no message on the mobile. Winterton must still be here. Then I spotted her green car tucked inconspicuously behind a telephone engineer's van near the low building that housed a small museum, café and toilets.

Desperate as I was to confront Winterton and snatch the cat-carrier from her, I sat in the car for a moment. Should I confront her? No, I couldn't predict what might happen. It would be better to follow my plan and keep safely out of sight till she'd driven off.

I curled up on the back seat, willing the mobile to ring with the message that Winterton was on the move again. When she'd gone, I could start the search for G. I saw myself forcing my way through the bushes, calling her name, hearing her answering mew....

But what if Gorgonzola was still in Câmara de Lobos? Or what if Winterton took G with her when she drove off from here? Would it be better to make a discreet reconnoitre, even at the risk of coming face to face with Winterton? Should I remain in the car? I didn't know it, but I was about to make what perhaps would be the most important decision of my life.

Time was running out. Winterton had already been here for half an hour. She might appear at any moment. The thought that G might be in the boot of the green car, only two hundred metres away, settled the matter. I couldn't just lie here and do nothing. I *had* to know whether Winterton had brought the cat-carrier with her. All I needed to do was to open the boot with my picklock. Even if that activated the car's alarm, I'd grab the carrier and be away.

Next moment I was out and running across the car-park. I peered through the green car's windows. There was no sign of the carrier. Putting my ear to the cold metal, I tapped the boot.

'G,' I called softly. 'G?'

217

No answering mew. No quiet thump of movement.

She might be lying in there, drugged or dead. I *had* to know. With shaking hands I fumbled with the picklock, inserted it in the lock and flung open the boot. Empty.

Had Winterton decided to hide the carrier on the viewpoint itself? I closed down the boot and looked around. The museum building and a small café stood between me and the paved area of the cliff top. From previous visits I knew that the centre of that paved area was taken up by a huge pine tree with spreading dark branches. Two large concrete blocks and a line of iron railings fenced off the drop to the sea. There was nowhere that a cat in a carrier could be hidden from the inquisitive pokings and pryings of the crowds of tourists who usually frequented the spot.

Perhaps she had taken the carrier from the car for safekeeping? G might be only a few metres away. My heart was pounding. I peered round the corner of the museum wall. Twenty metres away a lone figure was sitting with her back to me at one of the café tables. A woman, yes, but it wasn't Winterton. No flowery straw hat, no silk dress, the mark of the aristocratic Englishwoman abroad. The woman wearing a cheap cotton sunhat, voluminous psychedelic-patterned shirt and coarse, baggy, sack-like trousers was merely an American tourist from one of the cruise ships in the harbour. I could have wept with disappointment.

Then she turned her head. *Winterton*. The huge spectacles, as distinctive as a fingerprint, revealed her true identity. Cup, teapot and crumb-strewn plate were indications that she had been indulging in her habit of taking afternoon tea, and accounted for the length of her stay at the Cabo.

As I watched, she bent down, reached for something under the table and rose to her feet. In her hand was the cat-carrier. She'd be returning to her car. *Coming this way.* I ducked back round the corner. Elderly woman though she was, I'd have no qualms whatsoever in knocking her to the ground. I braced myself for the coming assault that would restore G to me.

When there was no sound of footsteps, I risked another peek. To my surprise, Winterton was walking away from me towards the railings that protected the 600 metre drop to the sea. It was the purposeful stride that signalled her intention.

In a sudden flash of insight it all became clear. She'd make that promised telephone call from South America telling me where to find G. In that sweet old lady's voice of hers she'd say, 'Your cat is at Cabo Girão, Deborah. You'll find her easily enough, I think.' There'd be a long pause to raise my hopes and make the next words even more devastating. 'Just look over the edge, my dear. The creature's at the foot of the famous cliffs, but quite, quite dead, I fear.'

With her every step the distance to the railings was narrowing.

'Sto—' The word died to a whisper in my throat. Alerted by my shout, she'd whirl round, make a dash and hurl the carrier over before I could reach her.

In desperation I whipped the ultrasonic whistle out of my pocket and blew it as hard as I could. I heard nothing, neither did Winterton, but all at once the cat-carrier took on a life of its own, rocking and twisting violently, tearing itself out of her hand. It thudded to the ground, the catch released and Gorgonzola tumbled out. I sprinted towards her, but was still ten metres away when Winterton saw me.

'Here, G! *Here*!' I screamed.

But dazed or drugged, she just crouched there. Seizing the chance, Winterton grabbed her by the scruff of the neck and, with surprising agility for one of her years, clambered up onto the stone bench beside one of the concrete blocks.

'*Back off*, Smith.' Her eyes were icy cold. 'Or your little friend here goes over the railings. The second highest cliffs in the world, aren't they? Six hundred metres of free fall, though I may be over-estimating a little. The creature will enter the *Guinness Book of Records*, posthumously of course. And don't think I'm bluffing. That fool, Mason, he got in my way, poked his nose in where it wasn't wanted.' A contemptuous snap of her fingers. 'Disposed of. Gone!'

I took a couple of steps forward, measuring the distance for a desperate lunge. *Now or never*. I threw myself forward.

'I warned you.' Clutching Gorgonzola tightly to her chest, she stepped nimbly up onto one of the concrete blocks, level with the top of the railings.

She should have known that cats, especially frightened cats, hate to be held in a painfully tight grip. Their instinct is to claw and struggle to escape. Alley cat genes transformed G into a spitting, clawing, biting fury.

Winterton staggered back, desperately trying with her free hand to fend off the slashing claws. One heel caught on the top of the railings.

I watched in horror as an arm flailed in a futile attempt to regain her balance. Then, clutching at insubstantial air, she fell backward and disappeared over the edge, taking Gorgonzola with her.

Still in nightmares I hear that fading scream. Even more haunting was the silence that followed. Filled with an awful dread and with tears streaming down my face, I rushed to the railings and forced myself to look down. Far, far below, two blue fishing boats were drawn up on the grey sand beach, beside them, a tiny patch of psychedelic-coloured cloth.

I buried my face in my hands. 'Oh, G,' I sobbed. 'G.'

If only I had backed off as Winterton had told me, perhaps, just perhaps, I could have negotiated some kind of deal. If only ... if *only* ...

People had materialized from nowhere as if a genie had rubbed his lamp. At first I was only dimly aware of the agitated voices behind me. Then a sharp elbow jostled me aside and I heard a shrill, 'Look, look, down there!' I couldn't bear to hear any more, had half-turned to push my way through the excited throng, when the words, 'Down there – something's in that spiky bush', stopped me in my tracks.

A spark of hope ignited in the darkness of my despair. I elbowed my way through to the railings and leant over as far as I dared. Three metres or so below, a fringe of aloes and blue-green prickly pear clung precariously to a bulge of rock before the cliff's sheer drop to the sea. I blinked rapidly to clear eyes blurred with tears. Then I saw G – a mound of reddish-brown fur wedged between the fleshy segments at the base of one of the biggest aloes.

'G,' I whispered.

She was safe for the moment, but any attempt to respond to me, *any* movement, might tear off that fleshy leaf or loosen the plant's shallow roots from the crumbling rock.

For a wild moment I contemplated climbing over the railing and somehow scrambling down to her. But that way lay death – for both of us: when I fell, as I inevitably would, G would be knocked from her precarious perch by my falling body.

What I needed was a rope and a ladder. And I'd seen one, not so long ago, on the roof of the telephone engineer's van in the car-park. I didn't stop to consider the practicalities of such a rescue. Heedless of the stares and comments, I shouldered my way through the knot of spectators and ran.

Please, please, let the van still be there.... I rounded the corner of the museum. I wasn't too late. There it was. Out of the nearside window rose a thin grey spiral of cigarette smoke.

Curled on my lap in my London flat, G shuddered and mewed softly in her sleep. After that traumatic experience at Cabo Girão I wasn't the only one who suffered from nightmares. I stroked her head gently.

'It's OK, G,' I murmured. 'You're safe now.' I pondered the irony of her rescue. 'Saved by killer nicotine, eh, G? If Jorge and Ricardo hadn't delayed their departure to take an unofficial smoking break, you wouldn't be here.'

I'd run up to the telephone van and gasped out my request. Galvanized by the very substantial reward I'd offered, the engineers had ground out their cigarettes, rummaged in their van for safety harness and rope and hotfooted it to the railings.

I'd thrust my jacket into Ricardo's hands as Jorge secured the rope. 'If the cat struggles to escape, you'll drop her. Grip her behind the head and wrap her up in this.'

Ricardo began his descent. I'd turned away, unable to watch. There was no way of telling how G would react.

'And you recognized my scent, fastened your claws in the material, and Ricardo brought you back with no bother at all, you brave little girl.'

I tickled her behind the ears. She purred and relaxed.

'It's been a long journey. What we both need is a good night's sleep.'

There had been no way, of course, that I could hide my involvement in Dorothy Winterton's death. The flood of calls to 112, the Portuguese equivalent of 999, reporting an incident on Cabo Girão, soon came to Comandante Figueira's ears. This, together with the message that Winterton's mobile phone signal, last location Cabo Girão, had been lost, was enough to bring her in person to the scene. She found me cradling a trembling G and downing a glass of *poncha* to get over the shock to *my* system.

Having interrogated the little knot of police and paramedics, she'd advanced on me, thrust her face close to mine and hissed, 'Winterton was our best lead. Our *only* lead. And it seems that you have once again blowed it. Please tell me, Sshmit, by what strange coincidence you are here when Winterton comes with the cat?'

Behind her Raimundo hovered anxiously.

'It is no coincidence, Comandante,' I said, all injured innocence. 'The fact is—' I caught Raimundo's eye. 'The fact is … I was in Câmara de Lobos,' – I searched for a plausible reason and came up with – 'hoping to find Haxby at her easel in her usual spot. You see,' I smiled guilelessly, 'a photograph of the painting she was working on would be evidence in the case HMRC is bringing against her for using fake art as a cover for her money laundering activities. And *then*, Comandante,' I injected a note of excitement, 'who should I see but Winterton driving past! I thought to myself, The mobile phone contact may have been lost. Perhaps the Comandante doesn't know where she is. I'd better follow her.'

Justinia Figueira's eyes narrowed. She knew a dodgy story when she heard one. 'Where Winterton went, it did not matter.' She stamped her foot. 'Idiot! We wait till she walks into the airport, and then we have the woman.'

I'll draw a veil over the rest of the scene – suffice it to say that Raimundo was detailed to escort me, and Gorgonzola, to the airport to catch that evening's London flight. For the second time within a fortnight, it had been an ignominious *adeus* to Madeira.

Ahead lay a debriefing session with Jim Orr. Judging from his terse note demanding my presence at the office, the *comandante* had already apprised him of my second ejection from Madeira. But my mood was buoyant – mission accomplished, drug ring broken.

I spread a thick layer of marmalade on my breakfast toast and propped up the newspaper against the teapot. 'What we both need, G, is a holiday somewhere quiet: a little country cottage, or a B&B that takes cats….' A newspaper headline momentarily halted my coffee cup halfway to my lips.

ART WORLD SHAKEN BY AUDACIOUS FRAUD
Michael Coggins, 36, owner of the prestigious St Ives gallery, Avant-Garde Art, appeared yesterday at Truro Magistrates Court

charged with forgery and fraud. He and co-accused, artist Celia Haxby, 43, are alleged to have sold works of art in the knowledge that the signatures of the artists were not genuine. All the paintings were passed off as the work of famous artists and were sold for considerable sums of money. Coggins also faces a second charge of money laundering.

The Crown opposed bail due to the serious nature of the charges and fears that the accused might abscond. Coggins and Haxby have been remitted for trial at Truro Crown Court at the beginning of July.

'What's the bet that Haxby's paintings of prison bars will pass for Modern Art and make her fortune, G?'

I looked over to where Gorgonzola was sitting, eyes closed, enjoying the warmth of the radiator and swaying gently to the melancholy notes of a Portuguese *fado* playing quietly in the background. Recalling how relaxing she'd found the Spanish *madrilena* music on that assignment in Tenerife, I'd bought her a *fado* CD at the airport.

And I too had received an unexpected present at the airport. With a conspiratorial wink, Raimundo had thrust a last minute gift into my arms in recognition of our little secret. Now, on my windowsill, five orange and blue strelitzia flowers pointed imperious beaks towards a grey London sky.

In a sense, Comandante Justinia Figueira was with me still.